BRAVE AS A WOLF

Blue Crescent

Book 3

SOPHIA MARTIN

Published by Blushing Books
An Imprint of
ABCD Graphics and Design, Inc.
A Virginia Corporation
977 Seminole Trail #233
Charlottesville, VA 22901

Brave as a Wolf
Sophia Martin

EBook ISBN: 978-1-63954-491-2
Print ISBN: 978-1-63954-492-9

For my favourite book buddy. He's yours.

Chapter 1

RAJ WAS no stranger to being hit. He'd spent enough time pitted against savage opponents in the Ring that he couldn't be, and before he'd found this place, he'd been in more fist-fights in his somewhat misspent youth than he could count. In truth, he didn't really mind it; he was so used to shaking off pain that it took someone special to actually make him feel the hurt when they managed to land a blow. The secret, he'd discovered, was to make sure he hit them back hard enough that they thought twice before doing it again.

To a certain proportion of the fierce, aggressive fighters that the Ring attracted, his size—over six and a half feet tall—made them view him as more target than threat; for one, they thought they'd be fighting some kind of slow, lumbering brute, and for another, there was always the draw of wanting to be the one to bring down the biggest man in the Ring. "Just means there's more space to aim for," he'd heard someone boast jokingly once before entering a bout with him. He'd hit the man especially hard to make up for the disrespect, not stopping until the guy had to be carried to the Ring's resident doctor on a stretcher.

His werewolf abilities gave him no special edge as a fighter here, either, since the Ring had a firm policy of no shifting and no magic, and almost all the fighters were were-wolves anyway—most of the Mystic City packs had a training scheme in place, following the centuries-old—and admittedly now, almost completely obsolete—tradition of keeping all their pack members of fighting age ready for a skirmish or invasion, just in case. So, they wound up with a bunch of well-trained fighters with no way to utilise their skills other than grappling with packmates, and a small proportion of those ended up somewhere like the Ring, showing off their skill to a mostly criminal audience and getting paid for each fight won. And they were good fighters, most of them.

Raj was, as his current winning streak demonstrated, better.

He had the advantage of his size, but other than that, very few of the benefits he was accustomed to in werewolf fighting—he could only fight in his human form, no teeth or claws allowed. All he had were his experience, his fighting instincts, and his fists, and somehow that made it all the more satisfying to be able to bring down an opponent. It was powerfully gratifying to know that just he, Raj as a man, without involving his wolf, was still one of the most formidable fighters the Ring had ever seen.

They called him The Librarian, because he'd foolishly let slip to someone that that was his day job, though most of the crowd that attended the fights probably just thought that the name had been allocated to him so they could follow it up with a variety of terrible puns about checking out books and paying fines. The people who watched his fights weren't exactly of the crowd that the library attracted, so he wasn't particularly worried about being recognised by any of them at work.

Tonight, he was fighting a wolf who was almost his size, though not as fast as Raj had ruthlessly trained himself to be. This one, referred to in the Ring as "The Professor" ("Time to get taught a lesson!"), was relatively new to the fights, but from what Raj had seen, he was ruthless in the way he fought, brutal and efficient to the point that his opponents were often taken to be looked after by the doctor who was paid a ridiculous amount to care for the victims of the underground fighting ring with the required discretion.

While the crowd roared and jeered, Raj stood in his position across the Ring from the Professor as they sized each other up, looking for potential advantages they might have missed. This was the part that Raj lived for—the adrenaline, the rush as his body prepared itself for brutality. The setting aside of societal norms and sinking into something more primitive. There was no pretension in the Ring, no layers of inference and implication, none of the political manoeuvring he was now used to as Beta of the Blue Crescent pack. It was almost unsettlingly easy for him, after all this time, to sink into the simpler, more brutal, instinctive version of himself— almost as if he was becoming his wolf, without actually shifting. Once the fight had begun, there was no thinking, no questioning, no uncertainty. Only winning, and losing, and pain.

And there was a part of Raj that relished the pain.

The anticipation of the fight blossomed in his chest as he surveyed the massive underground space that the Ring inhabited. It was a huge, excavated cavern, hidden beneath a warehouse complex that was perpetually under construction. The walls were raw rock, as were the tiers of seating that rose like an amphitheatre into the smoky darkness above. The Ring itself was raised on a platform that stood about three feet above the floor, a canvas-covered circle bound by ropes, and it was the only part of the cavern that was lit. The crowded tiers disappeared into the darkness, providing only the vague sense of rows of people packed together, smoking and drinking, money and far less legal things changing hands deep into the darkness of the crowd. The desire to bring pain reverberated through Raj as he watched his opponent playing to the spectators. Raj stood still, knowing that silence would momentarily fall.

The Ring's organisers, two sharply dressed men named Rod and Abram who Raj could only assume had a lot of experience with Mystic City's criminal underworld, climbed into the centre of the Ring and the anticipated hush fell over the crowd.

"Hello, friends," Rod and Abram said together, as always, their voices magically amplified to echo through the rough-hewn space, which then rang with cheers from the amped-up spectators. This time, it was the taller of the two —Raj still didn't know which one was which—who continued to speak after their joint introduction to the biggest fight of the night. They seemed to decide which of the two of them would give their customary speech with no pattern that he could discern, not alternating, but without one taking the speaking role noticeably more than the other. The speech was basically the same every time the Ring fight night was held, each time a few of a limited collection of phrases repeated just infrequently enough for the crowd not to get bored of them.

"Thank you, everyone, for your attendance at another of our informal gatherings!" Rod-or-Abram declared, a smile audible in his oily voice, and the spectators roared. "Another night of brutality and debauchery. A night for the strong to show what they are made of and the weak to fall to their superiors. Are you having fun, my friends?"

Again, the crowd screamed. Fuelled by adrenaline and alcohol and the witch-spelled pills and powders that were traded in high volumes at this event, they were desperate for this final, and likely most brutal, fight.

"Tonight, for our champion fight, we have something special for you," Rod-or-Abram continued. "A meeting of minds. Two lovers of learning, here to teach each other a lesson... or at least, to try." The sarcasm of his comments about their Ring names made his voice sound even smarmier than usual. "Our returning champion—you know him, you love him—the Librarian!"

The crowd yelled again, and Raj acknowledged their response with a nod. It felt like a veil had slipped over his vision, allowing him only to focus on his opponent and the fight ahead. Tension built in him, tension that he knew from experience would only dissipate after he'd bloodied his fists and taken some blows, relished the pain even as he shook it off like water from his wolf's coat.

"And tonight's challenger, the Professor!" Rod-or-Abram yelled, and Raj's opponent played to the crowd's answering roar, raising his arms and snarling at them as though he might imminently shift into his wolf form.

"Enjoy this night, my friends," Rod-or-Abram said. "You won't see a fight like this anywhere else."

There was another enthusiastic roar from the crowd, and then the small man who acted as announcer was back in the centre of the Ring, listing each of their fighting records and calling out final betting odds. Raj ignored him. His blood started to pulse in his ears, and he shifted from foot to foot, his muscles coiled for the moment he was unleashed.

Finally, the announcer stepped out of the Ring. There was a final hushed moment of anticipation, and then the bell rang. For once, Raj didn't wait for his opponent to make the first move. He leaped at the other male, his fists ready, and drove a blow straight into his jaw before the Professor could move to defend himself. The crowd roared, but Raj blocked out the sound. He didn't have room in his brain for the watchers, only for the man before him, who recovered with lightning speed and threw a punch at Raj's stomach. Raj punched him in the jaw again while he was distracted, copping the blow to his belly and blocking out the pain of that, too. The Professor, who seemed completely unfazed by the fact that Raj had just given him two blows that each, individually, would have been enough to lay another man out completely, spat blood on the ground and dove at Raj, tackling him to the floor. Raj took blows to his face and torso, moving and writhing in an attempt to get the smaller man off him, but he was well-braced, and Raj's position was hardly an admirable one. The announcer of the fights was usually fairly lax about ringing the bell that ended the fights, allowing them to go on much longer than a legal fight would have allowed—after all, people were here to see blood and pain—so Raj wasn't worried there would be a swift end to the match. He wasn't pinned—he was still striking the Professor as well as he could from this position—and he definitely wasn't finished. The next few minutes were a blur of fists and elbows and knees, of pain and satisfaction, smashing his forehead into the other man's nose, reaching for his eyes as if he'd claw them out right onto the dirty canvas. None of the rules of civilised fighting applied here; he could do whatever he wanted, as long as it wasn't irreparable damage, and with the benefit of the Ring's warlock doctor, there was very little that counted as irreparable. His blood pounded in his ears as he released the primal part of himself that was always just beneath the surface, howling to be let loose. This, it had quickly become clear, was not a fight he was going to win easily.

But hell if he was going to lose.

Raj had been attending lessons on how to fight both in his human and werewolf forms since he was a pup. And he'd been training, if you could call routinely getting into fights "training", for almost his entire life. In some ways, the lived experience was better than the careful sparring practice of Pack training. In those years of unofficial fights, he had learnt to fight the way he did now, without care for how much damage he was doing his opponent—or himself. He wasn't going to let one man with an absurdly high pain tolerance get in the way of the results of over twenty years of training. The Professor would not leave the Ring as victor.

The roar that left him as he finally managed to pin the other man to the ground was almost beyond recognition as human. Blood from a long cut on Raj's face was dripping onto his opponent even before he began pummelling him with all his considerable strength. He felt bones break under his blows, felt the man trying desperately to reverse their positions, but he held the Professor down under his weight, his knees pressing the other man's upper arms to the ground so he couldn't even try to land a blow of his own, and a single coherent thought managed to penetrate the animalistic haze that ruled his mind. *Who's getting taught a lesson now?*

The bell rang, loudly enough that even Raj, in his altered state of mind, could register it, and he climbed off the other man, swiping at the blood streaming down his face. It would heal soon enough; werewolves were lucky like that. One of his eyes was starting to swell, too, and based on the force of that blow, he'd be lucky to be able to see through it tomorrow if he left it.

He rarely went to be seen by the doc after his fights, unless he had a particularly obvious bruise that wouldn't heal within a day or two even with his werewolf capabilities, or he'd broken something and needed the warlock to magically mend the bone. It felt like a kind of cheating, to receive wounds like these in a fight he'd chosen to participate in, and then have them magically healed moments later. The cuts and bruises he received were like temporary badges of honour, and as long as they weren't going to be visible in the clothes that he wore for work or training, he kept them. As far as he was concerned, medical attention at the Ring was reserved for serious or obvious injuries only.

This black eye, though—he'd need to have that dealt with. He was already incongruous enough as a six-and-a-half-foot-tall, male, werewolf librarian, and somewhat intimidating to library users who just wanted to ask where they could find a book. Coming into work with a massive bruise on his face would not make him any less menacing to children trying to locate their favourite book of fairy tales.

He dragged in a deep breath, scenting blood and sweat and the heavy, thick scent of the large group of people currently cheering his victory or bemoaning their lost wagers, and... something else. Something... else. He couldn't quite put words to it—even he, a man who had words for everything even when they weren't wanted. It was... warm. It smelled like... like a fire burning in the fireplace on a cold winter's night when you were wrapped up in a blanket on the couch, safe and warm; but also, sweet, but at the same time, not. It was... safe.

And for some incredible, completely illogical reason that he had no hope of understanding, it was kind of turning him on.

He was literally standing over the bloodied body of a man he had just beaten to a pulp, only just coming out of the animalistic fury that had come over him when he was punching the Professor into what looked like borderline unconsciousness, and this completely incongruous scent was starting to make him worry he was going to get hard in a way that would be all too visible to the Ring's spectators in his loose workout shorts.

He stepped away from the man on the floor, and the

crowd thought he was pandering to their cheers, so they got louder, whistles and hoots coming from all around. The scent got stronger as the medical team approached, and after shooting a vague grin and a nod at the spectators so they'd think he cared what they thought, he looked over to see what he'd done to the Professor.

And in that moment, he saw her.

Her.

The tiny woman was kneeling by the beaten man on the floor, who was struggling to pull himself into a sitting position, though he was badly injured enough that he was practically leaving an outline of himself in blood on the floor of the ring. His face was already almost swollen beyond recognition. She was trying to keep the Professor lying down so they could put him on a stretcher, but he was having none of it. He kept trying to drag himself upright despite her protestations, even though she was trying to keep him in the position on his back that he'd been left in when Raj was through with him. As careful as her movements were, the words that drifted to him from her mouth were anything but.

"Stay down, you bloody idiot," she was all but yelling. "You might have damage to your spine, you dickhead, and I'm trying to keep you from making it worse. Fuck!"

"I'm fine," the Professor was insisting as he tried to sit up. "It's all just surface injuries."

"He's almost definitely fractured your cheekbone and at least a few of your ribs," the woman reminded him. "I saw your head snap back when he hit you. Just stay on the floor and let the doctor look after you."

When he tried to sit up again, she growled—actually growled, as though there was a little bit of wolf in her even though she was clearly human—and pressed on the side of the man's torso. He flinched, let out a groan, and stopped trying to get up.

No, this wasn't one of the assistants who usually helped Doc—the only name by which the other people who frequented the Ring knew their resident medical professional —with management of the injuries acquired in the fights. They were usually quiet and unassuming, helping with the basics of the healing process while purposely fading into the background. This woman was... *magnetic*. Even if he was wrong, and the scent that felt like it was filling his body with more adrenaline than the start of a fight *wasn't* coming from her, he would have been interested in her. But something was telling him that he wasn't wrong. Despite everything else in this room that should have overpowered any single scent, he was all but positive that it was her.

Maybe it was some remainder of the primitive state he had gone into during the fight, or maybe even his wolf coming closer to the surface than had happened unintentionally in years, but as he stared at her from across the Ring, watching as the Professor laboriously climbed to his feet despite her warnings, Raj was certain of one thing only.

He needed to know her.

Out of the corner of his eye, he saw Olivia sitting in one of the bleachers surrounding the Ring. She looked proud, a savage grin stretching across her beautiful face. Any other night, he'd have been happy that the woman he'd been seeing was accepting of the kind of fighting he did in the Ring. Initially, he'd been scared that the revelation of his somewhat brutal—and very illegal—hobby would horrify her, and he'd have to let the witches who protected the Ring reinforce the secrecy spells that magically prevented discussion of the Ring with the uninitiated. But Olivia had actually seemed to enjoy watching the initial fights. He'd sat with her through the first few, before he had to go and get ready for his own, and she'd picked a fighter to support in each bout and even considered placing a bet on one. She seemed completely okay with his secret, and normally, Raj would be thrilled by this, not to mention ready to expend some of his leftover adrenaline from the fight by dragging her into one of the back rooms of the facility and fucking the living daylights out of her.

Instead, despite her proud grin and the way she raised an eyebrow at him as though they shared a salacious secret, all he felt was… indifference. Suddenly, all he could think about was the doc's assistant who smelled like safety and sweetness and sex all in one.

In that moment, Raj knew he had done it. After all these years of hoping, he had found his mate.

And he was somehow going to have to explain that to his girlfriend.

Magnolia Gawler was a law-abiding person—well, other than her frequent jaywalking, which, in her opinion, didn't count if you did it sensibly. She didn't always take being told what to do particularly well, and she was highly independent, but she almost always followed the actual *law*.

Which made it particularly strange that she was here tonight, in an illegal, literally underground fight club, assisting Jeremy in magically healing the multiple injuries that had been dealt to this madman by the psychopath waiting outside the room to be treated himself.

There had been a number of times in Maggie's life when she'd looked around and wondered how on earth she had wound up in the situation she was in—the time she'd spontaneously booked a last-minute flight to Hawaii and found herself on a plane the next morning, for example, or when she drank too much at a college party and wound up in a room full of near-strangers being offered LSD with the laissez-faire attitude one might have when offering sugar for someone's tea. At this point, this situation was looking like it was going to go straight on that how-did-this-happen list.

She'd only been seeing Jeremy for a couple of months—long enough that she was no longer surprised to see him next to her when she woke up after he stayed over, but not long enough that she was ready to look particularly far to the future of their relationship. He was one of the doctors at the hospital where she worked as a nurse, and those pairings didn't always go well. Even though they were in completely different parts of the hospital—he was a trauma surgeon, and she was currently in the cardiac ward, so they rarely crossed paths at work—there was a power imbalance inherent in doctors dating nurses, and Maggie wasn't particularly good with being the less powerful one in that combination. Not to mention the fact that he was a powerful warlock, capable of magic that even most of his own kind could only dream of, and she was just a regular human. But Jeremy had never treated her with anything but the utmost respect, never acted like he knew more than she did just because he had "Doctor" before his name, so even though their interests tended towards different things, and his unassailable confidence and near-manic energy and occasional highhandedness sometimes bothered her, and she wasn't sure there'd ever be a future for them, she'd allowed their dalliance after a night at the pub to grow into something more.

And then the other night when they were eating dinner, he'd announced that there was something he hadn't been able to disclose to her until now. A secret that he'd been hiding from her. And he'd explained about the Ring. How the illegal fight club had needed a doctor, and he'd known one of the organisers, so they'd asked him and told him he could name his price—the Ring had an entry fee and got a cut of every bet the spectators made, so it raked in a lot of money. To have a doctor who could be relied upon for both his skills and his discretion, was so valuable to them that they'd pay him anything he wanted.

He'd been trying to pay off his sister's medical bills at the time, he explained—Maggie knew she'd had a car accident, though, from Jeremy's reports, it sounded like she was fine now—as well as his tuition from university, and it had seemed like too good an opportunity to pass up. He'd named a ludicrously high price, and they'd accepted it without blinking. So, on the night of the new moon every few months—they apparently didn't have a regular schedule, so they were less likely to be found out—he went down to the Ring and healed the injuries of the fighters who beat each other senseless for large amounts of money, and made a comparably large amount of money himself.

She was sitting there at the table, speechlessly staring at him, for a long moment before he added, "Since I finished with Nerida's bills and my tuition fees, I donate a big chunk of it to charity. I'm not just some greedy asshole."

"Jeremy," Maggie had said slowly, "you know you could lose your medical licence if anyone finds out."

"They're careful," Jeremy explained. "There are protection spells in place. They prevent people from talking about it with anyone who doesn't know—I had to wait this long to tell you because I needed to get an exemption made to the spell."

"And the people there are just... just beating each other up for fun?"

"And for a shit ton of money," Jeremy said, clearly trying to make light of the seriousness of the situation. He saw the look on her face and sobered. "Yes, for some of them, I think it's just the thrill of the fight. Nothing that brutal is allowed in regular boxing or martial arts matches."

"That... brutal?" Maggie asked tentatively.

"That makes it sound bad," Jeremy backpedalled. "What

I meant was, there are fewer rules in the Ring. The fighters are allowed to get a little more... primitive. And sometimes, that leads to injuries, so they keep me on staff in case anyone gets properly hurt."

"And in case one of these "primitive" fighters just goes on a rage? What do you do when someone starts beating someone else to death?"

He met her eyes evenly. "Maggie, I'm a surgeon. I could stop someone's heart just by spelling the right nerve if they got out of hand." Seeing her eyes go even wider, he added, "Not that I would. Unless there was an emergency. But that's not important." He looked a little wild-eyed for a moment, trying to work out how to keep her on his side. "Honestly, it's mostly healing bruises and minor breaks, to maintain the Ring's secrecy. People start asking questions if someone keeps appearing with black eyes or broken fingers."

"And when it's not just that—not just black eyes and broken fingers?" Maggie asked.

Jeremy shrugged, looking uncomfortable. "Well, some-times, it's something more serious. Never anything I haven't been able to manage on my own, but I usually have an assistant or two to help with the physical part." His expres-sion changed, as though he'd just thought of something. "Maggie, why don't you come and help me out next time it's on? I could use a qualified nurse. Most of the people I work with are just low-level witches looking to make a quick buck. I could really use your skills. You'll see it's not that bad, and you'll get paid well. Then you'll understand why I keep going with it—they need someone like me, and I can help them. If I wasn't around to heal the fighters, some of them could be stuck with proper injuries that need medical attention. And it's not as bad as you're thinking."

Hesitantly, and mostly, to her shame, thinking of the mortgage payment she had coming up, she'd agreed. She'd come along tonight, and it had turned out he was right. It wasn't as bad as she'd been thinking. It was significantly worse. The other fights, the smaller ones leading up to this all-guns-blazing finale, hadn't been awful; as Jeremy had said, it was mostly healing minor breaks and bruises that were going to become noticeable.

And then she'd seen what the Librarian had done to the Professor. Two ludicrous fighter names, but who was she to judge? She was here, wasn't she? His massive fists delivered blow after blow even when it became apparent that the other man was completely incapable of fighting back. Clearly, Jeremy had been right when he told her that regular boxing or martial arts matches didn't allow this level of brutality. They didn't even ring the bell for the end of the match until the Professor looked like he was inches from being beaten to death.

Her first concern had been for the man's spine, though he'd made it clear by refusing to hold his position on the floor that he didn't share her concern. She could see why Jeremy had been keen to have a trained nurse as one of his assistants in healing these people; the other assistant, a man who smelled strongly of old sweat and introduced himself as Ace when they met, might have had some training. Still, he was far from being a medical professional. He didn't even think to brace the Professor's spine, just helped him to the room where Jeremy, whom everyone at the Ring simply called Doc, had been ensconced all night, healing the broken noses, fractured fingers and black eyes of the other fighters.

Jeremy had clearly been preparing for some more significant magical healing to be required from this fight; she'd watched him race through the last of the minor injuries from the earlier bouts in the lead up to this finale match with none of his usual finesse. Her frustration at the lack of care both

Jeremy and Ace seemed to be taking had boiled over at Ace as he allowed the Professor to get to his feet.

"Are you nuts?" she spat at the other assistant. "He could have a cervical spine fracture. We need to keep his neck immobilised."

"If it's damaged, Doc will fix it," Ace replied, unaffected by her ire. "He's already beaten to hell; what does it matter if he gets a little more broken by walking to the medical room? Doc will fix it. They don't pay him this much to sit around and look pretty." His gaze flicked down over her, slowly enough that she figured she was supposed to notice it, even if he hadn't intended the rise of a wave of disgust that rolled through her in response. "I'm sure they would with you, though, if you offered," he said, grinning and raising an eyebrow, and she tried not to gag at the idea as she pushed past him into the medical room.

Jeremy was busy magically scanning the Professor's body for injuries—the battered fighter appeared to take the doctor's insistence with far more grace than he had Maggie's, because he was lying silently on the medical table as Jeremy worked.

"If you have a spinal injury," she told the beaten man bitterly, "I'm going to say I told you so."

"Whatever it is, Doc can fix it," the Professor replied, then started coughing. Jeremy placed a hand on the man's chest and the coughing eased. "You should see some of the shit he's had to heal in the past," the fighter continued. "The Librarian is not a man to fuck with. One time Doc had to regrow half of one guy's teeth, because he just knocked them right out."

"Then why the fuck did you want to fight him?" Maggie asked, feeling like she already knew the answer.

The Professor shrugged, then winced.

"Stay still, please," Jeremy said in a voice Maggie recognised from the few times she'd seen him in doctor mode in the hospital. "Nurse, could you please get the Professor some anaesthetic so I can get to work on some of these breaks?" She was a little taken aback by how distantly he spoke to her but figured it was to avoid letting the man between them know they had a personal connection.

She took the Professor's limp arm and inserted a needle into his vein, then injected the anaesthetic.

"Glory," the Professor said with a faraway smile stretching his battered, swollen face. It took her a moment to realise he was answering her earlier question—why would anyone fight the Librarian if he was such a savage? "Imagine if I'd won. I'd be a legend."

Jeremy made eye contact with Maggie and sent her a rapid nod as well as the universal hand movement for *keep going*. She assumed he was about to heal one of the Professor's broken bones and wanted her to keep him talking while the painkillers got to work, so Jeremy could stop magically blocking the man's pain and get to work fixing his injuries.

"He's that good?" Maggie asked, at a loss for what else to say.

"You saw what he did to me," the Professor said with something that could have been a laugh if it hadn't been as hoarse and rattling as his breathing. "I gave him all my best moves, I've been training for this fight for months, and I've been fighting for years, and he still put me on my back. I think it was last year... or maybe last month... a while ago..." Well, clearly the painkillers were kicking in and putting the man in a daze. Or rather, more of a daze, even as Jeremy was able to stop magically anaesthetising the man and focus on healing his injuries. She tried to subtly take his pulse, just in case.

"A while ago, anyway," the Professor continued unevenly, after a silence he didn't even appear to notice, "the Librarian had a bout with this fast little guy, can't remember his name. Running Robert or something like that." He snorted derisively, then coughed again. Blood flecked his lips. Maggie sent Jeremy a worried look, which he missed because he was focusing on the Professor's exposed flank, his hands moving as he worked his magic.

"So, everyone's betting on the Librarian, right, because this guy is little, looks like he'd go flying the second he got hit. But he's quick, that's his thing, fast enough to duck… and weave and… duck." The dazed Professor took another deep, rattling breath. "He's running circles around the Librarian, sneaking in fast enough to hit him then backing away and ducking and weaving again. Guess that's why he has that name." He chuckled and winced. Maggie wondered if she could give him any more painkillers, or if that would be dangerous. She tried to make eye contact with Jeremy again, but the warlock had his eyes closed, his hands now pressed to the Professor's chest.

"Goes on for a few minutes… a long, few minutes…" He faded away for a second, then blinked and seemed to come back to himself. "And the Librarian gets sick of it and lets the running man get a shot in, then sticks his arm out so the little guy smacks into it like a pole when he tries to run around him. Just *coat hangers* himself. The Librarian slams him down on his back and then it was on. The big guy had him pinned in half a second and just starts hitting him, face, chest, belly… now that was some damage. And that's not even unusual when you go up against this guy. What I got out of this fight was nothing compared to what the little guy took out of that other one. Doc could tell you; he was working on him for hours after."

This time when Maggie went to catch Jeremy's eye, he was looking at her, a trace of guilt on his features. "Black eyes and bruises, huh?" she asked acerbically.

"Mostly," Jeremy said quietly, then went back to the Professor. "All right, buddy, I've fixed your rib and the lung it punctured, but the bones in your face and all these bruises are going to take a minute. I need you not to talk while I'm working on your nose and cheekbones, all right? There's a hairline fracture in your jaw, as well, but that'll only take a second to fix."

Maggie took a step away as the hum of magic in the air increased, making her skin break out in goosebumps. She'd always been especially sensitive to the use of magic in her vicinity, and while it didn't make her uncomfortable—it would have been hard to work at the hospital, where someone was always being magically healed, if it did—she was always very aware of its presence. Even the protection spells that her best friend Della, who was a witch, regularly cast on her, since Maggie sometimes caught public transport home after night shifts and Della insisted she needed to be protected, always had a part of her almost... tingling. It was how she could tell when they needed to be renewed, though she hadn't told Della that part, since she didn't really think they were necessary. Maggie might be small, but she could take care of herself. It just meant that part of her was always aware that there was magic around her. At its usual low level, the vague psychic tingling was easy to ignore, but when someone like Jeremy was doing magic of this calibre in her vicinity, she felt it like pins-and-needles in her mind.

The Professor obediently maintained his silence as Jeremy worked on his battered face. The swelling and bruises were the last to go, but Maggie never got tired of seeing the evidence of physical injury fade before her eyes. Perhaps it was because, as a human, she'd never be able to heal someone this way, but she'd never lost her fascination with the speed, ease and reduced pain with which witches were able to fix damage to someone's body.

After a while, the Professor's battered face began to resemble a normal person once more, and Jeremy moved on to the bruises covering his torso and limbs. Maggie stood by the wall, presuming he'd call on her if he needed her, and watched as the quickly discolouring patches faded to the shade of the man's surrounding skin. The Professor was quite clearly still a bit loopy from the painkillers, occasionally attempting to engage the doctor or Maggie herself in conversation, but neither lasted very long. Eventually, he just lay there with his eyes closed as Jeremy healed him. She came around to stand beside the warlock.

"His spine?" she asked quietly.

"Minor fracture. Nothing serious. It's dealt with."

"I told him to keep his head still so we could stretcher him, but he insisted on walking," she said, feeling slightly validated. "Don't you have cervical collars in this place? Surely, you need them pretty regularly."

Jeremy actually cracked a smile. "These guys wouldn't be seen dead wearing a collar. They just assume I'll be able to fix whatever the damage is, so it doesn't matter if they make it worse coming in here."

"He could have wound up paralysed!" Maggie protested, forgetting to keep her voice quiet. The Professor opened one eye and went to turn his head, but Jeremy warned him to keep still while he finished the healing process.

"Wouldn't have been irreparable damage, with a little fracture like that," Jeremy said quietly. "I would have been able to fix it. I'm a pretty good doctor, you know." He sent her a smile that she didn't return, and she went back to her position by the wall. Such callous carelessness over worsening someone's injuries was completely antithetical to the way she'd been taught to practice medicine. The fact that Jeremy, of all people, displayed it this way was concerning, to say the least.

In truth, most of what they'd done tonight had been exactly what he'd described—healing bruises and small breaks, cosmetic issues mostly. While she didn't particularly like the Ring, she might have been able to set aside her qualms and continue working there just because of the amount they were paying her if not for two things.

The first was the baying for blood of the spectators. They might have pretended they were there just for a night on the town, that they appreciated the sport of the people in the Ring beating each other senseless, but she'd heard the way their cheers changed when someone was beaten drastically, when an obvious injury was inflicted rather than just the regular fist-to-face action. They *liked* the brutality of it, the animalistic nature of the conflicts, putting down bets on everything from who would win to how many bones would be broken in a fight, and that alone made her feel sick to her stomach. She'd stopped watching barely an hour into the night of fighting, right up until this final bout, which Ace had assured her was something she shouldn't miss.

And that... well, that was pretty much the entirety of the second reason right there.

The way the Professor and the Librarian, both with such respectable academic titles, had sunk into a deeper, more primitive animalism than she'd seen even in the other fights. The utter brutality with which they'd gone at each other, with no hesitation or concern that they might be irreparably injuring each other, no acknowledgement that this violence was by its nature unnecessary. The beating that the Librarian had delivered at the end, even when it was clear that he had the other man pinned and that the match could end there with an obvious winner. Whoever made the calls over when the Ring matches concluded had *wanted* to see the Professor violently injured, had allowed the beating to continue. A fracture to the cervical spine? It could have been so much worse. Even a warlock as strong as Jeremy could only do so much.

She'd seen the look on the Librarian's face as well, as he pounded his fists into the other man's unshielded face and torso over and over. He'd been relishing the violence of it, the pain he was inflicting. He'd *enjoyed* what he was doing.

They'd told her he was a werewolf, but she had plenty of werewolf friends who would never imagine sinking to that kind of blatant, brutal animalism, especially if it involved hurting someone for no reason. Was he some kind of psychopath, then? A man who so clearly took pleasure in the pain of others—a sadist, in the most brutal sense. A man who enjoyed inflicting injuries which, without magical intervention, could have killed his opponent. The Professor had had a punctured lung, for goodness' sake. If Jeremy hadn't been there, or even had been worn out from the rest of his work during the night, the Professor could have died from an injury like that.

The callous approach to pain and suffering, risking one's life for something as minor as the glory of beating an opponent, the joy taken in inflicting injury, was completely alien to Maggie. The very air of the facility was starting to make her feel sick, even knowing that the spectators were beginning to collect their money and leave, and the Ring was emptying. She needed to get out as soon as possible, before she threw up all over the patient bed.

With the Professor's healing complete, he looked like a normal man again. He sat up on the bed and swung his legs over the side, then gave her a smile that might have been attractively flirtatious under other circumstances. In this situation, it just made her nausea worsen.

"Thanks, Doc," he said to Jeremy, who was now washing his hands in the sink on the opposite side of the room. "Feels good as new." He took a deep breath as if to show off just how healed he was. "Perfect. And thanks for your help too, Nurse..." he trailed off, as though waiting for Maggie to tell him which moniker she'd chosen to stand alongside names like Doc and Ace and the Professor. And the Librarian.

"Don't worry about learning my name," she said quietly, starting to clean up after the man's healing. "I won't be back."

"Our loss, I guess," the Professor replied easily, standing up and stretching. He turned to Jeremy, who had moved to drying his hands. "Should I tell the big guy you're ready for him now? You might not have to do much. I don't know that I even did that much damage to the bastard tonight." He seemed now to have completely come to terms with his loss of the match, even giving Maggie a self-deprecating shrug as he spoke. "Have to train harder for the next time I'm up against him." He flexed a bicep. "No harm in good motivation, I guess." He tried to make eye contact with her, but she purposely looked over at Jeremy.

"Just give me a minute to get this cleaned up," she said to them both, and started wiping down the surfaces with antiseptic spray.

Jeremy walked the Professor to the door, clapped him on the shoulder as he left, and stood there for a moment talking to the man waiting outside for treatment, explaining that she was just cleaning the room before they could treat him. The Librarian, the sadist who had taken such pleasure in decimating his opponent—was she supposed to stand by and make small talk to distract him while Jeremy healed his wounds as she had with the Professor? Tonight, had felt like a bad idea from the very start, and somehow, none of it had felt as bad as the idea of seeing this man up close, knowing what he was capable of.

She finished cleaning the room and called out to Jeremy, "All right, ready when you are." Ace, who had been standing outside the room while they tended to the Professor, looked in as Jeremy and the Librarian entered, but made no move to come inside. *Lazy bastard,* she thought, but got into position on the far side of the bed in case Jeremy needed her.

The Librarian was a massive man, at least a foot taller than she was, dark-skinned and dark-eyed, with hair and a beard so black, they were almost blue, just slightly too long to look professional. Those eyes seemed to immediately shoot to her as soon as he entered the room, and she thought she saw his muscles bunch briefly when he registered her presence, before he came and took his place on the bed. Clearly, he'd done this before; he knew what was expected of him. The light caught his eyes as he moved to sit, then swung his feet up on to the bed, and for a second, they looked almost silver. His teeth were blindingly white as he shot her a smile, then winced. His response to the pain was a good distraction from having to sort out her own expression, which she thought might show her apprehension at being near this man.

"Yeah, we're going to need to sort out that cheekbone, as well as your eye," Jeremy said comfortably, as though the two men were lifelong friends. "From the looks of those hands, you might have taken out a few fingers as well, so do you think you can sit still for that long?"

The man nodded. His grin, though slightly reduced, was unflinching despite the pain that had made him wince before. He directed the smile to Jeremy. "Yeah, thanks, Doc."

"You and the Prof had matching breaks tonight," Jeremy commented. "Lie down, and I'll scan you properly, make sure he didn't do any other serious damage."

"The fucker packs a punch," the Librarian said in agreement. He was so tall, his feet hung well off the end of the bed as he lay down. Maggie stayed by the wall, figuring Jeremy would call her if he needed her to do anything. Their patient seemed to have transitioned to studiously not looking at her, as though he knew the mingled fear and disgust that his performance had brought up in her. As though he knew she'd have to force herself to treat him as clinically as she would any other patient, having seen what he cheerfully did to the Professor with that visceral, cruel enjoyment on his face. In her years as a nurse, she'd treated everyone from violent criminals to CEOs, including all kinds of supernaturals, but something about this man put her on edge. She'd never feared a patient before, but the air of barely constrained tension around this one made her almost afraid he would shift into his wolf form. Like he was actively restraining himself from leaping at her at any moment.

She shook her head to get rid of the weird thought and, at Jeremy's request, went over to the anaesthetics trolley to draw up some more pain medication before he started healing the man's broken cheekbone.

"Don't bother," the Librarian said, meeting her eyes for the first time in what suddenly felt like hours. She froze for a moment, feeling like she could fall right into those deep pools of silvery darkness and never feel the need to resurface. She blinked and looked back down at the tray, but not before she noticed his fists clenched into tight balls on the bed beside his body. "If I can handle the pain of getting the injury,' he continued, "I can handle the pain of it being healed."

"Sorry, I forgot about your tough guy tendencies," Jeremy joked, running the fingers of one hand over the Librarian's swollen cheekbone and making a complicated gesture with the other. The patient's *many* muscles briefly went tense, but he seemed to relax into the pain, almost welcome it. Maggie found herself looking at him closely now that she wasn't at risk of being seen doing it. He was fine-featured despite his size, his slightly crooked nose indicating that it had probably been broken at least once and not magically reset. His hands were the size of saucepan lids, currently curled into fists despite the relaxation of the rest of his body even with the pain of having his broken bone healed. This was a man with a pain tolerance so significant that punching him would likely have the same effect as punching a rock. It was no wonder he was such a favourite for those who frequented the Ring; surely, only someone of equal size and strength would even be able to come close to taking him down, and even then, they'd need to be as light on their feet and quick to respond as this man had shown himself to be.

Without warning, his eyes snapped open, looking even more silver than before as they met Maggie's own. She found herself frozen under his gaze again, caught in the process of examining him. Her hands still rested on the edge of the anaesthetics trolley, and she told herself she should look away, but she couldn't break the connection of that gaze. In his eyes, she saw the wolf he could turn into, the savagery and animalism that had come out tonight not even holding a candle to the kind of damage he could do in that other form. And yet, for some reason, the fear and disgust and borderline horror she'd had of this man when he entered the room seemed to melt away as their eyes held. Suddenly, she felt like she could also see beyond that, to the man he might be when he wasn't in this environment that idolised brutality.

Jeremy took his hand away from the Librarian's face, and the connection of their gazes broke. Immediately, she was aware of the tension that had crept into their patient's body during their stare-off, noticed the visible injuries that marred his bare torso and intersected some of the tattoos there, and the feelings that had evaporated while their eyes met rolled back in. How was it that all it had taken was a long stare from this man and she'd forgotten what she'd seen him do? What was she doing, allowing herself to stand out to a man who was so clearly savagely violent? She didn't want his attention. She should be trying as hard as possible to fade into the background and hope he didn't notice her.

Unfortunately, she felt like it might be a little late for that.

Jeremy moved to fixing the man's two broken fingers, then healing his bruises—the Librarian preferred that he only heal those specific bruises, he explained to Maggie as if it were a joke between them, which would be visible in business or training attire.

"I earned them," the Librarian said quietly. She felt like she could physically *feel* his eyes on her, though she'd studiously fixed her gaze on Jeremy's hands as he worked, to avoid getting lost in those silver-black eyes again. "It would feel like cheating to get rid of them all. And besides, they're hardly visible on my skin."

"Can't have you showing up to work with a face like you've got on the bad side of your Alpha, though," Jeremy said easily, then added to Maggie, "that's why we don't let any of the fighters leave the Ring with breaks or visible bruises. Have to preserve the confidentiality."

"I thought the spells meant you couldn't talk about this place to people who don't already know about it," she said quietly.

"Yes, but that doesn't mean they wouldn't get suspicious," Jeremy said. "And if someone starts digging, there's only so much you can do to keep a secret this big." He stood up from his position leaning over the Librarian. "All right, I think you're just about good to go. See you next time if you can't stop the next opponent from mangling your face again."

"I'll do my best," the man promised, sitting up from his position on the bed and swinging his legs back down to the floor. Even sitting, he was taller than Maggie was standing, and his height when he stood made her feel like she was the size of a doll. At a loss for what else to do, she started cleaning up.

"Thanks, Doc," the Librarian said as he walked towards the door. "And thanks for your help, um... Nurse."

"You're welcome," Maggie said, again refusing to look up from what she was doing even though she could feel him looking at her. The touch of his gaze on her felt like someone was tracing fingertips over her skin, even after he left the room.

Chapter 2

RAJ LINGERED for a moment outside the medical room before he left, some part of him hoping that he might hear the voice of the unnamed nurse—*his mate*—before he had to go and face the follow-up of the fight. Face the congratulations and the unwanted advice on how he could have done better, the spectators who wanted a piece of the winner of the night's biggest bout. Face Olivia, whom he'd been so thrilled about at the start of the night but now could barely bring himself to think of. The idea of another woman's hands on his skin was suddenly borderline painful. All he wanted was *her*. So, he loitered outside the door for a moment, just waiting, hoping to hear her speak.

He got his wish when he heard her say, "Are you seriously planning on continuing this, Jeremy?"

So that's Doc's real name, he thought distantly as awareness prickled his skin just from the sound of her voice.

"Tonight was busier than usual," came Doc's reply, sounding defensive. "That last match was the only one that came with major injuries. The rest were like I described to you—minor breaks, some bruising. Noses, fingers."

"That Professor guy had a fracture in his *spine!*" his girl-friend protested.

"Well, I didn't know the Librarian was fighting tonight," Doc replied. "Maybe we can organise things so you don't have to come on nights when he's on the list. No one else causes the kinds of injuries he does. If that's what you're worried about, we could try to organise it that way."

"I don't care if he's on the list," she snapped.

Gods, she was fierce. Despite being so small, he could probably pick her up with one hand. Suddenly, he was gripped by a desire to lift her smaller body over his and watch as she rode him, to lift her into the air so she wrapped her legs around his waist and fuck her against a wall, hard and rough. The shift of his eyes to pure lupine silver, which he'd been fighting the entire time he was in the medical room, surrounded by her scent, happened almost instantly. Blood started to rush to his cock, and he dug his fingers into one of the hidden, unhealed bruises on his thigh in an attempt to stop himself from getting a full-on erection.

"I don't care if one particular guy is on the list on one particular night," she was saying inside the room. "Did you see him fight? That guy is an *animal.* I've never seen someone go that... that savage. You saw what he did to the Professor's face. He could have killed the guy if the bell hadn't rung. And he was enjoying it."

"I thought you didn't care about one particular guy," Doc said.

"I don't," his mate snapped back. "I'm just saying this guy turned totally brutal, and everyone here was fucking loving it. They were cheering him on while he was literally punching the other guy in the face until his bones broke. He broke his own *fingers* with how hard he was hitting the Professor, and he was smiling the whole time, and every single gods-damned person in the stands was just cheering them on.

This place is so bloodthirsty, and they don't care who gets hurt."

"Maggie—" Doc started in a placating tone. Raj felt a shiver run through his body at the knowledge of her name. The piece of her he could now carry with him.

"Don't use that tone with me," she snapped. "I'm not some hysterical patient for you to calm down. I think this place is disgusting, and if you choose to continue working here, that's your business, but this isn't why I became a nurse, Jeremy. You can do your own thing with this place, but I am never coming back."

Never coming back? So, he'd never see her here again? How the hell was he supposed to speak to her, let her know that she was his mate? Convince her to see him again outside the Ring? Suddenly, his mind was whirling through ways to properly meet her, talk to her, disrupt this image she had of him as a brutal savage who revelled in other people's pain—though to be fair, that was the image he projected at the Ring—and make her see him as someone to get close to immediately and fall in love with as soon as possible. That's what being someone's mate was supposed to mean, right? Della, his friend Leo's mate, wasn't a werewolf, but she'd talked about the absurdly strong connection she'd felt to Leo and how quickly feelings had entered the game. It would be the same with him and Maggie, surely, as long as he could get close to her, and talk to her, and—

"Raj?" It was Olivia's voice coming down the hallway, and his head snapped around. He urgently dug his fingers into his thigh once more, wincing at the pressure on the bone-deep bruise, but felt his eyes begin to shift back to normal from the painful stimulus. A little bit of silver was fine, but he couldn't face Olivia with completely shifted eyes without having an explanation. An explanation he didn't have right now, not in a way that wouldn't hurt her, and he didn't want that. He didn't want to just announce out of nowhere that he'd found his mate so he couldn't see her anymore. Thanks for your time, have a nice life. He had to be more diplomatic than that—and despite his relatively new political position within the pack, pretty words had never been Raj's strong suit.

Olivia rounded the corner in the corridor and smiled when she saw him. She was beautiful, that was undeniable, blonde-haired and blue-eyed with curves in all the right places, a stunning smile. But even as gorgeous as he could still objectively admit that she was, Olivia suddenly looked all wrong. She should be small and feisty, with curly dark hair, not this golden-haired Amazon.

He walked down the hall towards her anyway, fearing that Maggie and Doc would hear it if they started talking right outside the door to the medical room.

"That was a hell of a fight!" Olivia said, reaching up to kiss him on the cheek. He almost forgot to lean down so she could reach the way he usually did. She took a step back and surveyed him. "And that doctor guy really got rid of pretty much all your injuries. That's an efficient way to do it. Make sure nobody has reason to ask any questions," she added with a cheeky grin.

"Well, I can't exactly go to the library looking like I've just been punched in the face," Raj said, trying to inject his usual good humour into his tone. "Even if, you know, I have been."

Olivia smiled up at him. "I've seen a million training fights and things, but that was on another level. I've never seen anything like it." She took his hand and squeezed it, and he made himself squeeze back. "You're a machine, honey," she added.

He forced himself to laugh. "Thanks. Years and years of practice, you know?"

"So, what's next?" Olivia asked.

"I have to go and get changed," Raj said. His voice sounded slightly dull even to his own ears, but Olivia didn't seem to notice. It was like she was riding the high of his win for him, while he couldn't get his mind off the woman he'd left in the room with the doctor. Being in such a small space with her and her incredible scent had been driving him so crazy even the pain of having his bones healed hadn't been enough to stop his eyes partially shifting. Shouldn't he be feeling some sort of rush of having found his mate? Some sort of endorphin high or adrenaline kick? Instead, he just felt empty because he'd had to walk away from her. Because he couldn't go back and sweep her off her feet like his instincts were telling him to do, like one of the men in the books he read would have done. That wasn't real life, he told himself. He had to find a reasonable way to do this. And if the universe had given him this woman as his mate, surely, it would find a way for the two of them to find each other after this. It wouldn't be so cruel as to give him a brief glimpse of her, then never allow him the opportunity to even try to be with her.

Or maybe it could. He'd dealt with the universe's cruelties before, as a foster child unwanted by family after family... But even then, the universe had provided, hadn't it? He'd found his family and his pack. Maybe the universe would help him find *her* too.

He swung into the large changeroom in the "backstage" section of the facility, Olivia still holding his hand. There were plenty of fighters now changing into their street clothes, checking in with trainers or even just sitting around chatting, even those who had fought each other tonight now swapping notes on technique and what had brought the winner to his victory. There was still an undercurrent of danger, as though one of these apparently friendly people might turn savage at any moment, shift into their wolf forms and start howling, but overall, the changerooms were a not-unfriendly place once the fights had been played out. He'd liked to have shown it to his mate, he thought, and let her see that the Ring wasn't all grim brutality and shattering bones.

Olivia clung to him as he moved through the fighters, accepting a few congratulations and more than a few dark stares. Of course, she noticed those more than anything else.

"Why are they looking at you like that?" she asked when they were standing beside his locker on the far side of the room. He'd chosen this one because it was farther away from the central area where the fighters tended to congregate, though that did mean he'd had a few brave souls try to play out the high school trope of beating up the loner in the locker room. Just a few months ago, it had happened again, a new guy looking to prove himself, and to Raj's shame, the other guy had got in enough hits that Raj himself had come home with a black eye he'd had to explain to his friends as a training injury. Of course, his assailant had had to be assisted to even be able to walk after Raj was done with him, so a black eye hadn't been too heavy a price to pay.

"They don't like me much," Raj said distantly as he collected his clothes.

"Why not? They seem to like each other well enough, even the ones who were fighting a few hours ago."

"I don't have much to do with them," he explained. "Prefer to keep to myself around here. Plus, you know, I've beaten a bunch of them up."

"They've beaten each other too, and that doesn't seem to be an issue," Olivia pressed.

"I'm just not really one of them," he said, closing the locker door. He was about to pull his shirt over his head when a tap came on his shoulder, and he turned to see the Professor standing behind him. He could feel the other fighters watching them. Raj braced himself for an attempt to recreate the fight they'd just had, immediately thinking through how best to shield Olivia when she was standing so close, but the man just shot him a wide grin. "Good fight, man."

Raj blinked, then relaxed ever so slightly. "Yeah, you, too. You can take a punch like nothing else."

"Years of practice," the Professor joked. "You've gotta teach me how to put that much weight behind a swing, though. And the wrestling? You have skills."

"Thanks," Raj said awkwardly after a beat.

"And this must be Mrs Librarian," he continued, giving Olivia a smile of his own.

She grinned broadly and laughed. "I think the Mrs part is a while off, but yeah, I'm the girlfriend. How are you feeling?" That was Olivia for you—she could hold up a conversation with a brick wall, and the wall would enjoy it.

"A lot better than I was before I saw Doc," the Professor joked. "That guy is a miracle worker."

"Is he here every time you guys fight?" Olivia asked.

"Yep. If he can't make it, the fights get postponed. He's healed just about every injury I've ever got in the Ring. Is this your first time here?"

"It sure is," she said with another winning smile. "It's pretty impressive. Maybe I'll get to come to the next one too."

"You'd better hang on to this one," the man told Raj. "Most women would have run screaming after seeing their man fight like that."

"Well, I'm not most women," Olivia said, arching an eyebrow. "I've seen the fights in our pack, so I'm used to a bit of savagery," she continued, looking over at Raj with a grin. "Bareknuckle fighting has nothing on claws and teeth."

The Professor shot Raj a look like they shared a secret or

something. Raj pulled his shirt over his head to pretend he hadn't seen the look.

"You have a good one, both of you," the Professor said, then clapped Raj on the shoulder. "And thanks for a hell of a fight."

As he walked away, the rest of the fighters who had been watching their interaction found other things to take their interest. A few kept looking at Raj and Olivia as Raj pulled a pair of track pants over the shorts he wore to fight in and shoved his feet into his shoes.

"He seemed nice enough," Olivia said.

"Yeah, when he isn't trying to put his fist through my skull and out the other side," Raj muttered.

"Hey, don't be like that," she said, a little reproachfully. "He was just trying to be friendly."

"I don't like to get friendly with the other guys here," Raj said quietly, knowing full well that some of them would still be listening. "It only comes back and bites you in the ass."

She gave him a confused look, but seemed to realise he didn't want to continue the conversation in this setting, and stayed silent as he collected the rest of his things.

They left the Ring through a crowd of lagging supporters who sent up cheers when they saw Raj coming. He was delayed by the occasional person who wanted to wish him congratulations, thank him for winning them money, or give him unwanted and unwarranted advice on how to win faster next time. He greeted them all with the same plastic smile and pre-prepared phrases and left every conversation as quickly as possible.

It was strange how, before a fight, when he had the energy of his wolf swirling in his blood and preparing him for the pain, the Ring felt strangely like home, or at least like a place he belonged. In contrast, after a fight and the usual messing around with healing and the other fighters, all he wanted was to get home and shower the place off his skin. He had no wish to talk to all these people, to be lauded as though his fight had been a choreographed performance for their enjoyment. He didn't want to be some kind of minor celebrity within the Ring. He just wanted to go home and get clean of the evidence of the bloodthirstiness that he knew still lurked inside him, despite Doc magically cleaning him of the bruises that had marred his skin.

When they finally got to the door, they had to go through the procedure of leaving; you couldn't have hundreds of people flooding out of a half-built construction site that was too small to hold them, or people would start to take notice. Many of the spectators were milling around, waiting to be allowed out in small groups. As one of the fighters, Raj took priority over the spectators, so he and Olivia were quickly shunted to the front of the line, where they waited at the discretion of the bouncers to be ushered out the door. One of the bouncers, Brian, punched Raj in the shoulder approvingly, and the other, Al, shot him a grin, opening the door for them. He'd made a point of getting to know them when he first started fighting at the Ring, and they'd clearly seen his victory tonight. They ushered Raj and Olivia out into the alleyway behind the building and they quickly moved towards where Raj had parked his car.

He almost asked if she wanted to be dropped home, but when they'd planned for the night, they'd decided for the two of them to spend the night together afterwards. *Resettling*, she'd called it, even though she'd insisted she wouldn't have any issue seeing the fighting or even seeing Raj himself tonight in the Ring. *Just fitting ourselves back together again now that I will have seen you in this setting.* Just the idea of having her in his bed, made him want to flinch away now that he had the memory of his mate—*Maggie*—in his head. The idea that Olivia might try to touch him, the way they had every other night she'd slept at his house... well, even the thought of it felt like a violation.

So, this was what Leo and Emmett had meant when they talked about their mating bonds.

Maybe it would be kinder for him to have this inevitable conversation with Olivia tonight. He could reveal that he'd caught the scent of his mate in the Ring and explain that he couldn't be with Olivia anymore, because it would be unfair to both of them to stay together when he constantly had another female in his head. He couldn't be with her when he was actively trying to find Maggie, wherever she was in Mystic City. Even if—gods forbid—he never found her, it was out of the question not to let Olivia know that they couldn't be together anymore. Surely, that was the best way to go about it. Raj wasn't known for being good with serious conversations; when things got tense, he tended to automatically start making jokes in an attempt to lighten the mood, which often didn't go down well. If he could mentally write himself something of a script that he could follow, though, he'd hopefully be able to break up with Olivia without completely fucking it up.

He was just summoning up the courage to ask if they could talk about something serious as they got to his house when she yawned widely. "I'm so tired," she said quietly, as though she was half-trying not to break his moment of silent contemplation. "That was pretty intense. I think the adrenaline rush might be starting to fade. I might go straight to bed when we get to your place."

"That sounds like a great plan," Raj said, half-disappointed that he couldn't get this uncomfortable discussion over with, and half-relieved by the reprieve from having to talk about his feelings, which was another thing he'd never been good at.

"No offence, but I think you might need a shower first,"

she said, laying her hand on his thigh as he continued to drive. It was a completely non-sexual movement, just offering closeness, but he still had to catch himself to avoid flinching away from her touch.

"Oh, definitely," Raj said in what sounded to his own ears like a poor imitation of his usual cheerful tone. "You don't fight like that then go straight to bed unless you want to throw out the sheets the next morning. And maybe the mattress."

There was a short pause as he turned into Blue Crescent Pack territory. The sense of homecoming that always came to him the moment he crossed the territory line was power-ful, but this time, it hardly touched the other emotions that had been roiling through him since the moment he'd caught the scent of his mate.

"Are you all right, Raj?" Olivia asked quietly. It seemed she was more observant than he'd given her credit for, or maybe he was just doing a crappy job of hiding what he was feeling.

"I'm fine," he lied. "The fight really took it out of me, and I-I don't love being in that place afterwards. So, I'm pretty worn out too."

"Why don't you like being there?" she asked.

"No more fighting to do, so what's the point of being there?" Raj said with a somewhat forced half-laugh, before turning serious. If he was planning on breaking up with her in the morning, surely, he owed her at least a bit of honesty now. "I don't know. Especially since we got Petra out of that underground cavern with the vampires, the whole place— being underground again in a space designed for spilling blood—just kind of makes me feel dirty. I don't notice it before the fights, I think because I'm jazzed up and full of adrenaline, but afterwards, it hits me. Most of the guys who fight there do it because they need the money to survive, and even if they didn't have Doc sending them home no worse than they came in, they'd still do it and deal with the injuries. It's just... brutal. Bloodthirsty," he added, thinking of what he'd heard his mate say when he left the medical room.

"And you're not?" Olivia asked with a laugh. "Raj, I saw what you did to that guy. You beat the shit out of him, and you were smiling the whole time!"

"Fair point," Raj said, even though he wasn't sure if it was, and more than that, whether he wanted it to be.

"I mean, you keep going back there. Why would you do that if you weren't a little bloodthirsty?" she asked.

Raj had no answer for her. How could he explain to someone who'd never felt it, the draw of the transformation from someone fumbling through learning to be a Beta with no relevant experience, into the unbeatable Librarian, who could be as brutal as he wanted? "Maybe you're right." He let the silence between them rise again for the short moment until he had pulled into the driveway of his house.

Olivia was clearly flagging as they entered, yawning what seemed like every ten seconds, but still, she climbed on to the bottom step of the stairwell to kiss him the way they had done every night they spent there since the first time they kissed, in that exact position. Raj's brain frantically spun into overdrive as he tried to think of a reason not to do it tonight, but she was already pulling him in and pressing her lips to his. The wrongness of it washed through him with the force of a tsunami, but he forced himself to kiss her back gently—not doing it would start that conversation about his having found his mate, and she was clearly too tired for him to put her through that now. So while it wasn't really fair to kiss her with his mind on someone else—someone small and feisty, with curly dark hair and hands that would feel perfect on his skin and a lush pink mouth that he wanted to be kissing right now instead of his still-somehow-girlfriend's—surely, it would be crueller to put her in a position where she had to hear the breakup spiel he was already mapping out in his head, when she was already exhausted. He'd do it in the morning, over coffee, when they could both be reasonable and explain their feelings. So, for now, he gave her a quick kiss, then looked down at himself.

"I've got to get in the shower," he said, as if explaining the brevity.

"Good plan," Olivia said, smiling softly. She turned and headed up the stairs, calling out over her shoulder, "I'll see you in bed, then."

At first, he'd loved how quickly she became comfortable in his space, loved that when he offered her the option of keeping a few clothes and a toothbrush there, she had given him one of her gorgeous ear-to-ear smiles and kissed him so hard, they'd wound up in the very bed she was heading for now. Had it really been so recent? Suddenly, it felt like years ago—everything that had happened before he saw his mate felt as though it had happened to another man. He'd been incomplete before, though he hadn't been aware of it, and finding his match, finding Maggie, even though he'd barely even spoken to her, and she'd said only two words to him —*you're welcome*—felt like it had caused some seismic shift inside him, rearranging him, until his greatest priority was… her.

Realising he was standing at the bottom of the stairs, staring into space, he stomped upstairs and threw himself into the shower, scrubbing his face and body until his skin was raw and he finally felt clean of the brutal version of himself that he'd become tonight, clean of the Ring and everyone in it. Werewolf healing meant the harsh cleaning only stung underneath the touch of the water for a brief moment, but he stood there until it started to go cold.

He tried to convince himself he wasn't imagining

Maggie's small body naked and warm against him, but his swollen cock told the truth of the situation. He'd never been with someone as small as her; werewolf females tended to be taller than average, and though he hadn't exclusively dated his own kind in the past, they were a clear majority. Would he have to be gentle with her, careful in the way he touched her, to make sure he didn't damage her? Despite those thoughts, the picture his mind produced had very little of gentleness in it. In his thoughts, the moment they entered the house, he would put her on her hands and knees on the stairs and fuck her from behind like he was trying to put them both through the staircase. He imagined her ass bouncing as he thrust into her, and suddenly, his dick was so hard, it hurt. With a curse, he turned the cold water back on—he could hardly get into bed with Olivia with an erection from thinking of someone else, even if he was planning on ending their relationship in the morning. If there was one thing that the books he read had taught him, it was that gentleness and respect were the way to go with females. Climbing into the same bed as the woman you were planning on ending things with, with your dick as hard as steel, was not a situation that would go down well in any scenario.

He had to find Maggie. Suddenly, that had become more important to him than almost anything. Somehow, he had to track her down and explain to her what was going on, what was destined to happen between them. Even if he had to go through every Maggie in the phone book, one by one, just to compare their voices to hers, he'd find her.

Olivia was already asleep when he climbed into bed, and he'd have been lying if he said he wasn't relieved by that fact. She liked to cuddle when the two of them were falling asleep, and he wasn't sure he could have handled her body pressed up against his tonight. He shuffled as close to the edge of the bed as he could and tried not to picture a very different scenario featuring his hands tangled in the hair of a small human woman as he held her as close to his body as two people could get. She had a prickly attitude, his mate—he'd seen that much tonight—but in his mind, after he'd pleasured her body into exhaustion, she'd be soft and sweet and curl in close to him just for the pleasure of feeling his skin on hers.

Just the thought of having her so close, worn out because he'd taken her so many times, had his blood pounding through his body like he was about to start another fight. He was never going to get to sleep like this.

With a sigh, Raj went back to the bathroom and took another cold shower.

In the morning, he woke to find Olivia gone from the bed. Again, part of him was relieved, because it meant he wouldn't have to find an excuse not to start their day with intimacy when, in truth, the idea of having any woman other than his mate touching him made him nauseous. He pulled on what he thought of as his Librarian uniform—trousers and a button-down shirt with the sleeves rolled up, the formality an attempt to look more like a staff member than a brawler who'd accidentally wandered into the library—and went downstairs. Olivia was sitting at the table with her breakfast and the day's newspaper.

"You're up early," he commented.

Olivia started slightly at the sound of his voice but gave him a warm smile. "I woke up and couldn't get back to sleep. How are you feeling after last night?"

"Right as rain," Raj said, pouring himself some coffee from the pot she'd made. "The doctor there is a great healer."

"You still had some bruises left after he was done," she commented.

"I don't tend to get all of them healed unless they're visible when I'm working or training," Raj said. "I came by them honestly, so I figure it's good form to keep them until I've healed them myself."

Olivia's brow creased like she was trying to work out a complex math problem. "That seems... unnecessarily masochistic."

"It's not because I enjoy having bruises," Raj said, wondering if he could find a better way to explain it. "They're a real pain, actually, no pun intended. It's just that I've been in a fight, and I made the choice to get in that fight knowing I'd probably come out of it worse for wear, and it feels like cheating to immediately have someone get me out of the consequences of it."

She shrugged, then drained the last of her own coffee. "It's your body, I guess." A smile took what could have been an insult out of her words. "I should probably get going. I need to pick up some stuff from home before I go to work."

Raj, who had been psyching himself up to tell her about finding his mate last night, felt the wind drain out of his sails. "Do you have a couple of minutes? There's something I wanted to talk to you about." The words felt hopelessly inadequate for what he was about to do.

Olivia's smile was unworried, like they shared some kind of secret, and his words had been an indication that he wanted to discuss it. "Can it wait? If I'm late again, my boss is going to get upset. We have that thing on Saturday. I could come over beforehand and we can talk." Without waiting for a response, she kissed his cheek and collected the handbag he hadn't noticed she'd already prepped to leave. "See you soon, hon." The door had closed behind her before he had time to collect himself enough to reply, let alone tell her they needed to break up because he'd found his mate.

This was not going to be a pleasant conversation. In fact, he was kind of dreading the whole thing. He wanted to plan it out, plot the way it would go as though he was drawing a map, but that would rely on her replying to things exactly as he anticipated, and obviously, that was unlikely. These were the situations that made him the most uncomfortable, the ones where he didn't know what was going to happen and couldn't plan out his responses so that he at least felt like he'd practiced slightly. Raj wasn't always the best with social situations, he knew that—he'd always been the big, slightly awkward, kind of silly one who made bad jokes to lighten the tension when things got serious. But that approach wouldn't work when he was telling this completely faultless woman that he had to break up with her because the universe had delivered one of the few things he'd held on to wanting since he was a pup.

He'd been the one out of his best friends who had clung to the idea of there being mates out there for them. When Leo had explained the feelings that he was experiencing towards Della, whom he had only met once, Raj had insisted it was because his friend had found his mate. The same had been true with Emmett and Petra. And now, it was his turn. Finally, there would be someone in the world who was just meant for *him*.

He just had to find her.

Chapter 3

IN TRUTH, Maggie wasn't much of one for parties. At least, not parties like this, where she didn't know many people and had to keep having the same conversation over and over. *How do you know Leo and Della/Wasn't it romantic how they got together/Isn't it amazing that he's the new Alpha/Isn't the work she does with the Council incredible?* She might as well have had her responses to each of the repeated questions tattooed on her forehead after the ninth or tenth run-through. If it had been a gathering of just her friends, it would have been different— despite her small size, she could drink with the best of them, loved a night at the pub with her close friends, and she had a bunch of people that she hadn't been able to see much since she started taking on more night shifts at the hospital. If it had been them at the party, she would have been having a ball. Instead, she was just starting to feel like a token human invited to balance out the group consisting of mostly witches and werewolves, even though, logically, she knew Della would never do that to her.

She'd been sitting with the few other humans invited from Della's workplace, with whom she didn't actually have a huge amount in common, but they'd kind of gravitated together after conversation with the larger group turned to the interrelationships between werewolf packs, and the precedent Leo was setting in Blue Crescent, the pack he now led, by having a partner who wasn't one of them. Apparently, their old Alpha, the one Leo and Della had defeated in the fight for Leo's leadership, had been kind of... well, racist wasn't quite the right word, but he had fought to keep anyone who wasn't a Blue Crescent werewolf from even setting foot in Pack territory. Emmett, one of Leo's two Betas —another new development, since most Alphas had only one—had also broken the old rules by finding his mate in a werewolf from a different pack. According to the gossip, Emmett's mate, a wolf with whom Della worked named Petra, was from the next pack over and had been kidnapped by a rogue vampire coven during their courtship, in an effort to cut off her work in interspecies integration. The group— Leo, Della, Emmett, their other best friend and Leo's other Beta, Raj, and Petra's sister, Francesca—had managed to save her from the vampires, and she had thankfully made it to the hospital in time to be magically healed from the wolfsbane with which they had dosed her, preventing what would have been a slow and painful death.

Honestly, these people had the most ridiculously complicated lives.

That didn't seem to stop them from having fun, though. According to Della, the Blue Crescent wolves seemed to almost universally admire Leo for kicking their unpopular former Alpha, James, out of the top job, but there was a degree of fear left over from the days when James had used Leo as his enforcer. Since he'd been Beta at that time, Leo had had no choice but to carry out the violent orders James had given him, and the Blue Crescent wolves hadn't forgotten that. These semi-regular gatherings at Leo and

Della's house were part of the way they were trying to help the pack see Leo as one of them, as much as respecting him as their leader, and showing them that he planned on being a very different Alpha than James had been.

Maggie would have considered leaving the party after the fifth or sixth near-identical conversation—which, after they'd exhausted the Leo-and-Della chat, almost always descended straight into a discussion of what she did for work and how great it was because nurses were *so* wonderful and *so* important—but she'd missed all the gatherings Leo and Della had thrown so far, including their housewarming, because of work. Della was so keen for Maggie to get to know the new friends she'd made since becoming mated to a werewolf that she'd gone so far as to request to see Maggie's work roster, so that this event could be scheduled at a time when Maggie would certainly be able to attend. So, Maggie stayed, even though she'd managed to exchange a total of two sentences with Della upon her arrival before the witch was engulfed by the larger group that Maggie herself had chosen to break away from. For a pack that had had a reputation for being very wary of outsiders, the Blue Crescent wolves certainly seemed to have taken to her friend. Della was constantly surrounded by people, both those Maggie knew were Della's own friends as well as Leo's werewolves. If she hadn't looked so happy at the integration of the two groups, Maggie would have tried to wade in and save her introverted friend from the constant interaction.

She sighed, looked down at her empty drink and excused herself from the somewhat boring conversation the human group was having, to grab another. Growing up in Mystic City, surrounded by schoolmates who could do magic or shift form at the drop of a hat, it had been hard not to feel like the most boring person in the room, but she'd thought she'd gotten over that feeling years ago. The flip side to growing up as a human surrounded by supernaturals was that, eventually, their magical capabilities did become somewhat commonplace. Humans in Mystic City still outnumbered supernaturals, after all, and even in professions like hers that were full of those who could heal magically, there were more humans than witches. She still sometimes wished she had the healing abilities of some of her colleagues, not to mention their ability to flick a finger and complete half a dozen menial tasks that she had to do by hand, but the jealousy no longer burned, the way it had when she was younger. Today, though, sitting in the corner of the party with her non-magical fellows, she kind of felt like the nerd at the popular kids' party. Even though she'd chosen to remove herself from the conversation she felt like she couldn't really contribute to, it was still a bit disappointing to be once again on the outside of magical discussions, the way she'd had to fight so hard not to be in her role at the hospital.

She collected the new drink and went to stand in a patch of fading sunlight over by the fence, enjoying the warmth on her skin. She had a cardigan in the bag she'd left inside, but she didn't really want to wade through the crowd to go and collect it. It was fortunate Leo and Della had a big garden, because more people were still arriving, enough that their little human enclave might eventually be absorbed back into the group purely due to lack of space. That would probably be a good thing, she thought idly, rather than allowing them to be separated by species. The witches and werewolves seemed to be integrating pretty well, judging by the talk and laughter that emanated from the groups, and they no longer seemed to be discussing purely supernatural topics. Why shouldn't the humans be involved too? Was it just that they were intimidated by being in a group where they were so outnumbered by supernaturals, as opposed to the normal way of things, where humans were the most numerous?

With that somewhat sobering thought in mind, Maggie left her patch of sunlight and went to find Della. She'd come to the party for her friend, after all; it would be wrong not to actually try to speak to her, even if it was just for a short time. Then, she decided, she'd make a real effort to talk to some of the other attendees, and maybe even make a friend or two. Then, and only then, would she allow herself to go home. Jeremy had raised the possibility of swinging by her place after he finished his shift if she wasn't out too late, so she could call him once she got back to her house and see if he was still interested in coming over.

Della was in the middle of a mixed group of witches and werewolves who were talking about some politician who had been called out for wearing a questionable Halloween costume some twenty years previously. She caught sight of Maggie and crowed, "Mags!" slightly tipsily before beckoning her in, and introduced her to each of the people in the circle, whose names Maggie immediately felt slipping out of her mind. She smiled at each of them and tried her best to contribute to the conversation—she knew about the incident; after all, there was a lot of time to sit and watch the news when you were on night shifts.

She was vaguely aware of the raucous greeting that one of the new arrivals had triggered as it happened but was a little caught up in the argument between two of her new acquaintances about whether making or promoting a racist comment meant you were a racist person. It was a few minutes before she could see over to who had engendered this response from the crowd, and by that point, whoever it was had been absorbed by the flow of people. She turned her attention back to the two people now arguing about whether the white privilege of one of them influenced his perception of what he thought could be called an acceptable mistake, and then she felt it. Like fingers running down her spine, the shiver rolled through her. It was like the feeling that someone was looking at her, but multiplied by a hundred, the sense of a feather-light touch caressing her skin somewhere between unsettling and... arousing?

Glad that she hadn't participated in the conversation enough that she'd need to explain this move, she pivoted in her chair, scanning across the people by the barbecue, the small human-only collective that she'd left, the werewolf gathering that she was pretty sure was comparing bicep size... and then she saw him.

The Librarian.

He was here.

And he was staring at her like he'd never seen a human before.

She jolted to her feet like a rocket had been set off underneath her, and fortunately, Della was standing at the same time so, to a casual observer, it might have just looked like she was standing up as her friend was doing.

"Oh, you don't have to come with me," Della said with the gorgeous smile that surely won Leo's heart. "I'm just going to say hi to Raj."

Raj. His name cemented itself in her memory the way the name of every other person she'd been introduced to tonight had failed to do. *Raj.* She'd heard Della talking about Raj, one of Leo's trio of best friends. She'd had a picture in her head of a fairly normal-looking guy, since all Della had ever really talked about was his role as the joker of the group; she'd presumed that only the sense of humour that Della spoke of with laughter and fondness was his defining factor. She hadn't pictured this Mr Universe candidate the size of the Eiffel Tower, with muscles on his muscles and a smile that could have stopped a moving vehicle. A smile that he was now directing towards her, as she found herself saying to Della, "No, I'll come with you. I might as well meet some more new people."

Della, who had been trying to integrate Maggie into her newly acquired group of friends since she met Leo, and been foiled almost entirely by Maggie's work roster, was thrilled by this suggestion. She paused before they got close to where the Librarian—*Raj*—was greeting Leo.

"You'll love Raj," Della said. "He's so much fun. He might look a bit intimidating, but honestly, he's a big softie."

Clearly, Della hadn't seen him beat a man halfway to death. Though if Maggie remembered right, wasn't it Raj whom Della had gone up against in the fight for Leo's leadership? Her respect for Della for winning that fight skyrocketed now that she'd seen Raj in that match in the Ring. She knew the story—Della, already half-exhausted by defending the border of the Apex River pack territory, had somehow summoned the enormous amount of power required to pull the energy from Raj's body into her own, where she needed to use even *more* power to destroy it, and almost burnt herself out in the process. She'd been admitted to St Philippa's Hospital, where Maggie worked. Fortunately, Maggie had been able to see her friend before she'd been released into Leo's care. From what Della had told her, that care had bordered on obsessive, with her friend's werewolf mate refusing to allow her to do things as simple as filling her own glass of water when she was thirsty. The new couple had argued over it several times, but in the end, Della had gone back to work exactly as she'd intended and, Maggie presumed, Leo had learnt to live with the repercussions of being bonded to a highly independent, incredibly powerful witch.

Della ran up to Raj without a hint of hesitation, pulling him into a hug and patting him on the back like the man was an oversized puppy.

"Mags, come and meet Raj!" she called over her shoulder.

Maggie had no choice. She walked forwards, fixing the closest thing she could muster to a smile onto her face. Unfortunately, the first words that left her mouth, entirely without the permission of her brain, were, "You're the Librarian."

"So, you *have* been listening when I talked about these guys," Della teased. "Yeah, Raj is a librarian, and he's just got a new job—very exciting!" She bumped him with her hip, but the man was so solid, he barely even seemed to notice.

"And you're the nurse," Raj said, his voice as deep as the Marianas Trench, as though Della hadn't even spoken. His eyes were fixed on Maggie's, his gaze penetrating her like a blade. She couldn't look away. She was trapped by his attention, and despite her best efforts, the focus of this magnificent specimen of masculinity was sending her own attention to places she didn't necessarily want it, in a crowd of people she didn't know. She was suddenly painfully conscious of her body, the dress she'd chosen, because it outlined her somewhat limited curves, her awareness inexplicably drawn to the press of her nipples against the lace of her bra and the sudden heat between her legs, and still, she couldn't pull her eyes away from his.

"Yes, I'm a nurse," she managed to confirm, as though she hadn't just been trapped in this man's attention like she'd been glued to the ground.

"That must have taken a lot of study," Raj, the Librarian said, sounding like he was working as hard as she was at keeping the conversation sounding close to what would normally take place between two people who had just met.

"It was worth it," Maggie replied quietly. "I get to help people."

"How come I haven't seen you at one of these things before?" he asked. "Della talks about you all the time. It sounds like you two are very close."

"I work a lot," Maggie said. "It doesn't always leave time for social commitments."

"Too many night shifts," Della said cheerfully. Her words seemed to remind both of them that she was still there, because Maggie saw Raj's eyes widen and snap to the witch just as her own did. "Didn't I say you should ask to be changed to working during the day more? Then you could come and hang out with us, not to mention it'd be safer travelling through the city." Her brow creased slightly. "I need to redo those protection spells on you soon, by the way."

"Why do you need protection spells?" Raj asked. He seemed to have swelled even larger at the suggestion that she might be threatened by something.

"Maggie doesn't drive," Della explained somewhat wearily. It was a discussion they'd had plenty of times before. "So, she finishes her shifts early in the morning and gets public transport home."

"Sometimes, I walk," Maggie said, purely to rile her friend. "I don't need to drive. I live fairly close to the hospital, and for anything farther away, there's public transport or a taxi." She raised the bottle in her hand, grinning at Della, who was rolling her eyes. "It means I never get asked to be the designated driver."

"Do you live alone?" Raj asked unexpectedly.

Maggie blinked at him for a moment before answering the odd question. "Um… yes?"

"So, no one would know if something happened to you, and you didn't get home safely."

This time, it was Maggie rolling her eyes and Della laughing. "You're not going to convince her, Raj. I've been trying for years, and she just doesn't want to learn to drive."

"I don't feel like I need to," Maggie said. "Cars are expensive, and I have no great need for one. Why would I bother when I can get everywhere I need without one?"

"It might be a good skill to have," Raj said. "Just in case you need it sometime."

"What, to drive a getaway car?" Maggie laughed. "I'm not like you guys, saving people from vampire lairs. I'm just a regular human. I can't see any instance where I'd be in an emergency situation that required me to drive a car."

"It would be safer than walking through the city at night."

"That's why I have protection spells on me," Maggie said sharply. Why was this guy so invested in her capacity to drive? She turned to Della. "Do you want to have a look at that roster I sent you and work out when's a good time for you to redo them?"

Della sent her a delighted smile. Normally, it was hard for them to find a time that was convenient for them both to work through the renewal process for the spells—Maggie with her convoluted and often-changing roster, and Della because she sat on the Witches' Council as well as working more than any single government employee should. Clearly, there was some benefit to this roster-sharing thing, Maggie thought. Maybe she should start doing it with her other close friends too. At least then, they might stop being disappointed when she announced, yet again, that she couldn't make it to whatever social event they were organising.

"That's a good idea," Della said, before something over Maggie's shoulder caught her eye. "Leo's trying to get my attention. I should probably go and see what he wants." The way her expression melted into a sweet, lovestruck smile when she talked about her boyfriend was one of the cutest things Maggie had ever seen. Della had been through a lot in her life—she was still sometimes recognised in the street from the news reports of the woman whose human boyfriend almost killed her in an attempt to reduce her powers—and seeing her so happy, so utterly in love, brought Maggie an indescribable amount of joy.

Unfortunately, this was tempered by the fact that she was now being left alone with this man she'd seen almost beat someone to death—but who, for some reason, she couldn't stop herself being fascinated by. He was looking at her again, in that way that made her feel his gaze like fingertips tracing over her skin, and after a long moment of looking at literally anything else in the vicinity to avoid making eye contact, she gave up and let her own gaze shift to meet his. Her breath caught in her throat, and she tried to stop the shock of her body's response from showing on her face, but wasn't sure she managed it. Just like in the medical room at the Ring, the moment their eyes met, it was like her concerns about him just... melted away. She could still see his savage grin as he pounded his fists into the Professor, sure, but there was also... more. It was like she was seeing into him, seeing the man for who he really was, beyond the savage face he'd shown those who paid to see him fight. The depth of him, the pain and pride and loneliness and love. And... she liked what she saw. More than liked it. Felt it echo like a siren song twinned to the beating of her own heart.

Especially when every single piece of it was focused on her.

She blinked herself out of her daze, unsure how long they'd been standing there staring at each other. "So, you really are a librarian?" she asked, for lack of anything else to say.

"Yeah," Raj said, finally looking away from her. "I made the mistake of mentioning it to someone there while they were trying to come up with a title for me, and they settled on that. I didn't really get a choice."

"It doesn't sound particularly threatening," Maggie said.

"I think they were just running out of professions they hadn't already allocated to someone as a title. The Ring's been going for a while now. There have been a lot of fighters. I think they've got to the point of just pulling something out of thin air, whether or not it applies. You didn't think the Professor was really an academic, did you?"

"He didn't exactly give off that vibe," Maggie admitted. "But then, I wouldn't have picked you for a librarian the other night, either."

He shrugged, full lips quirking upwards. "Some of the people at the library would agree with you. Until they need someone to put books on the high shelves, that is. Then I'm the most popular person in the building."

"I just can't picture you doing story time with children or something."

Raj shrugged again, looking more amused. "It's on Wednesday mornings. My week is next week if you want to come. Took some of the parents a while to trust me with their kids, but they're used to me now."

"I'd probably hesitate with a guy who looks like he belongs in a motorcycle club too, you know." Maggie bit her lip. As usual, her mouth had run away with her slightly, and she wasn't sure if that was going to be offensive to the big wolf.

Instead, Raj laughed. "What, the tats?"

"Well, that, and you're kind of massive," Maggie said, her mouth clearly still not under the control of her brain. Her own half-laugh echoed in her head. Was she... was she being flirty with this man?

"They're not motorcycle club tats," Raj said, grinning like he found the very concept ridiculous. He had a great smile, Maggie thought distantly. He held out his arm, and it took a moment before she realised that he was showing her the lines of script on the inside of his upper arm. She had to lean closer to read the cursive writing, and the proximity had her holding her breath before she realised she was doing it. *I have always imagined paradise will be a kind of library.*

"Is that a quote?" Maggie asked after a moment, trying to remember why the words sounded familiar.

He nodded. "Jorge Luis Borges. I don't have the names of my kills inscribed on my body. It's mostly just pictures I took a liking to, or quotes I like about books. There's a Dr Seuss one on my ribs."

"Dr Seuss?" she asked incredulously, almost laughing. "Seriously?"

"Seriously. From *Oh, The Places You'll Go.*"

"What does it say?" Maggie asked, intrigued despite herself.

He cleared his throat and fixed his gaze into the distance, as though he was about to perform a soliloquy for an audience in a theatre. He pressed a hand to his chest and put on a posh accent to recite, "'The more that you read, the more things you will know. The more that you learn, the more places you'll go.'"

Despite herself, Maggie felt her smile grow wider. "Why pick that one?"

His teasing expression dissolved into something she couldn't quite read, and she wondered what she'd said wrong. "Just struck a chord, I guess."

"There you are, honey." It was only at that moment that Maggie realised how close the two of them were standing as she examined the art on Raj's skin. She took a half step back, trying to make the move look natural, but unsure whether she managed it. The beautiful blonde who had joined them was exactly whom Maggie would have picked to be with someone like Raj. They were both fiercely attractive, but like two sides of the same coin, dark and light, savagery and gentleness. The woman tucked her arm through Raj's and fit into his side perfectly, but when she smiled up at him, the smile he sent her in return seemed slightly strained.

"Hi," the blonde said, turning to Maggie. "I'm Olivia. Blue Crescent pack. I'm Raj's girlfriend."

"Nice to meet you," Maggie managed in response. "I'm Maggie. I'm Della's friend."

"You look kind of familiar," Olivia said, tilting her head in a way that made it press against Raj's shoulder. Maggie was shocked by the spark of jealousy that kindled to life inside her. "Have we met before?"

If she hadn't been watching them so closely, she wouldn't have noticed the widening of Raj's eyes or the way he gave an infinitesimal shake of his head. *Oh*, so Olivia had been at the Ring that night—and for some reason, Raj didn't want her knowing that Maggie had too. Maybe he was right; after all, it was illegal. She probably shouldn't go around admitting her attendance to anyone who hadn't already worked out that she'd been there, even though Olivia herself had also been in attendance.

"I don't think so," Maggie said, wishing she was a better liar. "Unless you've been a patient at St Philippa's recently?"

Olivia's laugh was as beautiful as she was, and it made Maggie hate her just a little. Not just because she was gorgeous, and because everything *about* her was gorgeous, but because of the beautiful couple that she and Raj made.

What? Where had that thought come from? She didn't know this man—if anything, she should be *scared* of him. She'd seen what he'd done to the Professor that night, the pleasure he'd taken in inflicting pain. She'd watched him punch the guy so hard, he'd broken bones, both his and his opponent's. Why was she suddenly jealous of the woman who happened to be on his arm? Jealousy over Olivia's gorgeous silky hair and musical laugh would have been reasonable, but for her relationship with the Librarian? It made no sense for Maggie to be jealous of that.

"Not recently, no," Olivia was saying with a broad smile, completely oblivious to the thoughts rapidly unspooling in Maggie's mind. "Though I did get my appendix out there a few years ago. Would you maybe have been on one of the wards I was in then?" She added, "I'm presuming you're a doctor or a nurse. Correct me if I'm wrong."

"No, you're right, I'm a nurse," Maggie said. "I've worked all over the hospital over the years, so maybe we have run into each other before." She managed a smile to follow her words and was kind of proud of herself for it.

Olivia sent her another beautiful smile. "Well, it's lovely to meet you—again, maybe. I was just coming over to see if you wanted a drink," she added to Raj. "If you're done with that one, I can grab you one too, Maggie."

Maggie held up the bottle she'd forgotten was in her hand to demonstrate that it was still half full. "Thanks, but I'm good for now."

"A drink would be great," Raj said. "Thanks, Liv."

"No problem," she said and pressed a kiss to his cheek. To her horror, Maggie was suddenly profoundly aware of her own lips, as though something in her was longing for the right to be able to do what Olivia had.

There was a brief silence after she walked away, and again, Maggie found herself just looking at the man before her. In his well-worn jeans and blue button-down shirt, he was a far cry from the man she'd seen the other night. If it hadn't been for the tats, and of course, his size and the bulk of his muscles, she might even have said he looked like someone who could be a librarian.

"I didn't mean to tell you what to do," Raj said eventually. "What with, you know, not letting her know where she might have recognised you from. I just figured, the fewer people who know about that kind of thing, the better."

Though he hadn't been specific, they were both fully aware that they were talking about Maggie's presence at the Ring. He probably wasn't even doing it to protect her, she realised with something of a sense of disappointment. He was likely trying to stop Olivia from starting a conversation with a stranger about the illegal event they'd both attended. If Olivia wasn't a regular at the Ring, she might not be used to the required confidentiality of attending, especially if she'd only been there as a spectator. It was a leap of logic, but Maggie figured that those who had only been there to watch probably had less to lose in the event of the Ring being exposed than people like her and Raj, who had actually participated.

"I should go find Della," Maggie said finally.

"Maggie," Raj said, and his voice caressed the dual syllables of her name in a way that she'd never heard before, sending a completely unexpected bolt of heat through her body. She felt her eyes widen. Looking up at him, there was something like indecision on his face, like he was trying to work out how to tell her something he didn't know if she'd take well. Probably just a reminder to keep her mouth shut about the Ring, as though she didn't have a career that required confidentiality. Maggie was used to keeping the details of her patients to herself; she wasn't about to break that habit when it came to a secret of her own.

"I'll talk to you later," she blurted and darted off into the crowd.

Raj watched as Maggie walked away from him, slipping between groups until she was by Della's side again on the other side of the garden. The witch welcomed Maggie with an arm around her shoulders and introduced her to the man she was talking to, a werewolf from the Apex River pack that Emmett's partner Petra belonged to, Raj was pretty sure. As a relatively new Beta, he should probably be trying to make connections of his own with wolves from other packs, but the truth was he just couldn't summon up the energy. Not now, at least. Not tonight. Not while his mate was on one side of the garden, out of his reach and not seeming interested in coming back to him, and the woman he was dating was introducing herself as his girlfriend and bringing him drinks.

Most of the Blue Crescent pack was probably aware that Raj and Olivia were seeing each other; though the pack was large, gossip travelled fast, and Olivia had a lot of friends whom Raj didn't doubt—based partly on his own experience with women, and partly on what he'd read—she'd let know when the two of them had settled into something resembling a relationship. He'd been planning on talking to her about *the situation* today, before the party, but just as he'd been getting ready—he'd planned on sitting down together at the table so there was some distance between them, and he'd bought her favourite tea and some snacks that he knew she liked, hoping to make her comfortable and soften the blow somewhat— she'd called and apologetically let him know that a family issue had come up and she couldn't come over early. It had run even longer than she'd thought, so she'd rushed him out the door to get to the party as soon as she'd arrived at his house, apologising profusely and promising they'd have the conversation he'd asked for once they got home.

She didn't seem nearly as concerned as Raj would have been in her position, even cooing over the strawberry tarts he'd bought for her and swearing she'd eat them later. But she also didn't seem to have the faintest idea that the chat Raj kept asking for was going to be serious. Wasn't "we need to talk" supposed to be the most anxiety-inducing phrase in the English language for a woman in a relationship? And yet Olivia was cool as a cucumber and introducing herself as his girlfriend, as usual, behaving as though nothing could disrupt her unflappable, upbeat attitude. Her reliable positivity had been one of the things Raj liked about her in the beginning, but it was starting to grate on him a little bit, purely because *he* was so anxious about having this conversation.

She reappeared a moment later, with a drink for each of them, and gave him a wide smile. "Where did your friend go? Maggie, was it?"

"She needed to talk to Della about something." His words came out more curt than he'd intended, but Olivia didn't seem to notice.

"And you've just been standing here on your own?" she asked teasingly.

"Guess I just got caught up in my head," he said.

"For a change," she laughed, then tilted her own head to rest it against his shoulder. "You're okay, though, right?"

"Sure," Raj said, not sure if he was lying. "Fine. Just kind of tired."

She didn't seem to have heard his last sentence, because she crowed, "Look, Emmett and Petra just got here. I told you it wouldn't matter if we were a bit late."

"Well, they're always late," Raj said, glad the subject had changed. "I haven't managed to get Emmett to something on time since the two of them moved in together. I've started telling him anything time-sensitive Beta work starts half an hour before it really does, so he actually makes it before it begins."

"Well, you can't really blame them. When you live together, I guess it's easy to get distracted," Olivia said, giving him a smile like they shared a secret. *What was that about?* "I might go and say hi. Do you want to come?"

"You go ahead," Raj said. "I'll come over in a minute. Just need to..." He wasn't sure quite how he'd been intending to finish that sentence, but something in him objected to the idea of greeting one of his best friends with Olivia on his arm, like a couple, when he was planning on breaking up with her. Fortunately, she didn't seem to notice the slip, just squeezed his hand and weaved through the crowd towards the arriving couple.

"What's going on with you and Olivia?" asked a voice over his shoulder. Raj didn't need to turn to know it was Leo, but he shifted to face him regardless. It was the first time he'd actually managed to speak to his friend tonight—Leo's role as Alpha meant he was almost constantly surrounded by people either wanting his adjudication on something or trying to make an advantageous connection with a powerful member of one of the largest packs in Mystic City, even though he and Della had made it clear when they started hosting events like this one that, for the night, Leo was off-duty. And of course, if he wasn't doing the somewhat unwanted Alpha things, he had Della by his side; Leo was never happier than when he had his mate with him, and he kept her close as often as possible. The reminder of Maggie ducking away from him through the crowd left an ache in Raj's chest.

"Who says there's anything going on?" he asked.

"She's being totally normal," Leo said, taking a swig from his drink. "But when she's around, you suddenly look uncomfortable."

"Exactly how closely have you been watching me?" Raj asked, half-laughing.

"I saw you looking weird when you came in, and this is the first chance I've had to actually come over," Leo said. "I don't regret taking on the Alpha role, but sometimes, I wish I was like a superhero with a secret identity, and no one would

know it was me when I was just trying to be, you know, me."
He shrugged. "But we weren't meant to be talking about me
What's going on with you and Olivia?"

"Nothing," Raj said after a moment too long. He felt like
it would be insensitive to talk about finding his mate—who
was a different person to the woman he was dating—and his
plans to break up with Olivia with anyone before he'd actually done it. He didn't want Olivia to be surrounded by
people who knew she was about to have her relationship
terminated before she knew herself. She didn't deserve that.

"Raj," Leo said warningly.

"Don't put on your Alpha voice with me," Raj cut him
off. "I just can't talk about it yet, all right? I'll come to you
guys when I'm able to, but not yet."

Leo looked at him without speaking for a long moment.
"Is she pregnant?"

Raj reeled back like he'd been slapped. "*What?*"

"Okay, that's a no," Leo said with a laugh.

"Gods above, what made you think of that?" Just the idea
of Olivia carrying his child, ignited that same nauseous
feeling he got whenever she touched him, ever since the night
he'd found Maggie. If it was Maggie who was pregnant with
his child... well, that would be an entirely different story. Raj
desperately tried to restrain his brain from thinking about
what would be involved in getting Maggie pregnant, but the
fantasies unspooled in his head at lightning speed regardless,
picturing the two of them together in a hundred different
positions as he pleasured her.

"The I-can't-talk-about-it-*yet* comment," Leo said, dragging Raj's attention back to the present. "It sounded like
something was going on that you'll be able to discuss at some
point, but you can't yet."

"You've got pups on the brain or something?" Raj asked,
recovering himself slightly. "Anything I should know, Alpha?"

Leo laughed again. "Someday, hopefully. Not for a while yet."

Raj was somewhat shocked that his friend would speak so easily about having children, but then, Leo had already found his mate, had already won her love and had her sleeping beside him every night. He could only imagine how Leo's already protective attitude towards Della would be magnified if she fell pregnant, let alone towards a child they made together.

"It's not a pregnancy thing," he assured his friend. "Well, as far as I know, and I'm sure she would have told me."

Leo shrugged. "All right. Well, I'm here when you're able to talk about whatever it is."

"Thanks, man."

They clinked their bottles together, and then a petite witch Raj vaguely recognised as a friend of Della's sidled up to the two of them. "Sorry, I hope I'm not interrupting anything."

"Not at all," Leo said, his voice sounding just slightly tired as he seemed to realise what was about to happen. Raj watched his friend's facial expression shift slightly, as though he was putting on the Alpha mask over the real man.

"Leo, I was just wondering if I could introduce you to someone." She gestured, and a warlock with wild red hair shifted nervously behind her. "This is my friend Peter. He's a big fan of yours."

"A... fan?" Leo asked after a brief pause, sounding bewildered.

"Yeah, absolutely," the warlock said, a hesitant smile now breaking over his face. "I'm writing my PhD about progressive change in supernatural cultures, and the changes you're making around here? *So* impressive."

Raj took that as his cue to depart and clapped his friend on the shoulder with a grin. If this was the kind of thing Leo had to deal with at his own parties, Raj was glad as hell that he hadn't been the one who challenged James to be Alpha. It was hard enough managing the seemingly ever-increasing duties involved in sharing the role of Beta with Emmett, with his own work and his life outside of the two. He couldn't imagine trying to fulfil the full role of Beta and have a career at the same time, let alone a life as well.

He realised he'd finished the drink Olivia had brought him when he lifted it to his mouth and found it empty. He made his way over to the cooler to grab another and, as though his attention was being forcefully drawn there, noticed Maggie sitting slightly removed from a cluster of people over by the fence. She didn't look upset, or uncomfortable, or even lonely, despite clearly not being involved in their conversation; rather, she was watching the crowd like a scientist collecting data.

Purposely not examining his actions, Raj collected another fresh drink and made his way over. He sat beside her without speaking, partly listening to the voice in his head that said, "Words might not be welcome right now," but also, he had no idea what to say. Part of him wanted to blurt the truth out to her right that second, *You're my mate, and you smell so good that every part of my body is begging me to ravage you like the world is ending.* Fortunately, he managed to control that urge and simply offered her the second drink he'd collected.

"Thanks," she said, looking surprised.

"It didn't look like you had one," he said. "I thought you might need sustenance for your examination of the crowd."

That seemed to startle a laugh from her. "What?"

"You looked like you were analysing everyone, rather than joining in," Raj explained, wondering whether, as usual, he should just have kept his mouth shut.

"I guess that's one way to describe it," she said, still smiling as she took a sip from the beer he'd brought. The experience of providing something for her sent satisfaction shooting through him. "I was just thinking earlier, we wound up with a little group of all humans sitting over here, and the witches were mostly keeping to themselves, and the were-wolves too, I think even segregating themselves by pack. I was wondering how long it would take for everyone to start mingling. And whether the humans were keeping to them-selves because they were uncomfortable being in a group with such a big majority of supernaturals, when, normally, there are more of us than there are of you."

The way she drew such a stark line between humans and supernaturals, with her on one side and him on the other, made Raj feel like his hackles were trying to rise, even in his human form. Anything that separated him from Maggie, his wolf seemed to be saying, needed to be destroyed.

"Do you think that's what was going on?" he asked.

"Not consciously," she replied slowly. "I mean, the witches and the werewolves were staying separate at first too, so it's probably more likely that people just gravitated to the people they knew better at first, and they happened to mostly be the ones from their own pack or coven or whatever. But everyone seems to have integrated pretty successfully now." She gestured towards a group who had claimed a circle of chairs, where a human was shifting to sit on the lap of one of the warlocks in the circle, so that a werewolf could have her seat. "It's probably just me overanalysing things, as usual."

"It's an interesting hypothesis, though," Raj said, warming to the topic. As with many subjects, he'd read at least a few books about social division between humans and supernaturals. "I hadn't thought about what it would be like for a human who's used to being part of the larger group in the population to be in a scenario where they're in the minority."

"It's not so bad," Maggie said, reminding him once more

that she was, in fact, one of the group in question. "I work around so many supernaturals, I'm used to there being a pretty even split between them and the humans. Maybe not a majority as big as we're seeing here, but it doesn't bother me."

They were silent for a long moment before Raj managed to get up the courage to say, "Look, about the other night—"

"It's fine," Maggie said, turning to face him fully. He had the strange sensation that the two of them were enclosed in a bubble formed by the noise and bustle around them, their stillness keeping the two of them together in a space no one else could breach. "You don't have to worry about me telling anyone what you do on your nights off. I'm presuming the others don't know?"

"They don't," Raj confirmed slowly, wondering where he'd been thinking this conversation could go, because this didn't feel like the direction he'd have wanted.

"Well, like I said, you don't have to worry about me. I'll keep your secret."

"*Our* secret, now," he said, his voice low and a smile that felt false and uncomfortable spreading over his face, suddenly desperate to cement this one thing he had in common with her. Sharing a secret was supposed to be a cute, relationship-y thing, right? They could exchange secretive smirks and laugh about it behind other people's backs. This could be the start of something, identifying this thing they had in common. Maybe they could build on it, and it could grow into something between them that satisfied her human requirements for a relationship as much as his driving were-wolf urges to take her inside the house and bite his claim into the skin of her inner thighs, before pleasuring her until she forgot every word she knew, apart from his name. Because those urges were becoming stronger with every moment he spent in her company, and as much as he knew—from his own experience, as well as from romance novels—that he needed to provide a relationship that fulfilled both their needs, his needs were becoming pretty damned difficult to ignore in a way that would be even more obvious if he stood up.

Not that she looked like she was taking that comment in the way he meant it, though—trying to find something they had in common. Actually, she looked kind of horrified. What had just happened?

"Is that some kind of threat?" she demanded, and if he hadn't been so shocked, he might have found such immediate, vehement indignation towards him from someone so much smaller than he was kind of adorable. There was clearly a roiling tempest in his mate, despite her unflappable exterior and her cheerfulness with Della, and somehow, that strength of passion called to something in him even more.

"What? No, of course not—"

"What, if I don't keep your secret, you'll out me as well? Tell everyone that I was there, at your bloodthirsty fighting club?" She squared her body towards him, as if she was preparing for a fight. Gods, there was a good foot of height difference between them. What on earth did she think she was going to gain by squaring up like she was about to take him on? "I told you I'll keep your damn secret, *Librarian*. But I wasn't doing it because I'm afraid for my own reputation. I was being a decent person, which is apparently something you might benefit from learning more about."

"Maggie—" he started, not sure quite what he was about to say, and he was sure he didn't imagine the shiver that visibly ran through her body, or the way her lips parted, and her eyes widened just slightly. What was this, the second time he'd said her name out loud? The taste of it was as sweet as sugar, like honey spreading across his tongue, and he wanted to repeat it over and over. Preferably loudly, as her body moved over his, feeling her clench down as he thrust up inside her, his hands holding her hips, guiding her movements, making her take every single inch of his overwhelming desire...

"Maggie," he said again, just for the joy of feeling her name roll off his tongue, his body leaning down towards hers, over hers, purely because he couldn't hold himself back from the temptation of being close to her. But she stepped back from him as though her whole body was flinching from even the threat of his closeness. Their little bubble burst with her motion, and suddenly, Raj was aware of the clamour and proximity of all the people around them.

"Stay away from me," she spat, clearly furious. "I'll keep your damn secret, but I'll never be at that *club* of yours again, and if you do feel like telling people I was in attendance, I'd bet good money that it'd be damn hard to prove."

"Maggie, that's not what I was—"

But she was gone, disappearing into the crowd of people, which shifted to swallow her as though she'd never been there. Raj wanted to punch something. He wanted to chase her and hold her to him, explain that he hadn't meant to say that the way it had come out, that he was just trying to connect with her, because she was his *mate*, and wasn't she feeling just a tiny fraction of the drive to be close to him that he was feeling towards her? Della had said that, even though she wasn't a werewolf, the feelings she'd had for Leo once their bond had been established had been so intense and developed so quickly that she'd considered the possibility that she was under a spell. Shouldn't Maggie be feeling something similar, some draw to be near Raj, to talk to him and touch him the way he was desperately craving her? But no, she'd just explicitly told him to *stay away* when the thing he wanted more than anything was to get *close* to her.

Not that, he realised suddenly, he could have done any of

the things with her that he was longing for, even if she had been willing. He still had Olivia to consider. Olivia, whom he was planning on breaking up with tonight. Olivia, who would probably hate him afterwards, even though he'd wanted to do it gently—he'd wanted to do it before they had to come here as a couple, so she wouldn't feel like he'd been playacting the whole evening. Just being around her felt so inherently *wrong* now in comparison to the way he felt when he looked at Maggie. It was like his body and even his heart were rebelling against another woman thinking she had a claim on him, when he belonged to his mate.

He realised that he'd spent the last several minutes staring into the space where Maggie had disappeared when Emmett came up and nudged him with his shoulder. "You okay, man? You look pretty zoned out."

"Yeah, just tired," Raj lied automatically.

"Is this about the Olivia thing you can't talk about yet?"

Raj fixed him with the look he usually reserved for children messing with the library books with sticky fingers. "Have you been talking to Leo?"

"You'd been over here for a while, man. I asked if something was bothering you, and he told me what you'd told him."

"You two gossip like old women," Raj complained.

"And you don't? You're easily the worst of us. Don't you remember after Leo found Della, and—"

"All right, all right, I take your point," Raj interrupted, half-laughing. "Look, the thing with Olivia… it's not a huge deal. At least it won't be, after I get to talk to her. Tonight. I hope."

"It's nothing serious?"

"It won't be." He managed to put more conviction into the words than he felt, as if by hoping hard enough, he could make it true.

Almost as though she had felt them talking about her, Olivia appeared with another fresh drink in her hand. "I saw you standing all alone over here and thought you might need another one."

He remembered thinking just a few days ago that he loved making her happy because when she smiled, she was even more beautiful, but now he could only look at her face, feel her hand on his forearm, and think of the fact that she wasn't Maggie. Gods, it just felt so *wrong* to be with her, to know he had this plan to end things without having actually done it yet, and—

"I'm actually feeling a bit off," he blurted out, the words exploding from him almost without permission from his brain. *Because my mate is here but doesn't seem to want anything to do with me, while you want everything to do with me, but I can barely stomach your touch on my skin.* "Would you mind if I took off? You don't have to come with me."

"Of course, I will," Olivia said earnestly, her eyebrows pulling together in concern. "You stay right here, and I'll just put this back." She took back the beer she'd handed to him. "I'll go and let Della and Leo know we're taking off, and then we can be out of here. Two minutes, I promise."

"Thanks," Raj managed.

"You right, man?" Emmett asked quietly as she wound her way back through the crowd. "Or is this just part of The Thing We Can't Discuss Yet?"

"The Thing," Raj admitted. "We'll go home, we'll have a conversation, and then everything will be the way it should be."

Emmett shrugged, then bumped Raj with his shoulder. "Drive safe. Let us know when you get home. And when you can talk about The Thing."

Part of him was glad Olivia had volunteered to leave with him, because it meant they could finally have this conversation. The other part, possibly even the larger part, found the idea of leaving a party that Maggie was attending, with a woman who was not her, deeply distasteful. What he wouldn't give to be able to walk out of this place with the diminutive human on his arm, everyone who saw them fully aware that they were together, knowing he'd be able to take her home to his bed and worship her body with his own, to make love to her until the sun was coming up...

"All right, ready when you are." Mostly due to his inattentiveness, it seemed like Olivia had popped up out of nowhere, a concerned look on her face. "Are you feeling okay to drive?"

"Yeah, I'm not sick or drunk or anything," he replied as they made their way through the crowd and out the front gate. Raj caught Leo's eye as they were walking and sent him a wave, and the Alpha replied with a knowing look and two thumbs up.

"You're not?" Olivia asked, drawing his attention back to her.

He dug his car keys out of his pocket and unlocked the doors. "No, just didn't realise how tired I was, I guess. Wasn't up to a whole party. All those people."

"Well, if it's nothing serious, and you have the energy," Olivia said as she rounded the bonnet to the passenger door, "maybe when we get back to your place, we can have that conversation you were talking about." She smiled at him over the roof of the car.

Again, Raj was surprised by how positive she sounded after the threat of his saying, "There's something I want to talk about." Was it possible that she was in the same headspace that he was about their relationship and was looking forward to finding a polite way to end it? Considering her conduct tonight, the way she'd looked out for him and introduced herself as his girlfriend, that seemed unlikely.

They drove home in near silence. Raj lived close enough to Leo and Della that he'd been planning on walking to the party, after having the breakup conversation with Olivia, of course. When she'd arrived at his house late and suggested that they drive so they didn't exacerbate their lateness and that they push their chat until after they got back, he'd found himself in such a state of confused purposelessness that he agreed. He'd been so determined to talk to her before they left, and though the need to free himself from bonds to any woman who wasn't his mate was still roiling beneath his skin, nervousness was beginning to rise in his stomach. He wasn't good at breakups; in truth, he hadn't been the one who ended most of the relationships he had been in. It also wasn't something he'd done recently, and for a moment, a stray thought regretted that—that he didn't have more recent practice at how to do this properly, gently, kindly.

He unlocked the door and watched Olivia shrug off her coat as they walked through to the kitchen. He busied himself filling up the kettle. "Do you want a cup of tea?"

"Sure," she said.

"And I can get out those tarts I put away earlier. You didn't have much of a chance to eat while we were there."

"I can do that," she said, pressing a kiss to the back of his shoulder as she moved past him. The action made him feel slightly sick, like his body was objecting to any gesture of affection coming his way that wasn't from the female who, he guessed after tonight, would be happy to have nothing to do with him, ever again.

He waited until the tea was made, then carried it over to the table where the plate of tarts sat, minus one. Olivia was standing over the sink, eating it with a look of bliss on her face.

"Why don't you sit down?" he asked, and she pushed the

last bite into her mouth, then turned with a slightly sheepish look on her face.

When her mouth was empty, she smiled and said, "You know I can't resist these. Thanks for picking them up."

"No worries. I wanted you to have something nice... since I know sitting down for a serious chat can be awkward." Maybe he was saying too much. He closed his mouth tightly. It had seemed like the right thing to do, to make her feel like he was taking this seriously, but also that he was trying to make it as easy and painless as possible. Hopefully, once he told her that he'd found his mate and was ending their relationship, she'd remember that he'd tried to be gentle about it.

To his surprise, she smiled brightly. "Sure. That was very sweet of you. I love these tarts."

Raj let the compliment slip by, since, in a few minutes, she'd probably feel the exact opposite way about his actions in preparing the room for this conversation. He sat in the chair across from hers and folded his hands on the table, then separated them, worried he looked like he was delivering bad news. Which he was, but he didn't need to freak her out with his posture. "So," he started, feeling the nervousness once more roiling in his chest. He paused, swallowed.

"So," Olivia said, still looking inexplicably cheerful.

"There's something I've been needing to talk to you about."

Surprising him even further, her smile widened. "To be honest, I've kind of been expecting this."

He felt his brows pull down in confusion. "You have?"

"Sure. I mean, we haven't been together long, but everyone knows wolves tend to move quickly. We sure got serious fast. We get along great, and even when we're spending lots of time together, we don't get sick of each other. Hell, we spend more nights together than apart, so I guess it just makes sense to just remove the travel time between."

He blinked several times, completely blindsided. "I'm... I'm sorry?"

For the first time, Olivia looked slightly uncertain. "What are you talking about?"

"What are *you* talking about?"

"I thought you wanted to talk to me... hasn't all this, the tea and the tarts and making such a big deal of this conversation... hasn't this been because you were going to ask me to move in with you?"

Raj rocked back in his chair like she'd shoved him. "Olivia... Gods, I'm so sorry."

"You're sorry?" Now, she was starting to look properly worried.

"Olivia, look, you know I think you're amazing, right? And if it was up to me, this wouldn't be happening, but the universe kind of runs things by its own rules, right?"

"Raj..." She looked hopelessly confused now, her hands clasped together on the table in front of the remainder of the tarts, their bright pink colour suddenly looking garishly inappropriate. "What *are* you talking about?"

"Liv," he said and took in a deep breath. This would be the first time he'd said anything about this out loud to anyone, rather than just stewing over it in the privacy of his own head. He had to do it right. Delicately, like one of the charismatic heroes from the romance novels. They seemed to be able to break up with the women they weren't meant to be with in a polite, kind way. Surely, he could do the same thing.

"Liv," Raj's mouth said, apparently having entirely disregarded his plan, "we have to break up."

"*What?*" The look on Olivia's face couldn't have been more shocked if he'd admitted a sexual interest in cabbages.

Okay, so he hadn't exactly been delicate. Or, you know, in

any way even slightly diplomatic. Raj's problem was that, so often, he had the proper novel-worthy speech all but written out in his head, but it all came out wrong, like there was some kind of broken filter between his brain and his mouth that twisted his words.

"When we were at the Ring the other night," he said, and paused, hoping like hell he managed to actually say this properly, "I think I found my mate."

"Your *mate?*" she asked in obvious disbelief. "You actually believe that crap?"

"I guess I do," he said. "I just... I caught her scent, and it was just... " He mimed his brain exploding. "I can't get her out of my head. I can't stop thinking about her. And I thought... I didn't want to be the kind of guy who would string you along while I was looking for her. I wanted you to know, I wouldn't be doing this unless I thought it was the only right thing to do. Because I think you're incredible, you know I think that you're smart and you're funny and you're beautiful—"

"And yet, you're just going to throw me away because you caught the scent of some stranger at your fighting ring while you were halfway through beating some guy to death?" Olivia asked, fire blazing in her eyes.

"He didn't die," Raj protested, before realising that wasn't the most important point here. He reached for her hands, but she pulled them back. "Liv, please. I'm just trying to do the right thing."

"Do you even know who she is?" she demanded. "Or did you just scent *someone* in that crowd of fucked-up people and decide to pick through them one by one in the hopes that you'll find the right one? And that's if this myth of one perfect mate even truly exists, which I cannot *believe* you think might actually be true."

"I know who she is," Raj said.

Olivia didn't seem to have even registered his response. Her face had gone almost completely white as she considered what he'd said, the anger turning into something more like horror. "You kissed me that night. You slept in bed with me that night. Raj, you've been planning this since then?" She looked horrified, and in truth, he couldn't even blame her.

Reluctantly, he nodded. "I wanted to tell you straight away, but you were so tired, it didn't seem fair to drop something this big on you. And then I tried to tell you the next morning, but you had to go. This was… this was kind of the first chance I had."

She looked like she was about to cry. "Fine," she said softly, looking down at her hands clasped tightly together on the table's surface. "Go after this mate you think you've found." Her eyes came up to meet his. "But don't you dare come crying back to me when you realise there's nothing there."

Silently, he watched her collect her things and walk towards the door as if in a daze.

"Olivia," he heard himself say when she had her hand on the doorknob.

She paused but didn't turn around.

"I'm sorry," he said, wishing there were deeper words he could use to convey how bad he felt, the broken filter between his brain and his mouth once again twisting what he wanted to say.

"I don't care," Olivia said, and the door swung closed behind her

Chapter 4

MAGGIE HADN'T BEEN SLEEPING WELL the last few nights. Since the night at the Ring, actually, if she was being honest with herself. Even though after the party, she'd stayed long enough to help her friends clean up into the night, her body refused to relax and unwind enough for her to fall asleep. She was... dammit, she couldn't resist it. Somehow, she'd wound up in what could only be a hormone storm of *horniness*. She'd tried to distract herself, cleaned her kitchen and put away her clean washing and read a book for over an hour before she'd given in, turned the lights off, and let her hand slip inside her underwear.

The usual fantasies suddenly felt less than effective as she pressed a finger inside herself, feeling sudden wetness that she hadn't anticipated. And then, for some reason, she remembered the response she'd had to having Raj's eyes on her, and suddenly a new fantasy was unfurling in her mind, this one somehow far more powerful than those she usually went to. It featured the big werewolf pulling her away from the party to an imaginary secluded corner of the garden and pressing her back against a tree, as he knelt before her and peeled her underwear down her legs, exploring her with his fingers—*oh*—before positioning one of her legs over his impossibly broad shoulders so she was spread before him—*oh, gods*—and following the path of those wicked fingers with his even *more* wicked tongue. He wouldn't be silent as he pleasured her, she was somehow sure of that, and the idea of feeling the reverberations of his sounds of the pleasure he was taking in her own was almost enough to send her over the edge. Almost, almost, almost. She teetered on the edge of orgasm for just long enough for her imagination to provide the idea of him pressing a finger inside her and stroking, and then she was gone. The climax roared through her like a tidal wave, leaving her gasping for breath as she lay boneless on the bed.

As she came down from the pleasure rush, only one thought echoed through her mind.

What the hell just happened?

The man had intimidated her with the threat of revealing her presence at the Ring, and she just ignored it and focused on the way it made her feel when their eyes met?

Well, pretty much.

Because no one had ever had that effect on her before. No one had ever been able to make her so aware of her body and her sexuality with nothing but the connection of their gazes. Not even any of the men she'd actually dated, including Jeremy—

Oh, God. *Jeremy.*

Did this count as cheating, imagining another man pleasuring her while she touched herself, knowing full well she had someone who pretty much counted as a boyfriend, even if they hadn't officially had that conversation about titles quite yet? And of all people, the Librarian, whom Jeremy had some kind of weird working friendship with—not discounting the fact that the man had *threatened her with exposure* just a few hours previously.

With the post-orgasmic bliss that had enveloped her now well and truly dispelled, she'd sat up and reached for her book again. If nothing else, reading would stop her from stressing over something she couldn't change. She'd gone along with Jeremy's invitation, attended and assisted at the Ring, and she couldn't fix it now. If Raj were to expose her, she'd deal with that as it came.

She'd basically re-enacted that sequence of events every night for the last week. Her body seemed to view what she mentally considered bedtime as the best time to get supernaturally horny, and even when she tried to stick to the tried-and-true fantasies that usually got her off, somehow her brain was fighting to insert Raj into each one. It *was* starting to feel like cheating, or maybe some kind of obsession, though she wasn't about to mention it to Jeremy. He'd had a week of last-minute roster changes that had kept them apart but had offered to take her for lunch today, since they had magically managed to get the same day off. She knew he probably assumed they'd spend the afternoon afterwards the way they often did if they managed a midday date, entwined in bed, alternating making love and chatting about various unrelated topics. For some reason, though, the thought was suddenly unappealing to her.

With this man, at least. She could imagine enjoying it with someone else. Someone she could not stop imagining growling out praise and curses in the same breath as he moved above her, as he moved inside her.

Gods, there she went again. She needed to get her head examined.

She spent the morning compulsively cleaning her house to surgical standards of spotlessness. Midmorning, she sat down for a cup of coffee and admitted to herself what should probably have been obvious from the moment she woke up—she was doing this because she was nervous to spend time with Jeremy, after having these thoughts about Raj that she couldn't seem to help. That she wholeheartedly wished she could *stop* herself from having, after the way they'd left things at Leo and Della's party. No matter what all his friends thought of him, this was not a good guy they were dealing with. She'd thought about going to Della with what Raj had said, the way he'd all but threatened to tell her secret —*their secret,* she heard him say—but she didn't want to shatter her friend's view of the man. They all thought of him as this oversized, nerdy jokester. They'd probably never even imagine that he was secretly an illegal prizefighter who revelled in the pain of others, who would stoop to threaten her with exposure the way he had.

And anyway, she was now bound by the secrecy spells of the Ring just as much as any of the fighters. She couldn't talk to her best friend about this even if she wanted to.

Abruptly, she stood and poured the remainder of her coffee down the sink. The last thing her anxiety level needed was more caffeine at this point. She'd go out and get some things done; she had jobs she could tick off the list and, as a side benefit, get out of the house. Some fresh air, along with the satisfaction of getting some of her never-ending to-do list ticked off, would be good for her.

She visited the supermarket, picked up the parcels that were waiting for her at the post office, and dumped the heavy bags on her kitchen bench before glancing at the clock. If she unpacked the shopping now, would she still have time to return the books that were already a week overdue? She looked between the books and the clock twice more before deciding that she'd rather not rack up any more of a fine than she already likely had. She'd been meaning to return no fewer than seven books all week, and surely, even though they often waived her fines because she knew the librarians well, they would charge her if she didn't get them back to the library soon. She could return them quickly, in and out—and pay the fine, of course—and be home by the time Jeremy came to pick her up for lunch.

The library was one of Maggie's favourite places in the world. Unlike many of the public buildings in Mystic City, Northside Library had escaped the cult of modernising renovation and was still an old, multi-storeyed stone building with elaborately carved doorways between its rooms, enormous arched windows and high ceilings. It could almost have been a cathedral in another life, and as it was, she still thought of it as a place to worship the books it held. Some of her days off had been almost completely spent within these walls, finding a stack of books to read and settling into one of the deep, plush armchairs scattered between the shelves to start on them. She read everything from sci-fi to murder mysteries to philosophical treatises, loving the escapism and the learning that she found in them.

Today, she didn't have time to delve deep into the library's endless supply and stopped at the Returns desk with her pile of books in her arms. Most of the library's staff knew her by name; she'd been coming here for the best part of a decade, after all, even before many of them had worked at Northside. Most of them were used to her variable schedule and waived the late fees she accrued when her roster—and degree of personal motivation—led to her returning books late, so she willingly paid the fines she had to, knowing that she was getting off lightly with her regular late returns.

She was examining one of the books she was returning, a fantasy novel she'd particularly enjoyed and which she'd need to find the sequel to when she had time, when she saw movement in the doorway that led to the Returns desk. She looked up, and she saw him.

The Librarian.

They'd told her at the party that it was actually his job— a librarian, just like they called him at the Ring. He'd laughed off her slip when she'd blurted out his fighting title and hadn't Della mentioned that the guy worked at Mystic City Central Library?

And, her memory belatedly supplied, that he had just got a new job.

Which, clearly, was here.

The moment Maggie laid eyes on Raj, she was torn between wanting to run away and wanting to throw herself at him. It was kind of embarrassing, that immediate urge, but she'd been having those inescapable fantasies all week, and gods knew the man was attractive—what woman wouldn't want to drape herself across all that muscle? But somehow, this felt deeper, more visceral, as though she wanted to join herself to him like the aliens in the sci-fi book that she was returning could link themselves, sharing their entire sense of self. She wanted to dissolve into him, to meld them into one being, to hold his heart in her hands and keep him safe. She wanted him to wrap his massive arms around her and hold her to his warmth so she could finally feel at home.

And she wanted to run. She wanted to sprint away from this man who had threatened to reveal her secret if she exposed his, who made her feel things she had no business feeling, these strange emotions she'd never known before and didn't know how to control. She wanted to put so much distance between them that she never again had to lay eyes on him and feel the absurd degree of attraction, not just physical but *visceral*, that she felt to him. She wanted space to think through what she was feeling, but also to escape the aura of potential danger that he wore like a cloak around his massive shoulders. Physical danger, of course—honestly, just look at the man—but also a sense that he could destroy her emotionally if he chose. That getting close to him would mean walking a tightrope with nothing to catch her, just open air and a fatal landing when she inevitably fell.

"Maggie," Raj said, sounding slightly breathless, and the spell was broken.

"Hello," she said, her voice sounding strange even to her.

"Are you returning books?" he asked. It was a bit of a stupid question, given that she was at the Returns desk with a pile of books, but she allowed it. Perhaps he was as confused by her appearance as she was by his.

"Yes. These." She gestured stupidly to the pile she'd put down on the desk. "They're a bit late, I'm sorry. I'll pay the fine." He couldn't have been here long enough to know that most of the librarians waived her fines, because they knew that she had a slightly wacky schedule that often didn't align with library opening hours, and anyway, she'd be back in a day or two to collect more.

He stood unmoving before her for a long moment, and she took him in. He was wearing a white-and-blue checked button-down shirt tucked into jeans, the sleeves rolled up to his elbows. A brown belt, worn almost to the point of falling to pieces, wrapped around his hips. The sleeves of his shirt strained to contain his bulging muscles, and his heavily corded forearms—and the tattoos there, the lines of writing that encircled his left forearm, as well as the patterns and images that trailed across the right—were revealed entirely.

"I'll just scan these back in, then," he said eventually, and Maggie realised she had been staring. And that he was staring back at her. For a moment, she wished she was better dressed, something more impressive than a tired sundress, but she pushed the thought out of her head. What did she care if he thought she was stylish? The man had a girlfriend, and anyway, she had no business being attracted to a man who beat people up with a smile on his face, for gods' sake.

He reached out to slide her stack of returns towards his side of the desk, and she had to fight not to notice how big his hands were. Good hands, strong and callused, hands that, her inner seductress whispered, would know what they were doing on a woman's body. She snapped her attention back to his face.

"So, your new job is here?" she asked after a moment as he started scanning the books back in.

"Looks like it," he said. The words could have been harsh, but the smile he shot her made it a joke between them, rather than one at her expense.

The silence dragged just a little too long as she caught herself staring at his mouth. She felt heat rising into her cheeks, but for some reason, she wanted to keep talking to him. "It must be a bit different from working at the library in the city centre. That one is huge, and so... modern."

He looked up again from where he was processing her returns, and this time his smile spread right across his face. "This one isn't huge enough for you? It's practically a cathedral." She felt the surprise spread across own her face that he'd had the same thought she had about the building, but the smile somehow made it okay. Gods, but he had a great smile. "It's different, I'll give you that," he continued. "The building itself is much more complicated, all these smaller rooms instead of just big open spaces, so knowing where things are is a bit more of an issue. And two parents have pulled their kids away from me already today, like I was going to kidnap them or something."

"Well, we did go over the fact that you look a little threatening," Maggie reminded him.

"Me, threatening?" Raj said with pretend shock. "I'm

wearing a button-down and a name badge. I was shelving books when that little girl ran up to me. I'm hardly threatening."

"You're, like, nine feet tall, with a beard and a heap of tattoos," Maggie said with her own grin.

"And a staff name badge," Raj insisted, gesturing to his chest where it was pinned. She tried not to notice the swell of his muscular chest under the fabric but failed entirely.

"I'm sure they'll get used to you," she managed to reply.

"I should hope so," Raj said. "I don't plan on going anywhere anytime soon. This job is a godsend, truth be told. I applied for the transfer as soon as Leo named me Beta—I knew even with two of us doing the job, I'd need more flexibility, and this is so much closer to pack territory, it gives me a lot more freedom. They were pretty militant about schedules at Central Library." He seemed to realise that he was sharing a lot and looked down at the book in his hand. "So, *The Hobbit*, huh? Getting into *Lord of the Rings*?"

"I've read them before," Maggie said.

"Are you one of the people who loves *The Silmarillion* or one of the people who could never properly get into *The Silmarillion*?" Raj asked.

"Definitely the first one," she said, then looked down at her hands. Why was she worried that a librarian, of all people, might think she was a nerd for loving *Lord of the Rings*? She gestured to the copy of *The Hobbit* that he still held. "I had the audiobook of this one on CD when I was a kid. It was about eight CDs long." Well, that didn't make her sound any less nerdy.

"That sounds about right, knowing Tolkien." Raj grinned. "He's not exactly known for being concise. And you don't have a hard copy of *The Hobbit*, even though you're such a fan that you've read *The Silmarillion*?"

"Why would I buy books when I can get them here every

week, for free?" Maggie asked, raising an eyebrow with a smile. Hang on, was she flirting? Was she seriously bloody flirting with the Librarian? Was she insane?

"You're here every week?" Raj asked, and she couldn't read the expression on his face. Was that shock? Happiness? *Why?*

"I've missed the last two, because my roster got a little messy," Maggie admitted.

"That explains why I haven't seen you here before," Raj said. He sounded slightly breathless. A grin broke over his face, and he leaned forwards on the Returns desk. "I'm glad you're here. I was actually thinking of asking Della for your number. I felt like shit for how we left things at the party. I think I said something wrong. I do that sometimes, and—"

"Magnolia!" a cheerful voice, in a volume wholly inappropriate for a library, rang out behind Raj's broad back. Maggie leaned to the side to see past him and saw that Emily, one of the regular librarians, was coming towards them. Emily was a witch of indeterminate age, due mostly to the anti-aging spells that had all but frozen her face in an expression of polite welcome. Threads of silver ran through her blonde hair, but Maggie had never been sure whether they were natural or spelled to look that way. Emily always looked glamorous, no matter the time of day or how long she'd been at work, and never charged Maggie late fees. She ignored the Returns desk and came around to give Maggie a hug. "We haven't seen you in more than a week, darling. I was starting to think that hospital had swallowed you up completely."

Maggie laughed, returning the embrace. "No, just thought I'd bring you back all of these at once."

Emily turned to Raj. "The first rule of working here—we don't charge Magnolia late fees. She's a nurse, busy keeping people alive, and the poor thing has to work night shifts, so she can't always be here to return things on time. We have to respect that and look after her. First rule: Magnolia doesn't get late fees."

"I thought the first rule was making sure the desks were clear," Raj said with a grin. "Or was the first rule keeping food out?"

Emily gave him an indulgent smile, or as much as one as her frozen face could produce. "There are several first rules," she said archly, then turned to Maggie. "Darling, you've met our new librarian I see? He's one of the new Betas of the Blue Crescent pack." She sounded like a proud mother bragging about her child's achievements.

"We actually have some friends in common," Maggie said. "We've met before."

"Isn't that lovely!" Emily said, looking for all the world like Maggie had just announced she'd won the lottery. "Well, I'll leave you two to it. Or are you coming through to collect some more books?"

"Not today," Maggie said. "I have to run. Maybe tomorrow if I can."

"Well, flag me down when you get in," Emily said. "I have a whole stack of new recommendations."

"You just gave me five new recommendations," Maggie protested, laughing.

"Yes, and you weren't here last week, so now I have ten more." She kissed Maggie on the cheek and disappeared through the arched doorway behind the Returns desk.

"You weren't exaggerating about being here often, then?" Raj asked with a smile in his voice, still holding the copy of *The Hobbit* that she had brought back.

"You can never read too many books," Maggie said. "And if I had to buy them all to keep up with how fast I read, I'd be completely broke."

"When Emily asked me for recommendations for 'Magnolia' earlier, I didn't realise it was you."

"Not many people call me that," Maggie admitted.

"Why not? It's a beautiful name."

"It never really fit me," she said, wondering why she was admitting this to him. "I'm more of a Maggie. Mags, to my best friends, or anyone too lazy to say two syllables."

"Magnolia," Raj said, and the way he rolled the word around his mouth like a delicious sweet made Maggie's blood heat. His eyes fixed on her fully. "I think it suits you. Can I call you that?"

She tried not to show how much the comment affected her. "You can call me whatever you like, as long as you finish returning my books. I have to go." The words came out more harshly than she'd meant them to, but she stood by them. She had places to be. She had no time to be chatting with outrageously good-looking werewolves.

He looked back down at the books and started scanning them back in again. She couldn't read the expression on his face, and though she tried to tell herself she didn't want or need to be able to, it still grated on her.

Raj handed her the returns receipt once all the books had been scanned back in, minus the cancelled late fee, but didn't let go as she grasped it. She looked up at him, confused.

"Maybe I could take you out for coffee sometime," he said, and if she had had even a degree less control over her face, Maggie's mouth would have dropped open in shock. "Just to talk books," he said hurriedly, in response to what must have been a look of utter astonishment in her eyes. "And to finish apologising for whatever I said wrong at the party. I don't like you thinking I'd upset you on purpose."

"Don't you have a girlfriend?" she heard herself ask pointedly, ignoring the part of herself that wanted to immediately forgive and forget the fact that he'd—apparently unintentionally—threatened her at Della's.

"Broke up," Raj said, and he didn't sound particularly upset about it.

"I have a boyfriend," Maggie said, wondering why she was fighting this opportunity to go out and chat about one of her favourite topics with one of the best-looking men she'd ever seen. Other than the fact that she was sort of in a relationship, of course.

"That's fine," Raj said, but his smile looked slightly wooden, and was it her imagination, or were his eyes starting to shine silver? "I did just mean to talk about books."

"Oh," Maggie said. Some part of her had kind of *hoped* he was asking her on a date, even though she had a boyfriend, even though, by rights, she should still be scared of this man she'd seen grinning as he pummelled the living daylights out of another man. No matter that he seemed to love books as much as she did; no matter that he had held each of the volumes she was returning in those big, brutal hands like it was a baby bird in need of care and protection.

No matter that part of her was wondering whether he would touch her so carefully, or use those big hands to punish her the way she loved.

"I guess that would be all right," she said. "Look, I don't mean to be rude, but I really do have to go."

Raj gestured to the doorway. "Go for it. Far be it from me to make you late." There was a brief pause, where they both just looked at each other before he added, sounding almost hesitant, "Maybe I'll ask Della for your number after all?"

"Sure," Maggie said, and then, because her stupid mouth clearly had no filter on it, she followed it up with, "I'll speak to you soon, then?"

"I sure hope so," Raj said, and she could still feel his eyes on her until the moment the library's doors closed behind her.

Raj held his breath as he watched Maggie's retreating form striding away down the sidewalk with the confidence of a catwalk model. Today, her hair was pulled back in some kind of messy knot at the back of her head, and it showed off her cheekbones in a way that made her look almost feline. And every part of him was desperate to know whether she'd purr if he stroked her just right.

He looked down at his swelling erection, hidden from innocent library loan returners by the mountain of books that had been left on the Returns desk and trolley by librarians who either didn't have time to put them away or couldn't be bothered. He added Maggie's to the pile already on the trolley and was careful to keep it close in front of him as he rolled it through the doorway back into the rooms of the beautiful old building that held shelf upon shelf of books. If he couldn't stop himself responding to the woman, at least he could prevent the rest of the world seeing quite how intensely she affected him.

This was progress at least. She hadn't seemed quite as horrified by him this time as she had last time that they saw each other. A little reserved, yes, and he was pretty sure he hadn't imagined the look of shock mixed with a touch of horror he'd seen on her face when she realised that he was working in her local library now—a library that, if what Emily had been saying was accurate, "Magnolia" frequented every few days. And once they'd started talking, especially about the books themselves, the guarded look had disappeared from her eyes. She'd seemed to enjoy chatting to him about that, teasing him about the way his appearance affected the way the library's patrons sometimes saw him. It wasn't like he was handing out how-to-hide-a-dead-body books to teenagers and known violent criminals, even if that was what people, especially the parents of the small children coming to Story Time, seemed to think at first. She'd even laughed with him, just a hint of a chuckle, but it had lit him up to know he could bring that out of her.

He pushed the trolley into the History section, one of the most secluded areas of the library—he needed a minute to calm down enough that he wasn't going to take someone's eye out with his erection if he was walking through the library's more densely populated areas. Gods above, but the way he responded to her was intense. It was like every cell in his body was desperate to come into contact with every cell of hers. He wanted to know what every single inch of her skin tasted like, wanted to know if she'd shiver when he ran his tongue up the side of her neck, how she liked her nipples played with, whether she'd resist as he pressed her thighs apart to expose her to his gaze, to his touch. He'd have to be gentle—she was so much smaller than he was, so much more delicate, and a human on top of all of that, without the werewolf strength he was used to—but despite that, he couldn't get past the idea of having every facet of her body exposed to his eyes, to his hands, to his mouth. To his cock.

Gods all dammit, he was getting even harder now, just thinking about how she'd respond to his hands on her perfect body. Whether she'd keep spitting so much attitude, or if he could make her soft and sweet if he touched her just right. Whether Maggie, after he'd given her three or four orgasms, would be as much of a spitfire as Maggie before.

He picked up a book, found its spot and savagely shoved it into its place, so hard that the entire set of shelves wobbled. He heard a voice on the other side say, "What the hell was that?" and knew he needed to get himself in check, right now, or he'd have to explain an avalanche of knocked-over shelves in the History room.

The issue—and perhaps this was a mate-bonding thing,

or maybe it was just because it was Maggie—was that his interest in her went far beyond the physical craving dragging him towards her. He wanted to know why she chose the books she did—he'd heard Emily talk about all the different things the unknown Magnolia read when she was asking around for recommendations—why sometimes she was sweet and other times so fiery, why he'd seen her at Della and Leo's standing apart from all the other partygoers, watching them like she was taking notes for a science experiment. He wanted to understand this firebrand of a woman, almost as much as he wanted to take her to bed and see how many times he could make her scream his name. She was beautiful, to be sure, and he wanted to map out her entire form with his tongue, but beyond that, there was something in him that wanted to understand her, that wanted to know her so deeply, he could draw a map of her soul. Was that just the mate bond, drawing him closer to her in any way it could? Or was that something more?

Not that it really mattered. He was bound to her now, tied to her so strongly that, if the reading he'd done for Emmett when he was wooing Petra could be believed, ignoring the connection could literally drive him insane. And at some point, he'd need to tell her that she was his mate. He just had the feeling that, unless he could get to know her a little better beforehand and let her get to know him, she'd immediately laugh him out of the room. Or run away and refuse to ever see him again, which would be just as bad. Based not only on the experiences of his best friends, but also on the love stories he'd read and what he suspected their heroes would suggest he do in this situation, he needed to give her time to get to know him as a person, before he suggested that they were destined to spend the rest of their lives together. She was a human; she couldn't know the strength of a mating bond from the werewolf perspective.

She couldn't understand that it was near torture for him to spend time in her presence without being able to lay a claim to her, even one as simple as touching her when she came in to return her books. No matter how difficult it was, he needed to keep his distance for at least a little while, until she got to know him better, and then drop the bombshell of their connection. That way, she'd already, hopefully, like him as a person and know that she could trust him before he asked her to be open to more.

It would be difficult, and torturously painful, and he foresaw a lot of lonely nights in his future filled with jacking off to her image, but Raj knew he didn't have a choice if he wanted her to be open to the idea of having him as a mate. And hadn't Della said that what she'd felt for Leo, the attraction between them and how quickly her feelings for him had grown, had happened so fast she'd queried whether she'd been under a spell? If he remembered right, she'd gone to her firebrand of a grandmother—Raj had met Elise Greenbranch only twice, but she'd made an impression—who had informed her of the witches' version of the mating connection story, that the universe had chosen someone for Della, in ways beyond her understanding, and that fighting this higher form of magic would be useless.

So, there was hope, Raj thought. If Maggie was already attracted to him—though beyond the dilation of her pupils when she saw him today, which could admittedly have been fear at having a massive werewolf show up out of the blue, he had no evidence that she was—then there was a chance that this "supernatural magic", as the witches described, was affecting her too. So, his mission, now, was to woo her as a human might, to nurture the beginnings of those feelings he could only hope were blossoming in her too, and pray that the human version of the mate bond, if such a thing even existed, clicked into place for her. That way, when he finally told her about the bond—that he was tied to her for the rest of his life and he wanted desperately to please her in any way possible, and also would she mind if he kept her in his bed for a few weeks to work out the frustration of holding back for so long—she might be open to the idea.

Plus, there was the fact that he had to work around the minor detail that she had a damn boyfriend.

Just thinking about it, made red tinge his vision. Another man, touching what Raj couldn't help but consider his? Sickness threatened to roil in his stomach, and he realised he was close to crushing the small paperback he was holding. He dragged in a deep breath and relaxed his grip, leaving the book only a little worse for wear. He made certain to only push it gently back onto the shelf, to avoid crushing any unsuspecting library users with a domino effect of shelves falling over, and looked down at the piles of books on the trolley.

So, Maggie was still technically seeing Doctor Jeremy. The doc had to be the boyfriend. Well, Raj had technically still been tied to Olivia when he'd been mooning over his newfound mate at Della and Leo's party. A former relationship wouldn't get in the way of the true love that came from a mate bond—if all the romance novels he'd read, and the pack's ancient myths, could be trusted. Besides, her relationship status didn't mean Maggie was happy with the doc—hell, if the conversation he'd heard between them at the Ring was any indication, she had some serious issues with the way the man had been spending his nights. Besides, Raj had read plenty of books where the heroine started out with someone else. Even been in love with him, in some of them, but she always wound up with the hero she was destined to be with. It was just up to Raj to show her that he was the better choice; that way, once he deemed it the right time to tell her about their bond, having given her some time to get used to having him in her life, she'd have no choice but to realise the witches' "supernatural magic" had been drawing her towards him all along.

Hopefully.

At closing time, he swung past the liquor shop and bought a case of beer, then drove straight to Em and Petra's place. Now that his job had moved to a library closer to Blue Crescent territory, he was usually a little early for their tentatively agreed-upon time of arrival to watch the game together, but those scheduled times were never more than a formality. Emmett, Leo and Raj had been running around each other's houses since they were kids; they both had keys to his place, and he to theirs. It wasn't uncommon, if he was running late on game night, for him to come home and find both his best friends already set up in his own living room, watching the pre-match broadcast. If one of the owners' cars was in the driveway, he always knocked at the door of his friends' houses, but even Della and Petra were so used to his presence now that they'd usually just yell for him to let himself in. The idea of having a set "arrival time" for one of them to get to one of the others' places was governed only by whether they were trying to get a meal in together before the game, or settle straight into drinking, bullshitting and watching TV.

He could have gone home and changed into more comfortable clothes, he considered, but his Helpful Non-Threatening Librarian outfit was comfortable enough, even if the button-down shirts did tend to pull across his shoulders. He'd started wearing the more formal clothes, even though most of the library workers dressed very casually, once he realised that people weren't coming to him for help because they found him intimidating. The truth was, unless he was somewhere like the Ring or standing next to someone considerably smaller—*Like Maggie, for example*, his brain supplied unhelpfully—he tended to forget that he was taller than most people. His brain had clearly got used to it early on and no longer even took it into account. This was in particular an issue when he was walking through low doorways, and he had a scar that ran across the front of his hairline to prove it.

Petra and Emmett's cars were both in the driveway when Raj parked out the front. He collected the case of beer and knocked on the front door, knowing, since the two of them were alone and it was a day that ended in Y, that there was a not-insignificant chance that one or both of them would be lacking some clothing. Confirming his suspicions, he heard Petra's voice, somewhat muffled and frantic, call out, "Just a second!" Raj settled in to wait until they'd managed to separate themselves and put their clothes back on.

Fortunately, this time, the wait was only brief before Petra appeared, her hair mussed, and her shirt buttoned wrong, and welcomed him into the house. She sent him a slightly rueful smile, but Raj just winked and grinned and she relaxed, giving him a quick hug in greeting. "I was so sorry to hear about you and Olivia," she said, preceding him into the kitchen as per their usual practice when he came over for a game. "You guys seemed like you really fit each other. Did something happen?"

Raj really wasn't ready to start spreading around the fact that he'd found his mate, or who it was, so he just shrugged, hoping he looked appropriately upset. "It needed to happen. We wanted different things. Just weren't right for each other, I guess." *As in, she wanted to be with me, and I wanted nothing more to do with her in favour of claiming my mate, whom you also know, which is part of why I'm not telling you about it.*

"Still," Petra said, looking sympathetic in a way that Raj felt almost guilty for eliciting, given he'd been the one to end the relationship, "Breakups are never easy. We're here if you need anything, even if it's just to talk." Fortunately, at that moment, she seemed to notice that her shirt was incorrectly buttoned, and her face went pink before she stammered out an excuse and disappeared out of the room to fix it.

It wasn't the first time one of them had interrupted Petra and Emmett, and Raj was just glad that this time there hadn't been loud noises emanating from another room as there had been one night that he and Leo had been over, and Em and Petra had disappeared. Raj and Leo had had a very brief discussion of whether to leave, but both of them wanted to see the end of the game. Besides, Leo, having just experienced finding his mate, and Raj, having read a lot about the mate bond, were fairly sympathetic to the constant need humming between a newly mated couple. They'd simply turned up the volume and pretended not to realise anything untoward had happened when Em had eventually returned to the game, with barely three minutes left before the end, and excused his absence by saying Petra had "needed help with something."

Raj had felt like he'd almost burst a blood vessel with the restraint required not to answer with a joke when Leo asked faux innocently where Petra was and Emmett, clearly without thinking, responded, "In the shower." But with a wish somewhere in the back of his mind that they'd someday show the same respect when he finally found his own mate, Raj had kept his mouth shut and allowed the newly bonded couple to imagine they'd got away with their tryst without anyone noticing.

He tried not to imagine what would happen if—no, not *if*, he needed to stay positive, *when*—he managed to make Maggie his. How he'd be able to release this desperate craving for her touch that felt like it had been churning beneath his skin forever. Once he finally got her in his arms, the gods all knew he wasn't letting her go for a damned long time.

And there was the need roiling through him again, even as he unloaded his drinks into the fridge.

"Emmett just got home from work," Petra said, her blush still present. "He's just getting changed, he'll be down in a second. Make yourself at home, you know where everything is." She went and opened the oven, releasing a waft of deliciously scented steam into the air. "We're doing steak, garlic potatoes and salad tonight, but Em hasn't got started on cooking the meat yet. At this rate, you guys might need to watch from the balcony if you want to cook them out on the barbecue and see the start of the game."

"Well, we couldn't leave the poor man out there to cook alone," Raj said. "You know how it goes. Can't have a man barbecuing alone. Who knows what bad decisions he would make? It has to be a team endeavour."

"And we wouldn't want to risk the steaks," Petra said with a laugh. "I know how much you guys eat, so I got a couple of extras, but only a *couple* of extras. Try not to wreck any of them."

"I'm insulted you think so little of my barbecuing skills, my love," Emmett said, coming into the room with his wet hair slicked back.

"Can you blame me?" Petra shot back, clearly in the mood to challenge her mate despite the fact that—if Raj's suspicions were correct, and he was hovering around the 99.9% certainty mark—they'd been tangled up in each other only moments earlier. "After what you did to those ribs that time?"

"If you'll recall," Emmett said, wrapping his arms around his mate, "*Someone* was purposely distracting me the night I was cooking the ribs." The blissful contentment on his face as he pulled Petra towards him so that her back was against his front made Raj's chest feel hollow. Emmett looked like he had every single thing he wanted, right there in his arms. Raj wanted that for himself—hell, he could have it himself, if only he could find a way to win Maggie over so that she broke up with her boyfriend and chose to embrace the traditions of a culture that wasn't even her own. He could only hope that she was feeling the same lack of his presence that he was experiencing in her absence, though she might not understand what it meant. But he had time, he reminded himself for what must be the thousandth time. He had plenty of time to win her over, to ease her into the knowledge that he needed her to be a part of his life if he wanted to retain his sanity. If he could keep his raging physical attraction to her under very strict control and win her over like the hero from a book.

Before the silence could become strained with Raj as the third wheel to his friends' display of affection, another knock on the door sounded, and Petra excused herself to let Leo in. Raj passed Emmett a beer and grabbed one for himself, digging the bottle opener out of the drawer. He was almost as comfortable in his friends' houses as he was in his own, though it had taken a minute to get used to each of them again after the women had moved in. Leo and Della had waited an almost, though not quite, acceptable amount of time before deciding to cohabitate, but Em and Petra had proven correct the time-honoured joke that werewolves moved faster than lightning, seemingly desperate to share space. Neither of Raj's friends had lived in the archetype of the completely spartan bachelor pad, but their houses were definitely different after their mates had moved in. Raj had never lived with a partner, so assisting in the moving process for each of his friends' mates was his first experience of what it looked like, and the main thing he had taken away from it was that women had a phenomenal amount of *stuff*. Not just clothes and books, the things he would consider essential, but furnishings and ornaments and kitchen appliances. In the end, in both cases, he'd left much of the unpacking to the people the house actually belonged to and gone to get pizza so all of them could take a break to eat.

Leo strolled in with his own case of beer, as usual—they rarely finished the two cases in the night, but it took a lot more than sipping on beers, even a lot of beers, to get a werewolf drunk. Of course, when the werewolf in question was a certain former-Beta-now-Alpha who had just found his mate and mixed about twenty of the beers with a serious dose of questionable liquor, it was possible the combination would have an effect… not that Raj was talking from experience or anything.

Emmett turned the TV on and opened the French doors between the living room and the house's wide back veranda, where the barbecue sat. They had to have the volume up inordinately high to hear it while they were out there, but fortunately, Petra didn't mind the noise.

They stood around the barbecue, beers in hand, chatting about what still seemed almost ridiculous, that the three of them had wound up in charge of one of the largest werewolf packs in Mystic City. There were a few pack issues that they needed to iron out, but strangely, the whole thing was running relatively smoothly, even under their inexperienced control. James, the previous Alpha, had basically let the pack run itself and had very few protocols or systems in place, other than the ones that forced other pack members to stroke his enormous ego or do things that benefited him. Still, even though Raj, Emmett and Leo had needed to almost start from scratch in that department, things were not moving too badly as the pack worked through the transition from their previous leadership team—if you could call anything James had led either *leadership* or a *team*—to the current one.

Emmett put the steaks on to cook, and though he seemed to be paying close attention to them, he still managed to take Raj completely by surprise when he asked, "So, down to business. What the hell happened with you and Olivia? Was that the Secret Thing you couldn't talk about at the party?"

Had he really managed to go this long without explaining what was going on to Em and Leo? He'd gone over the situation in his own head so many times, he had somehow neglected to tell them what was going on. In his mind, it felt like everyone he knew should know about it already, because it had been occupying so much of his brain.

"Oh, yeah," he managed to say lamely. "That."

"Yeah, that," Leo put in. "Della was so weirded out by it. She said you guys looked like a 'perfect pair'—her words, not mine. And why the hell would you do it just after going to a party together? Did she do something that was a total deal breaker?"

"I just didn't want everyone else knowing I was planning on breaking up with her before she did. I meant to do it before the party, so it didn't come right after we presented a relationship to everyone, but she was running late, and she didn't really give me a chance. So, I did it afterwards, and it was uncomfortable as all hell. She thought when I asked if we could talk about something important that I was about to ask her to move in with me. It honestly made me wish I hadn't ever started it with her, just so that scene could have been avoided."

"That bad?" Emmett asked, looking almost impressed. He had been something of a hook-up king over the years, until he met Petra, not least because he had a bad habit of falling in love with every woman who so much as bought him a drink, though those liaisons rarely lasted beyond a night or two. It had got the three of them into more than a bit of trouble over the years, trouble that Leo had frequently honed his now-laudable negotiation skills by talking them out of, and when that failed, had been a big part of how Raj learnt to fight. If anyone knew how to manage a breakup, purely based on breadth of experience, it was Emmett.

"That bad," Raj confirmed. "I felt like the world's biggest asshole, even though I knew it was the right thing to do. The only thing to do."

"Why was it the only thing to do?" Leo asked. "Della was right when she said you two seemed good together. I never even picked up a hint that there was something off between you guys until that night."

"Though the fact that she wanted to jump straight into moving in together so fast might have been a bit of a warning," Emmett put in.

The words startled a laugh out of Raj. "Dude. You don't think that's a little hypocritical, coming from you?"

Emmett brushed off the comment with a grin. "It's different when it's your mate. You just want to be around each other *all the time*, to the point that being apart becomes almost painful. You'll understand when you find yours."

"Well," Raj said, then hesitated, and he could practically see the lightbulbs light up above his friends' heads as they realised what he was trying to work out how to say.

"Are you serious?" Emmett exclaimed, so loudly that Petra stuck her head around the door to the TV room.

"Everything okay?" she called out to where they stood on the balcony.

"All good," Em called back. "Raj just said something I didn't expect."

Petra fixed the three of them with a benevolently bemused look. "Okay. Don't forget those steaks, all right?"

"Shit, the steaks," Emmett muttered, turning back to the meat, giving Raj a reprieve from his accusatory glare.

"So, you found your mate," Leo said. His face broke into

a massive grin. "I'm happy for you, man. This is what you've always wanted."

That, at least, was accurate. Even though both of his friends had dismissed the story of finding one's perfect partner as what they called the "mate myth", considering it just a story told to pups, Raj had always hoped it was true. Had always, if he was being honest with himself, loved the idea of finding someone who could belong to him as much as he belonged to her. Coming from years as a child in the foster care system, the idea of having someone for whom he'd been made to fit had a dizzying potency to it.

"So, who is she?" Emmett demanded, turning back to them with his barbecue tongs in hand like some kind of weapon. He pointed them at Raj. "And I'm not done being mad at you for not telling us straight away, for the record. I told you practically the minute I found Petra."

"In case you haven't noticed, we've been a little busy running the pack," Raj protested.

"No excuse," Leo said with the air of a decree being issued. "So, who is she? How did you find her?"

Raj paused and took a deep breath. Saying this out loud, would make it more real, more tangible. Once someone else knew, he was letting down a kind of barrier, a protective shield that kept him safe from the thoughts and opinions of others. Once other people knew, he'd have to justify his choices, the path that he'd decided on. And perhaps most importantly, once other people knew, it became a secret that the group of them were keeping from Maggie, who was one of Della's best friends.

"It's Maggie," he said, hearing himself that his voice was muted. It was also, in a way he hoped his friends couldn't read, full of a kind of desperation that he'd never felt before he'd caught the scent of her.

"Maggie? Do we know—" Leo cut himself off as understanding dawned. "Maggie, as in Mags, Della's best friend Mags, came to our party Mags..." His eyes lit up once more. "Don't tell me you found your mate at my afternoon barbeque," he told Raj with a wide grin.

"All right, I won't tell you that," Raj said, returning the smile and knowing his friend would take it as confirmation that he'd first caught Maggie's scent in Leo and Della's backyard.

Unfortunately, Emmett was too quick to be fooled by Raj's dishonest implication. "Wait, if you met her at the party, how come you were planning on breaking up with Olivia before it?"

"I didn't meet her at the party," Raj managed to cover for his slip. "That's what I'm trying to say. She comes to the library, and I didn't realise that the Magnolia my boss is always collecting book recommendations for was the same Mags whom Della talks about, until I actually met her in both contexts." There, that was all true, though he'd implied a timeline that wasn't accurate.

"But she's your mate," Leo said, still apparently needing confirmation. "Maggie, Della's friend, is your mate."

"Yep," Raj said.

"That's fantastic!" Leo crowed, to Raj's surprise. "She's already one of the gang. We're not introducing anyone new, we already know she gets along with anyone. None of that new-girlfriend-meeting-the-friends awkwardness. Francesca says she's good people," he added, referring to Petra's younger sister.

"She's pretty funny," Raj confirmed.

"How the hell are we supposed to deal with someone else with a sense of humour compatible with Raj's?" Emmett asked, grinning.

"Big talk from a man who can't even remember that he's cooking steaks," Raj shot back.

"Shit, the steaks!" Emmett swore, turning back to them.

"So how did she take it, when you told her?" Leo asked.

"I haven't yet," Raj said. "I mean, I know she saw the mate bond process when it happened with you and Della, but she's a human. I don't want to throw something as serious as 'you are my destined partner, and if I spend too long without you, I might actually lose my mind' on the poor woman when I've only met her a couple of times."

"All right," Emmett said, taking the news a lot more evenly than Raj had thought he might. Then again, Emmett had dealt Raj in on his own difficulties with his mate bond with Petra in the beginning, so maybe he was just waiting to hear how Raj was going to deal with it.

"At the very least, I can get to know her a bit, let her get to know me. Hopefully, the witches' 'magic of the universe' is affecting her as strongly as it is me and she feels the draw towards me that Della talked about," he added with a nod to Leo.

"You're going out, then?" the Alpha asked.

"Not... exactly," Raj hedged.

"What, then?"

"I thought I'd ask her out for coffee first, just platonically to talk about books, since she's at the library so often," Raj said. "Have a conversation, try to feel out where her head is at. Do it a couple of times, let her get comfortable with me, then, hopefully, the attraction builds, and she breaks up with her boyfriend for me."

Both of Raj's friends made sympathetic faces when he mentioned the boyfriend, Emmett blowing out air like he'd just taken a blow.

"I'd forgotten Mags had a boyfriend," Leo said. "Some doctor at her hospital, right?"

"Yeah," Raj said, deciding not to mention his own connection to Doc.

"That's got to be rough," Emmett said. "Knowing your mate is with someone else. And she's a human, so you don't even have the guarantee of a mutual bond to ensure she'll pick you over him in the end—ow!"

Leo had reached over and punched him in the arm. "You didn't have to say it like that, dickhead."

"Yeah, fair enough," Emmett said, turning back to the steaks. "Sorry, Raj."

Raj shrugged it off. "It's nothing I haven't thought already."

"Well, these are just about done," Emmett said, "And I don't appear to have burnt the living hell out of them like Petra was worried about. What do you say we take them inside and settle down to the game, and leave Raj to come up with his own love story?"

Belatedly, Raj realised that the game had started while they were talking. He'd been completely unaware of it. "Sure," he said, straightening his shoulders. "I've probably talked enough about this for one night."

"Just promise you'll come to us if you need anything," Leo said, clapping a hand on Raj's shoulder. "You were there for both of us when we were going through what you're experiencing right now, and the circumstances might not have been exactly the same, but that doesn't mean we won't be able to help if anything comes up."

Leo's words struck a chord in Raj that kind of made him want to pull his friend in for a hug, but he had a feeling that would make him uncomfortable. Instead, he offered his hand out in front of himself, and Leo returned the gesture so they were grasping each other's forearms. It was a move they'd performed hundreds of times since beginning it as a mark of their friendship in their schooldays, but the potency of the gesture had never stopped hitting Raj. That these people accepted him, really *wanted* and *valued* his presence, instead of just putting up with him... sometimes, he couldn't understand how the hell he'd become so lucky.

Instead of voicing those thoughts, though, he shot Leo a cheeky grin. "Whatever you say, Alpha."

Leo groaned, but he was smiling too. "Are we any closer to you getting sick of annoying me with that title?"

"Not even a little," Raj said, opening the door for Emmett, whose hands were full with the massive plate of meat, so he and Leo could both precede Raj through into the living room.

Chapter 5

MAGGIE GOT the text while she was getting ready to begin one of her late shifts. It was simple, unadorned. *Hey Maggie, it's Raj here (your librarian friend). Still up for that coffee sometime? I've got book recommendations for days.*

Of course, he'd said he'd get her number from Della or Leo or whomever, as she was stumbling out the door after their strangely intimate-feeling conversation over the Returns desk. She was suddenly struck by the urge to call him, to hear his voice in her ear. He had a beautiful voice, deep and mellow, and just hearing it sent a shiver through her whole body that coalesced into heat blooming at her core.

Not like that afternoon with Jeremy. He'd tried to initiate something sexual, and she'd been unable to summon even the slightest hint of attraction towards him. While he wasn't the most handsome man in the world—*he couldn't hold a candle to Raj,* her traitorous thoughts giggled—they'd always been highly compatible. Maggie had found herself lying silently in bed after she had pushed him away—Jeremy had taken her rejection somewhat gracefully, though he didn't hide that he was disappointed—and they had watched a movie together instead. There was a polite kiss goodnight, and then she tucked herself so deep under the covers that he couldn't imagine she was looking to cuddle. She hadn't been able to stop her thoughts from turning to Raj. It was only then that the warmth had started to roll through her body like a tidal swell, and it felt like such a betrayal of the man on the other side of the bed that she'd rolled away to stare at the wall and wonder whom she was turning into. What had triggered this fierce attraction to a man she knew full well was dangerous, a man she barely knew? Worse, why had it seemed to overcome and destroy her ability to be attracted to any other man—including her boyfriend?

She wasn't going to see Jeremy for a few days because of her run of night shifts and his own gruelling schedule, and she planned to use that time to think through what might be happening to their relationship, if she could use that word to describe it. Was this just the end of the honeymoon period? Was it just a blip that would soon be overcome, and they could return to their usual healthy, if not mind-alteringly spectacular, sex life? *Sex with Raj would be mind-alteringly spectacular,* said that same traitorous voice inside her head. *You'd never want anything else again.* Or was this sudden loss of attraction to Jeremy something more serious, a symptom of a deficit that was only just revealing itself? What if this failure of attraction never went away and she couldn't bring herself to be with Jeremy anymore? The only logical thing to do would be to break up, but surely, she didn't need to do that immediately. She could give herself a little more time to work out whether this was just a brief deviation from the norm. Maybe these few days apart would be good for them, and she'd return from her run of night shifts re-energised and ready to jump his bones once more.

Even thinking about returning to physical intimacy with him made her feel slightly nauseous, though that might also have been due to the anxiety she felt when she considered what she should be doing with this text message sitting in front of her. Was it even a good idea to converse with someone—to develop a friendship with someone—to whom she felt this absurd combination of extreme attraction and something like fear?

Add to that, that she couldn't work out if she was actually afraid of him or just felt like she should be. She'd seen him completely destroy the Professor at the Ring with that savage grin on his face, but when they'd spoken at the library, she hadn't felt like she needed to fear him. If she'd had time, she might even have stayed longer, just to talk with him, to chat about books and enjoy his sense of humour. There'd been no sense of purposeful intimidation; if anything, it had been as though he'd been intentionally not acknowledging the secret they shared for the joy of having something that connected them. And Maggie found that she liked that idea, far more than she should have, the idea of sharing something with him that no one else knew about. Something binding them together beyond what those around them could see.

She had to admit it. She wanted to see him again. So, reading over his text message for what must have been the sixth or seventh time, she finally pulled herself together and spent an inordinate amount of time constructing a response.

M: *I'm always looking for new recommendations as I'm sure Emily has mentioned. A coffee sounds great.*

She'd sent it before she remembered to include the difficulties with her schedule and quickly tapped out a follow-up.

M: *I should mention I'm on nights for the rest of the week. Would next week work for you?*

The reply came back quickly, almost as if he'd been waiting for it. *Don't be silly,* she told herself. *He was probably just already looking at his phone.*

R: *Looking forward to it. Let me know which day works well for you, and we can set something up.*

Suddenly, almost violently, Jeremy leaped back into her mind. She would never cheat on a boyfriend, but the wave of guilt that washed over her as she realised that she hadn't even considered what *he* would think about her texting Raj made nausea roll in her stomach. As far as Jeremy knew, she had just had a couple of nights of not wanting to have sex. Would he feel as awful as she did now if he found out that the reason for that was the very man she was now exchanging messages with and arranging to meet? He couldn't possibly be upset with her for catching up with another man to go over book recommendations, but then, that didn't consider the fact that her attraction to Raj appeared to have destroyed her interest in her boyfriend. Even worse, she thought, was this how something started that Jeremy *would* have a right to be upset about? A casual coffee with a nice guy she wanted to be friends with... but that wasn't all he was, was it? It also just so happened that she got hotter just thinking about him than she did with her actual boyfriend's hands on her body. Could something like that ever be casual when she was so militantly holding back her own attraction to him?

It had to be. Purely platonic, nothing more. She did actually want to spend more time around him, even if just to feel that strange sense of insight and connection that struck her when their eyes met.

And if nothing else, her logical side reminded her, it was probably a good idea to stay on the good side of the man with whom she shared the damning secret of the Ring, just in case he decided that it wasn't in his best interests to keep it a secret anymore.

Are you free Saturday afternoon? she found herself typing out.

I'll have had a chance to sleep by then and might be halfway capable of holding up a conversation.

Maggie took a deep, steeling breath, and pressed send.

What did this make her? Some kind of pre-cheater, not quite a scarlet woman but not quite *not* one, either? She wasn't doing anything that, on the surface, was wrong, but she also knew full well that she was following the letter of the law rather than its spirit.

It wasn't right to be dating one man while actively working to spend more time with the man to whom one was substantially *more* attracted.

But somehow, she couldn't stop herself.

Chapter 6

MAGGIE WASN'T sure she'd ever been so nervous in her life. Which was ridiculous because it was just coffee. Just two people who loved books cementing a tentative friendship to discuss them. He'd even specified, that day at the library when she had no doubt looked shocked at his invitation, that their interaction would be *just* to talk books. They were, after all, bound together by the secret of the Ring, though after their conversation, she felt that more as a connection she could imagine herself *wanting*, rather than one that was being held over her head as a threat. Was there any reason not to make the best of the connection, to make it an enjoyable one now that they knew they had something in common?

Any reason other than the twinge of guilt she felt when she thought about Jeremy at least.

She hadn't mentioned to him that she was meeting a man for coffee, and especially not *this* man, with whom Jeremy had his own relationship. She'd just told him she was catching up with a friend of Della's to talk books. Jeremy had glanced around her bookshelf-lined bedroom and the teetering pile of novels on her bedside table and gave her the gently amused grin that had once made her entire body shiver. Now, she actually felt slightly annoyed, seeing that smile. What had once seemed so sexy now seemed vaguely patronising—*You go discuss your little stories, dear, I'll just be off saving lives*. Confused by her own thoughts, she'd given Jeremy a weak smile of her own and moved off to climb into the shower, taking clothes with her so that she wouldn't have to be naked in front of him. The rush of exhibiting her bare body to him and, of course, his response had once brought her such a delicious, wicked pleasure. Now, she didn't even want his eyes on her, let alone his hands. And there was a strange kind of loneliness which she'd never felt in the presence of another person before, something oddly akin to the feeling she'd had as a child when she realised that, despite being surrounded by magic, she'd never be the one wielding it. A kind of longing for something that she knew full well would never be there. Or, maybe, for someone.

And it wasn't Jeremy.

And why was she doing this now? This casual meeting between unexpectedly linked people, who had found something they had in common? Why was she choosing to spend time with someone like Rajesh Lewis, who seemed to have inspired this strange, unwanted, completely inexplicable longing in her?

Well, mostly, because it seemed that she couldn't *not* do it. At least three times, she'd picked up her phone, meaning to text him and cancel with some trite comment about work, but each time, she'd hesitated with her fingers hovering over the screen, unable to go through with it.

And now, here she was, lurking outside the sweetest, most stereotypical backstreets coffee shop she'd ever seen—Raj had suggested it, calling it "ideal" for the discussion of books —waiting for a massive man with eyes full of understanding to appear. He was ten minutes late, and she'd gone over and over whether she should just go inside and claim a table but decided to wait on the footpath between the large pots of blooming flowers that decorated the café's entryway, surveying the quiet street and wondering if she was out of her mind to even do this. Hadn't Raj, at least kind of, threatened her with exposure at Della and Leo's barbecue? Well, she now thought, that seemed a bit extreme—he'd kind of apologised for it at the library, when he suggested he'd said something wrong unintentionally. Hell, from what Della had said about Raj's routine awkwardness, it was more likely that he was just being awkward and had tried to make a connection with her in the wrong way—he constantly seemed to be policing himself for saying the wrong things, so maybe it was a habit of his, and she'd been on the receiving end. She couldn't, now, properly imagine that he'd meant to intimidate her into spending more time with him, or threaten her. It just didn't fit with the parts of him she'd seen—and the parts that, she couldn't help but admit to herself, she had a strange sense of just from those periods of extended eye contact, when she could have sworn a connection was formed between them.

The bell over the door to her left jingled as she was scanning the quiet back street for Raj once more, indicating that someone was leaving the café. She almost jumped out of her skin when a deep, resonant voice called, "Magnolia, is that you?"

She spun to see Raj leaning out of the doorway, which seemed like it should be far too small to contain his bulk, that gorgeous wide grin of his contrasting his white teeth with his dark skin. "I was starting to worry you weren't coming, and then you moved, and I could half-see you behind one of the armchairs," he said. "You couldn't have been better hidden out here if you'd tried. Have you been waiting out here long?"

"We must have missed each other arriving," Maggie said, her face creasing into a smile of her own even though the rest of her body suddenly felt heavy and unwieldy, in a particularly noticeable kind of way, as though just by looking at her, he'd be able to tell that she suddenly had no idea what to do with her hands.

"I was a bit early," Raj said, an expression she couldn't read briefly crossing his face. "It didn't occur to me that you wouldn't come straight inside. Come on, get in out of the wind. I think you'll like this place." He shifted so it was his hand rather than the bulk of his shoulder holding the door open and gestured her through.

The moment she passed through the door, she knew he had been wrong. She didn't just *like* the little coffee shop—she *loved* it. It was all wood panelling and overstuffed armchairs, little tables wedged in between, decorated with brightly patterned cloths and coasters. And the *books*—everywhere she looked, there was another cleverly crafted bookshelf fitting a nook that no ordinary set of shelves could have conformed to, or a pile of books on one of the small side tables, whetting her appetite to read like nothing else could.

"I hope that's an awestruck silence of approval," Raj said from very close to her, and she realised she'd paused in the doorway right beside him, and as such, his body was so close to her that she could feel the heat radiating off him.

A full-body shiver went through her, and she couldn't keep the sheer, breathless joy from her voice when she replied, "It's *perfect*—how could I have not known this was here? And so close to me?"

Somehow, despite the limited space, Raj managed to manoeuvre around her and lead her to a table tucked away in a corner. He claimed the seat he must have been in before she arrived—the one with a great view of the doorway, but with its view of the space to the right of the door, where she'd stood blocked by another armchair, she noted distantly —and she sank into the other, feeling like she might almost disappear into its well-stuffed cushions.

Almost immediately, a waitress appeared, expertly moving between the many chairs and tables. She was exactly what Maggie would have expected from this place, the far side of sixty, grey hair in a bun, wearing a pretty floral apron suited to a Stepford wife.

She gave Raj a wide, familiar smile. "Your lady friend finally arrived then, Rajesh?" She shot them both an over-done wink.

"Oh, no, she's not—" Raj started.

"I was just waiting outside," Maggie said at the same time, not wanting the friendly lady to think he'd almost been stood up.

"No need to get defensive," the waitress told them merrily, her smile getting even wider. "Tea or coffee for you, honey? I know Raj's order by heart, as I should after all these years."

As if by mutual decision, Raj and Maggie's eyes met, and they burst into a strange kind of almost-awkward laughter, saved from being uncomfortable by the sweetness of their connected gaze. Maggie decided immediately that she would not do any further examination of this phenomenon and ordered her coffee. Raj smiled fondly when the waitress confirmed he'd have tea, as usual, and she manoeuvred her way back through the clustered furniture without writing a thing down.

"So, I'm guessing you come here often?" Maggie asked into the silence left in the waitress' wake. She was still trying to reconcile the image of the massive prize fighter with the fussy, grandmotherly coffee shop; and yet, somehow, at the same time, just the presence of so many books seemed to make it so that he fit into the space perfectly.

"A time or two," Raj admitted. "I put the books back on the highest shelves for them, so sometimes they give me free cake. I wasn't about to let that kind of offer go to waste. Too much of a sweet tooth." He grinned unrepentantly.

"I can't believe I didn't know this place was here," Maggie repeated, almost to herself. "It's so beautiful, like something out of a fairy tale."

"I used to come here on my days off and just read and drink litres of tea all day," Raj said.

"And you don't anymore?" Maggie asked.

"I don't have as much time as I used to," he said with a slightly rueful grin. "Ever since Leo made me Beta, there are always more things that need doing. I only do four short days a week at the library now, too, because there's so much that needs doing as Beta, even with two of us doing it. I don't understand how Leo did the whole job on his own, and he was working a bit on the side. Especially with an Alpha like James."

"He wasn't a good Alpha?" Maggie asked tentatively, not sure how to phrase it, and then rebuked herself. *Tentative?* What was that about? She'd never been tentative a day in her life.

"James?" Raj asked with a bark of a laugh. "Absolutely not. He should have been rousted years ago, but most of the pack was too scared to challenge him, not to mention that they would've had to beat Leo in the fight as James' Second. No one backed themselves that hard—Leo is a beast in a fight."

"As are you, if I remember correctly," Maggie said with a sidelong look, wondering where she got enough courage to mention their heretofore mostly unmentioned Ring connection.

Raj laughed again, and it felt like the sound of it lit up her whole chest from the inside, and what was that about?

"Maybe so," Raj said through his laughter, "but I'm not the one they were taking on as Second, or at least I wasn't, until Leo was James' challenger and he picked me to try to hamstring Leo's potential advantage."

"What's the deal with having a Second in an Alpha challenge anyway?" Maggie asked, steering the conversation away from the traumatic fight Raj, as James' selected Second, had been forced to have against Leo and his Second, Della, despite her desperate curiosity to know more about it. "Surely, the new leader just needs to be able to beat the old one?"

Raj shrugged. "It's always been that way. Maybe to make sure no one can win just because they got lucky with their first opponent, choosing to seize power at a particular point just because the current Alpha is unwell or has an injury. Plus, it's usually the Alpha and Beta fighting as a team, so maybe to demonstrate their fighting skill working together?"

"You had to fight as the old Alpha's Second, though," Maggie prompted, her curiosity getting the better of her now he'd given her a second opening to ask. Pre-empting his answer, she added, "Della told me a bit about it. Pulling all your energy from your body without compromising your life force—not many witches could do that and survive."

She almost regretted asking, seeing the haunted look that passed over his face. "Yeah, James picked me as his Second, mostly as a fuck-you to Leo, so I had to fight for him even though it was the last thing I wanted."

"Why couldn't you say no?" Maggie asked.

Raj looked down at his hands, then up with a rueful grin. "Them's the breaks, unfortunately. When I swore myself to the Pack, I swore to follow all their rules and laws, and that's one of them. I'm not sure the people who wrote the laws realised they might be condemning someone to fight for a cause they completely opposed, but the laws are there, regardless. Once you've been named as a Second in a challenge, you can't back down. Werewolves are big on tradition."

"It must have really upset the apple cart, then, when Leo named Della as his Second."

To her surprise, Raj chuckled. "She kind of announced it herself, actually. And once the words have been spoken in a ceremonial setting like that, you can't take them back." The amusement faded from his eyes as the haunted look returned. "I know I was bound to fight to the best of my ability, but in all honesty, I was terrified coming up against her. She looked so small and tired and alone, and there I was, a trained fighter, forced to protect a regime I'd rather have torn down with my teeth, against the love of my brother's life, and all I could think was that I would rather violate my vows to the Pack than destroy her the way the Alpha wanted me to..." He took in a deep breath and let it out, and then his lips quirked up in a smile. "And then she absolutely handed my ass to me, so I guess all that worry was for nothing. Teach me to underestimate Della—she's got a fighter's spirit to rival any wolf I've ever known." His good humour returned with his last words, but a hint of the shadow remained in his expression. It reminded Maggie of nurses she'd seen in their early, more idealistic days, when they lost a patient and realised that even with the absolute best of care, the best of intentions, sometimes circumstances were beyond their control. Briefly, her mind shot to how it must have felt for Raj to stand up against his best friend's mate, knowing that he had no choice but to beat her to a pulp according to the laws of the Pack to which he'd sworn himself. Seeing her apparently defenceless against his training... and then the strange relief he must have felt as the energy was drained from him as he collapsed into the dirt, knowing he didn't have to hurt her, but also knowing that even *having* that feeling was betraying the laws of his Pack.

She knew she sometimes wore the same expression—surely, all nurses did—and without thinking, she lay her hand over his where it lay on his knee. She only meant to offer comfort, but he jumped like she'd shocked him, or maybe dragged him from a deep reverie with her light touch. But he'd been looking at her, and talking, so was that even possible? Still, she didn't flinch away, just looked down at her small, pale hand against his large, dark one.

"Asked you here to talk about books, and here I am, wasting your time with ancient history," he said, removing his hand from beneath hers to pour the tea that she hadn't noticed being delivered. Gods, how wrapped up in this man had she been? She collected her coffee and sipped at it, savouring how delicious it was, trying to hide that her hands were ever so slightly shaking.

"I don't mind," Maggie heard herself say softly, her voice throaty, then swiftly brought herself back to reality and cleared her throat. "So, what are you reading at the moment?"

"A couple of things," Raj said, taking a drink of his tea. The cup looked impossibly dainty in his big hands, hands that she was suddenly unable to prevent herself from picturing tracing lines on her skin, making her look and feel as dainty as that teacup in his grasp. She swallowed, hard, and tried to pay attention to what he was saying.

"...a book about ancient woodworking techniques and the first in a sci-fi series where the author seems determined to use as many words as possible to describe every little insignificant thing the characters see or do. I swear, I know as much about the construction of their vessel as I do what each of them are thinking. Reading it feels like I'm wading through quicksand just to get to the actual plot."

"Are we talking Tolkien-describing-trees level, or..." Maggie asked, leaving the question open.

"Firstly," Raj said, "Don't ever insult *Lord of the Rings*, or I'll be forced to rescind my invitation to talk books. I don't fraternise with heathens."

"Noted." Maggie laughed, putting her hands up in mock surrender. "But I will respectfully point out that I wasn't insulting him, just referring to his descriptive capacity."

"And second," Raj said, laughing, "definitely worse than Tolkien describing trees. We got a multi-page description of a part of one city—one of many cities they've visited, I might add—where the characters spent a single night. I know more about the cobble-stoning pattern of this region than I do about Mystic City's planning system."

She faked a horrified gasp. "No!"

"Completely irrelevant to the plot," Raj said, "And absolutely no respect for Chekhov's Knife."

"No one even twisted an ankle on the cobblestones?" Maggie asked.

"Not a one," Raj confirmed.

"Why didn't you stop reading it?" Maggie asked, laughing.

"I try never to leave a book unfinished," he said with a shrug.

"Even if it's awful?" Maggie asked.

"Even then," he replied. "I don't like unfinished business."

For the briefest of moments, she imagined she saw a heated look come over his face, thought she might have caught his eyes flitting over her body. But then it was gone, and he was reaching to refill his tiny teacup.

"They really didn't account for the size of men like you when they were ordering their crockery, did they?" she asked, feeling inexplicably off-balance.

He sent her a look with laughing eyes. "Is this a bad time to say, 'There are no men like me'?"

Maggie blinked, recognising it as a quote. "Where is that from? I know it, but I've forgotten."

"No, think about it. I'm sure it'll come to you."

"Now, that's cruel," she protested, and then, like lightning, proving him right, she realised from where she had recognised it. She snapped her fingers, like that could light up the lightbulb she could all but feel switching on above her head. "It's from *The Avengers*, isn't it? Loki says it. I love those movies."

"A woman of taste," Raj said with a grin. "I think Jaime Lannister said it too, but I can't remember whether it was in the *Game of Thrones* TV show or the books. Which is a little embarrassing to admit, as a librarian," he added, seeming not the least embarrassed.

"I think you can be excused for not remembering every single word from *A Song of Ice and Fire*," Maggie said. "Now, there is a writer who's unafraid to explain and describe things irrelevant to the plot."

"A little more embarrassing for me than most, since I have a quote from the series as a tattoo," Raj said breezily.

"Which one? Where?" Maggie heard the eagerness in her own tone and realised she was sitting practically on the edge of her chair, leaning towards him as he was her, like twin trees growing to form an archway. Still, she couldn't bring herself to move more than a little, repositioning herself to sit upright a little farther back on the chair. "You know, if you're comfortable sharing," she added lamely.

"Wouldn't have mentioned it if I wasn't," he said blithely. "It's a bit of story, though."

"I love a good story," Maggie said, unable to deny her eagerness to know.

"Well," Raj said, settling into his chair, "Like most of my

stories, it starts with Leo and Emmett and me getting into trouble."

He was a born storyteller, this man, Maggie thought distantly. His tone had immediately changed into one that suggested whispered confidences, or perhaps being tucked into a cosy armchair by the fire with a book while a storm raged outside.

Maggie blinked at the direction her thoughts had taken. How could just his tone of voice bring forth such a strong reaction in her? Even her skin felt extra-sensitive, like the smallest touch would shatter her completely.

Raj had noticed her response to her own thoughts. "Is something wrong?" he interrupted himself.

"Oh, no," Maggie floundered. "I was just... surprised, that's all—the three of you getting into trouble. You all seem like such upstanding citizens. A hereditary Beta, now an Alpha, and his two Betas too." She thought about it for a moment, and her brow creased. "Other than the fight against your incapable Alpha, that is. And rescuing Petra from that mob of homicidal vampires." She looked up from her hands to see that his eyes were dancing. "All right, maybe 'upstanding citizens' was stretching it."

"Just a little," Raj agreed cheerfully. "We were in trouble more than we were out of it as kids... and for a few years after that. In hindsight, Leo was probably rebelling against the role he'd inherit as Beta, and Emmett and I... well, we were just trouble. How do you think I learnt how to fight?" He raised an eyebrow, holding her gaze as if in acknowledgement of their shared secret, but his grin made it a fun secret, like they were hiding something together from the rest of the world, and together, they would get away with it.

"I just assumed... you know, most packs have fighting classes for their young werewolves..."

"And we were just a couple of boisterous young males

looking for practical applications of the noble art of self-defence," he said, winking. "Too much testosterone, the inability to hold your tongue and a rowdy wolf beneath your skin do not make for a trio of quiet young pups, that's for sure. So, we were in trouble a lot, fought a lot, at least when Leo couldn't talk our way out of it—no wonder he's such a diplomat, he's been training for it since we were kids—and eventually, we got good enough at it to win, at least most of the time.

"The time I'm thinking of, if I'm remembering correctly, was shortly after we were old enough to drink. It's hard for a werewolf to get drunk—increased metabolism and all—but we were down at the pub giving it our best shot. We weren't getting into fights quite as regularly, partly because some of the pack noticed and enlisted us to get it out of our systems in a healthier way, by helping teach some of the fighting classes, and partly because, by then, we had a reputation for being good fighters and fewer people wanted to take us on.

"Anyway, the guys we wound up going up against had been at the pub a few hours longer than we had and were definitely giving their wolf metabolisms a challenging night. Emmett struck up a conversation with a female which because he's Emmett, immediately turned to flirting, which led to her boyfriend seeing another male's hand on her arm and losing his ever-loving mind. He took a swing at Em. Leo and I jumped to his defence, the other guy's friends came to back him up... complete chaos ensued. Broken tables, shattered glasses, screaming patrons. It was like something out of a movie. Thank the gods none of us risked shifting, or we might have brought the whole building down.

"Anyway, they were a bit off their game as they'd been drinking for longer than we had, and as I said, the three of us were decent fighters even then. Clearly, one of them must have realised we were winning and decided to take things to the next level. He grabbed a piece of broken glass and stabbed me with it." He indicated the right side of his body with an almost lazy gesture. "I guess realising what he'd done brought some sense into him, because he and his friends ran for it. Em and Leo got me to the hospital. They repaired the damage and cleared out all the blood that was in the wrong places, and I healed. But I was reading one of the *A Song of Ice and Fire* books at the time and was inspired to put the quote 'Not Today' over the scar on my side, in honour of the close call. Because, what do we say to the god of death?" He gave her as much of a bow—including flourish—as he could while seated, and Maggie realised she was once again on the edge of her seat listening to him tell his story.

"Wow," she said, feeling kind of stupid but unable to come up with a better response.

"Thanks," Raj said. "I'm sorry, I've organised this to talk about books, but I've managed to derail it by telling you my entire life story."

"I enjoyed it," Maggie said honestly. "You're a hell of a storyteller."

"Years of reading fairy tales to children at storybook hour," he said with a grin. "You learn how to do that when you have to do it every week."

"Don't pretend you don't enjoy it," Maggie teased. "I can tell just from your face that you do." And, to her surprise, she wasn't lying.

Raj's smile turned a little embarrassed. "You've caught me. Nothing like a good fairy tale. And the kids just come alive if you read them properly." He cleared his throat. "I mean, we all know they're ridiculous—like, what are the odds that Cinderella had a unique shoe size? And isn't it creepy that Aurora's prince felt entitled to kiss the Sleeping Beauty without her consent? Still, there's something about them that I've never been able to get over, even as an adult. A kind of…

magic." He met her eyes, completely unashamed, and a strange kind of cord seemed to tug at something in her chest, pulling her towards him. Then he smiled, a gentle one this time, and the spell that his words had cast between them faded, at least a little. "So, Magnolia, which one's your favourite?"

"I don't have one."

"Come on, everyone has a favourite fairy tale," Raj said.

"Not me," Maggie said. "I loved them all, of course, because I loved hearing stories. But I wanted a story that I could picture myself in, and all the girls in those stories seem to be meek or stupid, and maybe I'm flattering myself, but I like to think that I'm neither."

"Definitely neither, after that exposition," Raj said with a laugh. She must have looked taken aback because he added, "That's a good thing, you know. At least, it is to me."

She couldn't help the smile that spread over her face in response. "It just meant that I never really related to the regular fairy tales, you know? But stories about the fairies— well, those, I loved."

Raj looked confused. "What do you mean?"

"The stories about the fairies themselves that didn't feel like parables convincing young girls that as long as they were beautiful and well-behaved, a prince would sweep in and change their lives. Good fairies, evil fairies, fairies that stole away children, that left pieces of gold for poor families. At least, they were self-determining; they thought for them-selves and acted on their own moral codes, however skewed they were. I still like to read a lot of fantasy novels, but it all started with those fairy stories. It seemed like once the need to teach girls to be subservient and hard-working to earn the right to be saved was taken out of the picture, you got much richer, more detailed characters who weren't just purely Good or Bad to further the story. And I could see pieces of myself in both of them." She blinked, wondering if she should have revealed that much, but Raj still looked interested, so she continued. "There are lots of good Young Adult fairy stories too, only they're normally called *faeries* with an A-E, or *fey*, or something like that. I liked that they were often viewed by humans as evil and Other, and then once you got to know a few of them, you'd realise they were actually just like the humans themselves, each one different and nuanced and usually just trying to get by under the rules of their own society. Not to make them into parables too, but it kind of makes you think, as a kid reading those books, about the importance of not tarring everyone with the same brush just because they're different to you." She shrugged. "Pretty relevant, for a teenager living in Mystic City."

"I'll have to get you to write a list of the best ones if you're up for it," Raj said. "That way, I'll have it on-hand for the times teenagers ask me for recommendations and I immediately forget every YA book I've ever read."

"Is it the teenagers or the asking that's the problem?"

"Both," Raj said. "Have you seen teenagers? They're terrifying."

"I can't say I have all that much to do with them," Maggie said. "We get nursing students every now and then, but they're usually in their early twenties. They're either utterly terrified or convinced they know everything."

"Which one is worse?"

"Oh, definitely the know-it-alls. They're impossible to teach, because they're positive that the way they think things should be done is the right way."

"It doesn't sound like you mind the teaching so much," Raj said, his voice sort of... soft? Maggie looked into his eyes and once again was all but overcome by the feeling that she was seeing beyond the surface of the man, down into the very core of him, and something in him seemed to call to a matching piece of her.

"No," she blurted out, then realised what she was supposed to be saying. "I mean, I don't. Mind it, that is. It was the best part of my training, actually getting to be on the wards with real patients. Doing all the things we'd been taught so much about for years, and finally putting some of those skills into action. Not that anyone really has any noteworthy skills at that point in the training, but you get to start developing them in real situations. But teaching them, seeing people start to get the positive feedback of making a difference to the patients, can be a really beautiful thing."

"You love it, don't you?" Raj asked. This time, his voice had definitely gone soft.

She ducked her head to hide a smile, feeling unaccountably embarrassed. "Yeah, I guess I do. I mean, there are awful parts, of course—I've never met a nurse who actually enjoyed dealing with bodily waste, or patients who won't listen, and of course, it can be hard being with people who are really unwell. But you get to do so much that's worthwhile, it makes up for the bad bits."

"Della mentioned you do a lot of night shifts," Raj said. "Why not take the day shifts, when you actually get to talk to the people more? It's just, it seems like the people are really your favourite part of it—helping them, that is."

"I'm still doing a lot of that at night," Maggie said, her voice coming out sounding defensive. "It's not just sitting around doing crosswords."

"I didn't mean it was."

She steadied herself with a breath, unsure of the wisdom of how much she was about to reveal, but for some strange reason wanting to do it anyway. "I started doing it when I was working in Palliative Care. Lots of people hold on through the days, when there are lots of things happening and plenty of people around, then slip away in the night, when it's quiet. I guess I just wanted to make sure they knew there was someone there who cared about them at the end. Lots of the patients in that specialty have been hanging on for years, often just for the people they love. I wanted them to know that love was reflected back on them, even when they didn't have family or friends gathered around them."

There was a long moment of silence, and Maggie couldn't hope to read the look on Raj's safe. "You probably think that's kind of strange. Or silly. Or—"

"Not at all," Raj interrupted. "Not even a little. You've got a lot of heart in you, Magnolia. That's a beautiful thing. Not silly at all."

They sat in silence for a moment—though strangely, Maggie thought, it wasn't an uncomfortable silence—before Raj said, "We're not doing at all well at keeping this to talking about books, are we?"

The completely unrepentant look on his face, that grin that might have looked cheeky on someone who wasn't so damn tall, startled half a laugh out of her and somehow encouraged her to continue the blatant honesty. "I think the books someone's read tell you a lot about that person. Even if we'd just sat here and recited Shakespeare's soliloquies at each other, I'd still know you better than before by the ones you chose. Stories lead to more stories, whether they're ones you've read or ones you've lived, and at least in my experience, talking about one type tends to lead to talking about the other."

When she looked up from the now near-empty coffee that she barely remembered drinking, he was watching her with that strange, inscrutable expression. Surprise, maybe. Trepidation. Determination. And maybe even something that looked like... longing?

"I like that," he said after what must have been a long

moment but felt like time had stopped moving completely. "'Stories lead to more stories.' It's completely accurate, but I've never heard anyone phrase it just right before. In the library, people always tell me about what different books mean to them, the stories they've read and the ones they've lived."

A wide smile split her face before she could help it, a warm glow blossoming in her chest at his approval. "Well, I'm glad I could help."

"It'd look good as a tattoo, don't you think?"

Maggie felt her eyes go wide. "You're not seriously thinking of—" She caught the twinkle in his dark eyes and her breath left her body in a rush. "Oh, thank the gods, you're joking."

"Would it really be that bad?" Raj asked.

"To have some throwaway comment of mine preserved forever on your body?" She tried—and failed—not to picture that big, strong body the way she'd seen it in the Ring, heaving tattooed chest, skin shining with sweat, blood running in rivulets. A body that could take complete control of anyone else's, whether that was in a fight, or... She realised what she was thinking and immediately shoved the thought out of her head, bringing herself back to the conversation. What had they been talking about again? Oh, right. "Of course, it would be that bad. Tattoos are supposed to be something special, to mean something. You can't just put a sentence that I rambled out over coffee on your skin forever."

"But it did mean something special to me," Raj said, his voice perfectly even.

"I can't even tell if you're joking," Maggie said, starting to feel desperate.

"Am I?" Raj asked, cocking an eyebrow. Then he winked, and another laugh burst out of Maggie. Despairing of the ridiculousness of men, she rolled her eyes, and in doing so caught sight of the clock on the wall behind them.

"Oh, shit."

"What?" Raj asked, his posture immediately losing its casual laziness as he sat forward.

"Don't worry, nothing serious. I just hadn't realised the time. That went so fast—I really have to go. I told Jeremy I'd see him after work." She felt her face heat and, for some reason, added, "Jeremy… uh, Doc, you know, from the, um, other night."

"I know him," Raj said. His expression still made him look perfectly at ease, but there was something in his posture than Maggie instinctively thought belied that casualness. Maybe he and Jeremy didn't get along? Strange, since they'd seemed quite friendly that night at the Ring. She pushed the thought from her mind—their relationship was none of her business.

"Can I ask you one thing before you go?" Raj said suddenly.

"Of course."

"How did you wind up, uh, *there*, the other night? You really didn't seem to want to be there."

Maggie paused. "It was a long night. It wasn't anything personal." *That was a lie.* "Jeremy finally got approval, I guess, to breach the secrecy spells and tell me about it, and he wanted me to see that it wasn't as bad as I was thinking it was."

"And was it?"

"Not until your fight," Maggie said without thinking. "No offence," she added after a moment. "You two were just a lot more, um, injured than most of the other people. Jeremy was trying to convince me that it was mostly just black eyes and broken noses, minor stuff, but the Professor had a punctured lung and a fractured vertebra. He could have been paralysed. He could have died."

Raj had the good grace to look slightly uncomfortable. "It was a bit more violent than most. He didn't go down easily, and they held off on ringing the bell for longer than I expected. You have to keep going at that point. You're not allowed, as one of the fighters, to announce that you've won already and can they just ring the bell so you can stop punching the guy."

"I don't even know why you do it," Maggie said. "I can't imagine wanting to hurt people like that."

"It's not like that, really," Raj said. "Believe it or not, I actually am a pacifist."

"Then how did you wind up there?" Maggie asked.

"Same as everyone else. Someone heard I was a good fighter, scouted me, got permission to breach the secrecy spells with me, and there I was."

"You couldn't have said no to them?"

"I could. Even now, I could say no if I wanted to stop. They wouldn't be happy to lose their champion, but there's no contracted length of time I have to keep fighting." The look on his face was inscrutable.

"And why don't you?" Maggie asked.

Raj looked at her for a long moment. "I don't want to tell you that," he said.

"Why?"

"Because I'm worried you'll look at me the way you did that night. Like you're scared of me and disgusted by me all at once."

"I don't like violence," Maggie said, then added, "but I don't think I could go back to thinking that of you."

"Why?"

She answered the question with her earlier one. "Why don't you stop?"

"Because for one night every few months, I get to be all the things I can't be in my real life," Raj said. "I have to be measured and thoughtful and supportive and kind, especially now Leo's Alpha, and we're the support team. I can't lose my temper or get in an argument or, gods forbid, a fight. If I even raise my voice in public, people look at me, see what I look like, and assume I'm a danger to them. When you're a foster kid, especially one with a history like mine, getting moved between houses over and over, you spend all your time trying desperately to prove that you're worthy of being kept with that family. For years, other than pack training sessions, I've been leashing every single negative part of myself to avoid fulfilling the worst assumptions people make of someone like me. In the Ring, I can stop working so hard, I can let the worst parts of me out, and no one cares."

Maggie was silent for a long moment as their eyes met and held. That same feeling of connection seemed to tug at her as if urging her closer to him. For a moment, it felt like time had stopped, like there was nothing in this world but the two of them. Out of nowhere, Maggie had the thought that, somehow, she had found someone whose soul made sense to her.

Someone dropped a teacup, and the moment shattered with it. Maggie looked down at her hands, abruptly uncomfortable with how much of him seemed to be visible to her from just a few sentences. "I didn't know you were a foster kid," she said eventually.

"Not a very nice one, either," Raj said with a crooked smile. "Penchant for fighting, picking on smaller kids. I became Blue Crescent after my parents adopted me. The pack changed my life."

"Is that why you feel so strongly about it?"

"The pack? Absolutely. Leo and Em, too. I'd be a very

different person if I hadn't found them." He cleared his throat. "You said you had to go."

Maggie sat bolt upright. "Crap! Yes. I had totally forgotten."

"Maybe we can do this again sometime," Raj suggested. "And maybe, next time, try to actually talk books a little more."

"Stories lead to more stories," she said with a smile, and with a deep breath, she took the leap. "I'd like that. I'm still waiting on those book recommendations you promised."

His laugh seemed to warm her to her very core, sending heat shooting through her body. "Return your books on time this week, and I'll have some ready for you."

She rolled her eyes. "Ugh, if I have to." Impulsively, she leaned in and kissed his cheek above the line of his beard. A feeling like an electric spark passing between them made her pause, just for a moment, before she remembered that she was running late. She'd made this date with Jeremy days ago. Why was she now so reluctant to keep it?

"I had a lot of fun today," she said, pulling back to collect her bag. "Message me, and I'll work out my roster so we can find another day that works for both of us. Oh, and let me give you money for the coffee—"

He put his hand on her arm as she reached into her bag for her wallet. Again, the feeling like electricity passed between them, like they were parts of a circuit that closed when their skin touched. Maggie jerked away.

"I can afford to buy you a coffee, Maggie. Go on, I wouldn't want you to be late."

They both stood, and even knowing she was out of time, Maggie wanted to wait and marvel at him. So big and strong, with all those muscles and tattoos giving him just a hint of savagery... the man was drop-dead gorgeous, she had to admit, and in that moment, she wanted nothing more than to stare at him until she'd committed every inch of him to memory.

One of the café's other patrons sneezed loudly, and again, the moment snapped like an over-stretched rubber band.

"I'll, um," Maggie said into the quiet, "I'll just be going, then."

"I promise not to get any tattoos of your quotes without your permission," Raj said. "At least until I see you again."

"Until then," Maggie said with a smile at his goofy sense of humour, then wound her way out between the overstuffed armchairs and small tables, feeling in a strange way both heavy and as light as air.

Raj waited until Maggie was out of the shop before dropping his head into his hands. Sitting across from her, talking and laughing like this, had somehow been both so easy and, yes, *so goddamn hard*. Had he ever found it so easy to just sit and talk to a woman about things that mattered? Sure, they'd started with books, but it had flowed so easily into stories of his life and hers. Raj was good at chatting, usually, even with women, though his tendency towards humour could some-times mean an inappropriately timed joke ground things to a halt. Maggie didn't seem to mind his jokes, though—she'd laughed with him, and the sound of her amusement had sent what felt like tiny bolts of lightning running through him, lighting him up and heating his blood with arousal, all at once. He'd immediately decided he wanted to hear that sound every day, forever. He wanted her, needed her, so badly that it hurt, but she'd seen him fighting in the Ring and had been so tentative towards him when they'd met. Maybe she understood why a little more, now they'd talked about it.

But still, he needed to show her that he wasn't a threat, that he would only ever use his size and strength in service of her —his blood immediately heated further at the thought of *servicing* her—but never, ever against her. He needed her to see that he wasn't a danger to her before he could ever think of trying to seduce her.

The problem was that was taking time, and right now, everything in Raj was begging him to jump straight to the seducing stage. He'd been as hard as a rock for almost their entire conversation, trying not to shift in his seat too much, in case it drew her attention to the erection he was doing his best to hide. Even the faint scent of her that remained, diluted by the smells of coffee and baking in the little shop, was enough to keep him harder than he'd ever been in his life.

He glanced over at the over-stuffed chair that had almost enveloped her small frame, and realised there was a small, dog-eared notebook almost hidden by the seat's cushion. Had it fallen out of her bag when she was preparing to leave? He flipped the cover open, wondering if this counted as an invasion of privacy, and saw her name and phone number printed in small, neat handwriting. He was on his feet before he knew what he was doing, rushing out of the shop with only a quick, "I'll be right back, I promise," to Lucille, the owner who treated him so well.

Maggie had turned left—did she know where she was going? His blood thrummed with satisfaction at finally being able to *do* something for her, however small, her little note-book clutched in his hand. What was it, a journal? Did he have all her secret thoughts in the palm of his hand? Part of him wished he had time to pause and flick through the pages, to see if she'd written anything about him, even knowing what a violation that would be. Instead, he kept walking, so fast, it was almost a run down the sidewalk. How damn far could a little thing like her have gone in such a short time? He breathed deeply, following the trace amounts of her intoxicating scent that still lingered on the path she'd taken, knowing he was on the right track as it became stronger.

Finally, he caught sight of a flash of red the same shade as her shirt, turning down another alleyway. It was the wrong one if she was trying to get back to the main road, he knew from experience. "Maggie," he called and swung into the alley at speed, only to collide with the woman herself, who'd presumably turned to see who was calling her name. She stumbled backwards with a small "Oh!" of surprise, and Raj reached out and grabbed her as she started to slip on the refuse littering the laneway, holding her close so she could regain her footing.

For a moment, they just stared at each other, her body pressed close to his. Her eyes were wide, deep, dark pools that he wanted to drown in for the rest of his life; her perfect pink mouth was still open in a sweet, shocked O. Arousal once more surged through him, and he realised that she was pressed up against *all* of him—including his still-straining erection, which he hadn't spared a single thought as he'd chased her down the street. It might have gone down a little from the rock-hardness he'd been sporting all through their conversation, but it was now back to full attention, just from the press of her body against his and the sweet look of surprise on her face.

He saw the moment she realised, when her eyes went even wider, and her mouth snapped closed. Could it be arousal that had her pupils dilating, or was it fear?

Her eyes dropped to his mouth. Was it just his imagination, or did her own lips purse just slightly, as though imagining a kiss?

She pulled back a little and Raj let her go immediately

Maggie checked the ground around her feet and stepped back.

"Raj—" she said, and though his name had never sounded as sweet as it did on her lips, he cut her off.

"I didn't mean to shock you," he said, speaking as much about pressing his hard-on to the softness of her body as he was about running into her. "Just, you left your notebook. And this is the wrong street; you want the next one if you're going back to the main road."

"Raj," she said again, but he couldn't seem to stop his mouth from running.

"And this one's pretty foul besides, most of the businesses that back onto it just throw their rubbish out here. And there are stray cats and rats in places like this, so you never know what you're going to step in. I speak from experience."

"Raj," Maggie said for the third time, putting her hand on his arm. The contact of her soft, warm palm against the skin exposed by his rolled-up sleeve shut down his entire brain, and, fortunately, shut up his rambling mouth.

"I have a boyfriend," Maggie said softly. She didn't even avoid his eyes when she said it, and for a moment, his brain supplied the image of her as a warrior queen.

"I know," Raj said and then found he couldn't say anything more.

"It's not... we're not... lately, I can't—" she started, but he just laid his hand over hers where she touched his arm.

"It's okay," he said, then forced himself to add, "I really do want to be your friend."

"I don't know if I can," Maggie said, still staring up into his eyes.

"Why not?" He forced a grin and gestured down at the erection that seemed to be trying to claim all the blood in his entire body. "This doesn't matter. Ignore it."

"I don't know if I can," Maggie repeated, and then,

suddenly, her hands were grabbing at his shirt and dragging him down, and her mouth was meeting his in the sweetest perfection he'd ever known. Her kiss was desperate, furious, her hands rushing over his neck, his hair, down to clutch at his shoulders, like she was trying to memorise as much of him as possible, as fast as she could. With a growl that he felt more than heard himself make, Raj wrapped her in his arms and lifted her. Her legs wrapped around him, and he felt the purest jolt of pleasure he'd ever known at the feeling of her core pressed against him, even shielded by her jeans. She kissed him like she was dying of thirst and he was water, and her addictive scent filled his entire being. Her tongue sought entry to his mouth, and he gave it willingly, tasting only her, intoxicated by her. She tasted like coffee and cherries and nights under the stars, and Raj gave everything he had to the kiss, drowning in Magnolia.

Until, suddenly, she pulled away with a strangled gasp, her legs releasing their grip on him in the same moment, so she slid down his body, right over the place his swollen cock was begging for the chance to touch her.

"I can't," she started, seemingly mostly to herself. "I don't... I shouldn't..." Finally, her tortured gaze met his once more. "I have a boyfriend," she repeated; again, it seemed in large part to herself.

"I know," Raj said, knowing his voice sounded hollow.

"That's why this was a mistake. That's why we can't do this again," she said, and those beautiful eyes looked halfway to tears, so he didn't argue. Didn't tell her that she was his mate, that she was everything he'd ever dreamed of and more, that he'd cut off his own hands if it stopped her from experiencing even a moment of pain.

He stepped away from her, to give her space, to stop his riotous body from bothering her with the evidence of the effect that their kiss had had on him.

"Maybe not do that last part again," he said in a vague attempt to lighten the mood, "but I really would love to talk books with you some more."

"Raj," she started, but he didn't stop to let her demur.

"Just the books part, Maggie, and that's all. Do you know how hard it is for me to find someone who loves to read like I do and is actually capable of holding up a conversation? I really do want another chance to just sit with you and talk books, and this part... we can just call it momentary madness, and leave it behind."

There was a long silence before she eventually said, "I'll think about it." She slipped past him and picked up her notebook from where it had fallen on to the ground—thankfully, a relatively clean part—during their kiss. "Thank you for returning this," she added, not meeting his eyes, and within a moment, she was gone.

Raj fought the urge to lean against the filthy, stained brick wall and *groan*. His first kiss with his mate and it had been in a dirty back alley of all places. And all his ideas of being gentlemanly had flown out the window the moment her lips had touched his. But then, she'd hardly been maintaining a restrained distance herself, yanking him down into the kiss, seeking his tongue with her own, wrapping her legs around him when he lifted her up, shamelessly grinding her core against his abs. Well, at least he knew now that he wasn't the only one drowning in arousal. She wanted him too, even if she didn't *want* to want him, and he could work with that. Dr Jeremy was an obstacle, but surely, if he and Maggie spent some more time together—to discuss books, of course—she'd realise that what was between them was far more important that whatever meagre attraction she felt to Doc.

He wandered back to the coffee shop, deep in thought, and paid Lucille for their drinks. "Come after work tomorrow," she urged him. "I'm making that pear and raspberry bread you like." She gave him a sly sideways look. "And you can take some for your lady friend too if you want.

"Oh, she's not... we're not... she won't be..." he stumbled over his words in an attempt to say... what? He took a steadying breath. "Thank you, Lucille. I'm sure she'll really appreciate it. And if she doesn't, you know I'll eat it."

"I have faith in that, at least," Lucille said with a gentle smile. "You've caught yourself a very pretty one."

He gave up on the idea of trying to convince her that he and Maggie weren't an item, feeling like every protestation just made her believe it more strongly. "She is, isn't she?" he said finally.

"Especially when she smiles. Make her smile more, Raj, there's a good boy." She reached up and patted his cheek.

Of all the women Raj knew, only his grandmother and Lucille would think it was reasonable to reach up his six-foot-six frame to pat his cheek, let alone call him 'boy'. He grinned, and the grin widened when she pressed a wrapped package into his hands. "Banana bread, too," she whispered conspiratorially. "For all those books you put up for me earlier. I put a piece in for your girl, too."

"Thanks, Lucille," Raj said, leaning down to kiss her cheek. "Now, I just have to convince her to eat it with me."

Maggie had no idea what to do. She paused in a recessed doorway off the footpath several blocks down from where she and Raj had... *whatever* that was... and tried to catch her breath, to still her heartbeat from its racing pace, and steady her still-shaking hands before she even tried to make it to the bus stop. She couldn't see Jeremy like this. She couldn't see *anyone* like this, because the only person she wanted to see her like this was Raj, and the naughty part of her that craved that didn't just want it to be while when they were fully clothed in a cute little café. She wanted him to see her like this—to *make* her like this—when they were alone, just the two of them, somewhere better than a dirty alleyway, somewhere private with a bed, or hell, even a table. A space of clear wall. Any flat surface would be acceptable, really.

Dammit, she had to stop thinking like this. Just the idea of his huge, muscled body covering hers, his exposed skin pressed against her own, was enough to speed up her already thundering heart, to go the opposite direction of steadying her shaking hands. She balled them into fists and pressed one to her still-tingling lips.

She must have temporarily lost her mind there for a moment. It was the only explanation. It just felt like, after that long session of trying to ignore her attraction to him every time he smiled or cracked a joke or, hell, even *looked* at her the right way... And then feeling his erection, the undeniable evidence that Raj was as attracted to her as she was to him... It was like something in her just *snapped*, some tether tying her to sanity. And suddenly, the good-girl Maggie Gawler who did the right thing and followed the rules and looked after people and made sensible decisions... it was like that Maggie just didn't exist all of a sudden. Like that version of her had fallen away like a snake's shed skin and, in her place, was left standing the woman he called Magnolia, a woman of power and desire, who would do what she wanted and create her own fate.

But in reality, that woman didn't exist. In the real world, *consequences* existed, especially for things like kissing one man —and grabbing at every part of him you could reach and practically climbing his body—when you were dating another.

She wanted to call Jeremy and tell him she couldn't see

him today. Maybe that she couldn't see him *at all*, that this had gone far enough, and it had been long enough now since she'd felt even an inkling of attraction to him that she was pretty sure it wasn't just a short phase, and she'd now proven graphically that she was still capable of attraction, just not to him. Not the perfect Dr Jeremy, the man many of her co-workers had cooed over before he asked her to dinner, the man she'd surely be insane to allow to get away.

Was it crazy to cut him loose over one kiss and a period of reduced attraction between them?

Maybe she just needed to give it some more time. Time when she was completely and totally, one hundred percent faithful, and not just because to do anything else would be stomping all over her values. Maybe she'd even see Raj again, to prove to herself that today had just been a fluke, momentary madness, and that she was so much stronger than her physical impulses.

The truth was she'd loved sitting there today sharing stories they'd read and those of their own lives, even if she subtracted the attraction that had simmered in her through the whole endeavour. She wanted that friendship—the *friendship* part, she told herself, nothing more—too much to risk it over a stolen kiss in a back alley. Even if the moment his lips had met hers had felt so damn *right*, it was like all her misgivings had evaporated. Even the guilt hadn't hit until afterwards—after she'd tasted his tongue and run her hands across the breadth of his shoulders and clutched at his hair and ground her core against him like she was trying to meld her body into his. It had all felt so *right* when they were touching, as though she was exactly where she was supposed to be.

But that wasn't right. It couldn't be. She and Jeremy hadn't had the official boyfriend/girlfriend conversation, but they'd been seeing each other for a while now. It was probably reasonable, at this point, to assume that exclusivity was part of the deal. And she wasn't, she *couldn't* be, the kind of girl who kissed one man while another had his toothbrush in the holder in her bathroom.

She didn't want to lose what she and Jeremy had created, the instant understanding of each other's work, the easy banter. But all of that was starting to feel more like a close friendship than a romantic relationship, now that she'd all but eliminated the sexual aspect of the time they spent together. If only he felt the same, it would be so easy to end the romantic part of it but keep the friendship. But other than his confusion when she started moving away from his touch, Jeremy still treated her like his girlfriend. He still kissed her hello and goodbye each time he saw her, still reached out for her in his sleep, even though lately, since she'd stopped enjoying his touch, she had to fight not to go rigid every time his skin touched hers. And she didn't want to lose that, the reliability and comfort of what they'd created together, especially not on some kind of wild gamble on a man who, if she was looking at things through a purely logical lens, she should still be at least somewhat terrified of. Raj was the wild card here, and Maggie wasn't someone who enjoyed making high-stakes bets. Even if some part of her was repeatedly insisting that she couldn't imagine ever wanting anyone more than she'd wanted Raj in those all-too-brief moments in his arms.

Maybe she'd been right when she said she just needed to give it some time. A week, maybe just to see if anything changed with Jeremy now that she'd maybe broken whatever psychic barrier had been blocking her off from her sexuality. *You've had no trouble thinking sexual thoughts about Raj all this time,* an internal voice said slyly. *It's just Jeremy whose touch you don't want.*

Maggie steadfastly told the internal voice to shut the hell

up and laid out her plan. She'd see Jeremy tonight, see if things had changed, maybe even talk to him about what was going on between them. That was probably well overdue. Maybe if they could see each other once or twice more during the week if their rosters lined up.

And then... make the choice.

Was she going to keep trying with the safe option, or risk it all—risk her *heart*—on the wild card?

Chapter 7

RAJ CALLED an emergency summit of the boys that evening, after poring over every romance novel he could think of where the heroine started off with someone other than her eventual hero and coming up blank on what to do. He'd been in a simmering state of semi-arousal ever since their kiss, which hadn't been helped by skimming sordid stories and, unavoidably, getting stuck on the parts where the leading lady and her real beloved finally got down and dirty. Before he rang Leo and Emmett, he gave in and had a very hot shower where he wrapped his fist around his aching cock and pretended it was Maggie's hand stroking him as water drew paths down her curves, pretended she was the one jacking him off as she pressed her body to his side and whispered everything he so desperately wanted to hear from his mate. *I've been waiting so long for this. I need you inside me. I want to put you in my mouth. I've been imagining this while I touched myself.* The idea had sent him over the edge, the image of his mate picturing him as she pleasured herself seared forever into his brain. He'd told her after the kiss that they could pretend it never happened, but the truth was, even being near Maggie without touching her had been torture, and that was before he knew how her lips tasted. Going back to that, knowing that she was at least somewhat attracted to him, was going to be torture. But if the romance novels had told him anything, it was that patience was key in this scenario. He had to let her find her own way to him.

Although this genre did feature a significant number of books where kidnapping a woman was viewed as a romantic overture, so maybe he shouldn't take them as gospel truth.

Emmett arrived at Raj's place before Leo, took one look at the books scattered across the table, and groaned. "Really? You're back to these?"

"What's wrong with them?" Raj asked, a little offended. He'd given Emmett a bunch of relevant romance novels when he was trying to convince Petra to be with him, and while Em had never explicitly stated that they'd helped, Raj had chosen to believe that they'd provided his friend with at least a little assistance. And it had worked, hadn't it?

Leo walked in then and also saw the books and laughed. "Really, Raj? You're using these for research purposes?"

"What's wrong with them?" Raj repeated. "Most of them are written by women, for women. What better way is there to work out what women want?"

"Because they're not exactly written as real life women would want something to go," Emmett said. "Can you imagine how mad a woman would be if you actually interrupted her wedding, instead of telling her how you felt beforehand? She might like it in a book, where everything is for effect, but in real life, that shit would get you blacklisted for sure."

"Seriously," Leo agreed. "At least if you told her beforehand and she chose you, she could probably get part of the cost back when she cancelled the wedding. Do you know how expensive weddings are?"

Raj fixed his gaze on his friend. "Not really," he admitted. "Do you, though?"

Leo, realising he'd been caught out, didn't even try to deny it. He grinned unashamedly. "All things going according to plan, I might have a reason to find out pretty soon."

Abandoning the books, Raj skirted the table and wrapped Leo in a back-slapping hug. "That's amazing, man."

"Fantastic," Emmett agreed, giving Leo a one-armed hug of his own. "I'm guessing from your phrasing there, you haven't asked her yet, though."

"Not yet," Leo admitted. "I keep thinking, I'm only ever going to do this once. I want it to be perfect for her. Plus, what with it being a witches' ceremony, I'm a little worried about what it'll entail. What if they want us to dance naked under the moon while they cast spells on us?"

"Then I'll be there to take your commemorative wedding photos," Raj said in his solemnest voice, but he couldn't hold the straight face.

Leo punched him in the arm.

"It can't be that different from our partnering ceremonies, right?" Emmett said. "Wear a nice suit, make your vows, kiss the bride, she throws the bouquet. Big party with your nearest and dearest afterwards, and save the naked dancing for later."

"I don't know," Leo said. "The witches tend to have their own ways of doing things. I just want it to be perfect for Della. She's only going to get one of these. Gods know, I'm never letting her get away." The male-in-love look on Leo's face was unmistakeable, and for a moment, Raj let himself wonder if he looked the same when he was looking at

Maggie. And if he did, how could she possibly have failed to realise how he felt about her? How could she have just walked away after that earth-shattering kiss?

"Oh, no," Emmett said, breaking into Raj's reverie. "Leo, he's got the look."

"Oh, no," Leo echoed.

"The look?" Raj asked.

"The moony-eyed thinking-about-my-mate face," Leo said. "I've seen it in the mirror, and I've seen it on Em, so don't think you can pretend it's something else. What happened with Maggie?"

Raj gave them the rundown of what was going on, sparing only the details of the kiss. The three of them had discussed many of their exploits in the past—mostly Emmett's—but this felt different, like he'd be betraying a confidence if he told them any details of the way Maggie's mouth meeting his had felt like she was branding her owner-ship on to his soul. Instead, he just gave the barest details of their back-alley embrace and the way she'd practically run away from him.

"Petra walked away from me after the first time we kissed," Emmett reminded him. "It feels shitty, but it's not exactly a death sentence. I mean, look at us now."

"No disrespect," Raj said, "but I'd rather not have to go through what you did to get my mate. The kidnapping by subversive vampires really isn't my ideal dating scheme."

Emmett shrugged off the comment. "Hey, at least I get to go home to her every night. More than worth the troubles."

"So, am I supposed to do what you did?" Raj asked. "Help my mate try to get rid of me until we fall in love?"

"Does Maggie want to get rid of you?" Leo asked.

"I honestly don't know," Raj said. "I think if it wasn't for the boyfriend—" *And the fact that she saw me go full savage in the*

Ring, he added silently, "—I might have at least some kind of chance. A kiss like that can't have been an accident, can it?"

"Well, from what she said to you, it definitely sounds like she's attracted to you," Emmett said levelly. "And really, that seems to be where most mate bonds start."

"Della said she worked out what was going on because she was feeling so strongly so quickly, and she cast a spell to see if someone was using magic on her to make her feel that way," Leo added. "Witches refer to their version of mating as 'supernatural magic' that draws two compatible people together. Maybe something like that'll affect Maggie too, even though she's human."

"So, what the hell do I do?" Raj asked again, starting to get riled at his friends' even-tempered answers. They weren't the ones dealing with the fact that their mate had a boyfriend who, from how violently she'd reacted after their kiss, Maggie still felt strongly for. Who, for all he knew, was still getting to touch her in all the ways Raj was dying to, all the things that his instincts as a mated male were demanding that he claim as his own. "Am I just supposed to wait on the sidelines and hope she breaks up with him?"

Leo and Emmett looked at each other, then both shrugged.

"Only thing you can do, really," Leo said.

"Keep spending time with her," Em advised. "Show her you're the better choice in whatever way you can. Just don't push it, and wait until she comes to the right conclusion."

"Maybe I would rather go through what you guys did," Raj groaned, dropping his head into his hands. "Even with the near-death experience. Leo, Della was all over you basically from the moment you guys met. I'd sell a kidney to have that with Maggie."

"I hate to tell you this," Emmett said, gesturing to Raj's

spread of reference books, "But real life isn't always like these stories. Sometimes, the best thing you can do is *not* have sex with the girl."

"You did," Raj pointed out sourly.

Emmett didn't even try to hide his grin. "That's not the point. And besides, it's not like the gods didn't make me wait a while too.'

"Not like this," Raj said, pain spearing through his chest. "Not knowing she could be with someone else."

There was a beat of silence. "Yeah," Leo agreed softly. "You're not wrong." He clapped a hand on Raj's shoulder in what felt like a cross between sympathy and solidarity.

"So, I just wait?" Raj asked into the beat of silence that followed. "I just have to be her friend and wait until she realises it was me all along?"

"Can't hurt to get to know her if you're planning on spending your lives together," Leo pointed out with annoying logic.

"And if the whole hanging out thing had her so worked up that she wanted to kiss you, maybe doing that same thing repeatedly will speed up the process," Em suggested.

"I hate the fucking process," Raj grumbled.

"Yeah," Emmett agreed without a hint of humour. "The process is definitely the hardest part."

Maggie was fairly sure that Jeremy was trying to seduce her. Back before that night at the Ring—*before she'd seen Raj,* corrected the snide voice inside her head—maybe it even would have worked. It seemed the way she'd been holding Jeremy at arm's length the past few weeks was getting to him, and it seemed he had a plan to break their drought.

She'd been on her way home after a long day shift, ready to spend the evening with her feet up and some mindless reality show, but he'd rung while she was still on the bus. Though she didn't like talking on the phone while on public transport and generally disdained those who did, she'd picked up.

"How was work?" he'd asked.

"Busy," Maggie had replied truthfully. "We're still getting heaps of those weird werewolf cases in from Cardio. The ward's filling up. Have you been getting an abnormal number of wolves through?"

"Unless they're trauma cases, I can't say I have much to do with them," Jeremy said, but she'd clearly piqued his interest. "I've been on to the cardio ward a few times, though —we've had a couple of unusual cases wind up there. I missed you, unfortunately, since you've been doing so many nights, but it does seem like there are a lot of wolves there. I see a lot of them anyway—always pups taking stupid risks to prove themselves, and the adults don't grow out of it. There's always something savage in them." Something in his voice sounded slightly off, like he didn't like the idea, but she hoped it was just a doctor's response to the over-filling and chronic under-staffing of the ward. She'd never thought of Jeremy as racist. "You should think about cutting back on nights," he added, his tone returning to normal. "They could really use someone as skilled as you during more of the days. It's chaotic there."

"They need me on nights, too," Maggie said, unwilling to get into this argument she'd had a hundred times before, especially while she was sitting next to a stranger on a bus.

"Anyway, I'm glad I caught you before you settled in for the night," Jeremy said, and Maggie had the sense he hadn't even heard her response. "I thought I'd take you out for dinner tonight since we're both off, somewhere nice. I'll pick you up in about an hour if that works?'

She could hardly refuse him that, not with the guilt of the kiss she'd shared with Raj still weighing heavy in her belly. She'd agreed, and instead of the relaxation she'd been hoping for, spent the next hour choosing a dress appropriate for 'somewhere nice', and going through the complicated process of turning the face of a nurse finishing a long shift into a happy-to-be-treated-so-nicely girlfriend face with full hair and makeup. The dress was a deep red, cut in a way that emphasised her curves and, somehow, with its below-the-knee length, actually made her look slightly taller. She was just blinking on mascara when she heard Jeremy's knock on the door and called out to let him know she'd be right there.

She knew she'd made the right choice to dress fancy when she saw him. He was wearing black pants and matching jacket with a blue button-down shirt, and carrying flowers. *What is that about?* asked a voice in her head. He hadn't brought her flowers since they'd first been dating.

"Great dress," he said after she ushered him inside so she could strap on the heels she'd chosen.

"Thanks," Maggie said with a smile that felt false. Hell, this whole situation felt oddly false, as though she was acting out a part in a play, rather than living it. How could she not, when while she'd been thinking about whether they should break up, Jeremy had been planning this fancy date? The guilt weighed heavy on her chest, but she tried to ignore it, tried to pretend it wasn't there with every breath.

'Somewhere nice' hadn't been an overstatement of the place Jeremy took her to. The waiters all wore waistcoats and ties, and the food was excellent. Their conversation flowed easily, as usual. Having someone who understood the troubles faced when working in a hospital was in some ways a relief, not needing to explain the difficulties of patient-staff ratios or the edicts handed down by the administrators or the inevitable hierarchical politics, all to someone who had never experienced it. And if she was a little more stilted, a little more awkward than usual, well... that didn't have to ruin the night. She decided to push down the guilt at least for the length of their date, to just ignore it and enjoy the delicious food and the company of this man who, if nothing else, she still liked. All relationships went through troubled patches, right? When the honeymoon period faded, and the realities of meshing two lives set in. Maybe that was all this was, all this needed to be—a blip for them, after which everything would go back to normal. A new normal, where maybe they weren't tearing off each other's clothes every time they were alone, but their attraction maybe became more mental. Maybe she could use tonight to kick-start her body into wanting him again, overcome the block in her mind that had cut off her attraction to him.

She resolutely did not think about a certain librarian even when Jeremy asked what she was reading at the moment—he didn't love books the way she did, but still every so often tried to discuss them. It should have made her happy that he was interested, but he always seemed to expect some kind of reward for discussing something she cared about, like he was doing her a favour, like he was wearing a sign saying, *look how good a boyfriend I am, paying attention to her interests*. A stray thought made her consider whom she'd rather be talking to about her reading choices. She shoved the thought out of her brain and told him about the Jeffrey Archer novel she'd picked up at a garage sale, trying not to notice when his attention started wandering partway through her explanation.

He drove them back to her house, one hand on the steering wheel and the other on her fabric-covered thigh, a move that had once brought her skin into goosebumps with growing desire. Now... sure, it was suave, but she felt no surge of heat as she once had when he'd touched her. She tried to focus on kick-starting the blossoming burn of want, imagining times they'd been together in the past and how good he'd made her feel, but her body remained resolutely un-aroused.

When they got to her house, she bustled around making tea for herself. Jeremy refused when she offered him some, openly running his eyes down her body as she moved around the kitchen. She found herself chattering inanely about work and friends and more books she'd read recently, until the kettle boiled and she had no choice but to take a seat with him at the table, her tea steaming in front of her. He was going to try to touch her again, she could feel it taut in the air between them, try to break the drought she'd put them into with her lack of interest. She took a sip of too-hot tea and sputtered as the near-boiling water seared her tongue.

"That was amazing food," she managed after her eyes stopped watering, reaching desperately for anything that would break his focus on seducing her. "I feel like I'm about to fall into a food coma."

"Maybe I can give you a good reason to stay awake," Jeremy said and leaned forward to kiss her.

She couldn't help it, she flinched away, unintentionally knocking over the mug of tea. It spilled, mainly over the table, but some splashed on to both of them. Maggie leaped to her feet, heedless of the pain from the hot water soaking through her dress, and grabbed a couple of tea towels from the drawer. When she returned, Jeremy was magically bringing most of the tea back towards the cup while grimacing, presumably from the pain of being splashed himself. She felt a little like laughing at the absurdity of it all, but instead, she spread the tea towels over the remaining mess before he could fully return the liquid to the glass, needing the activity to keep from focusing on the look on his face, which firmly removed any trace of humour from the situation.

She bit her lip and kept cleaning up the water, carefully keeping her gaze fixed on the tea towels in her hands even once she'd finished. "I guess I'll just go and put these in the laundry."

"Maggie, what was that?" Jeremy asked, his voice loud and sudden in the quiet.

"I just spilled it," she said quietly, knowing she was avoiding the real question. "I didn't mean to. I'm sorry. Are your legs all right?"

"That's not what I mean, and you know it. Mags, you *flinched* when I touched you."

She risked a glance up at him, then immediately looked down again, unable to stand the pressure of the concern and confusion in his gaze. "I didn't mean to," she repeated.

"Is this still about that night at the Ring?" Jeremy asked, and she looked up in surprise. "Practically ever since then, it's like you can't stand to have my hands on you. You don't want to have sex, you hardly kiss me anymore, you move away when I touch you... Was it really so awful, seeing what I do there? It's not like I'm the one hurting anyone. It's practically the same job I have at the hospital, and I know that's never bothered you."

"It's not that," Maggie said.

"Then, what? Did something happen?"

"No, it's not like that."

"Then, *what*? Tell me how to fix this, Maggie, and I will, but I can't keep doing this, wondering what I've done so wrong, you barely even let me kiss you goodnight." His words cut deep, knowing she had been hurting him with her distance.

Her next words came out in a blur, surprising even her. "I think we should break up."

There was a moment of silence where Maggie felt she might be almost as stunned as Jeremy looked. What had happened to her plan of giving it a week? Deep down, she knew the answer—she knew that, in truth, she wasn't going to somehow magically overcome this revulsion she felt when he touched her, knew after that incredible kiss with Raj that it wasn't some issue with her ability to want a man. Knew that it was just about what was between Jeremy and herself. Or more importantly, what wasn't anymore.

"*What?*" Jeremy could hardly have sounded more surprised if she'd smacked him in the face.

"You're right," she heard herself say, feeling the truth she was finally forcing herself to face ringing through her chest. "We can't keep doing this. It would be unfair of me to ask you to. And I don't know what's going on with me, what's causing it—" Except that it revolved around a certain man whose kisses made her long for everything she could no longer stomach with Jeremy. "—but until I have it figured out, I think we should break up."

For the first time since she'd known him, it appeared Jeremy had been rendered speechless.

"I'm sorry," Maggie said quietly. "I didn't plan this, and it feels awful, especially after you went to such trouble tonight, but you're right. What we're doing right now just doesn't feel... right." She took another deep breath, wondering if she should be crying or something, but inside, she felt only a strange sense of relief that she would no longer be playing a role in Jeremy's life that she didn't feel like she fit anymore.

"Maggie, what the fuck?" Jeremy said, apparently having overcome his stunned silence. "Where is this coming from?"

"You can't say this hasn't been coming, in one way or another," Maggie said, her tongue apparently freed by the

intense sense of relief. "You're right, that night at the Ring...
something changed. We can't deny that, and we've been
fumbling around with it until now, but it's not fair to either of
us to continue a relationship where I can't even stand you
touching me."

"You can't..." Jeremy trailed off. Again, he looked like
she'd hit him or something equally unexpected. "Jesus,
Mags."

"I'm sorry," she said helplessly.

"I didn't know you felt like *that*," he said, apparently not
even registering her apology. "I just thought it was some kind
of slump, just a sex thing." He drew in a deep breath, like he
was fighting for control. "Can't stand me touching you?"

"I'm sorry," Maggie said again. "I'm so sorry." Suddenly,
she found that the absent tears were threatening as she took
in his shock and pain.

"Maggie," Jeremy said, reaching out for her as if to pull
her in towards him. They both seemed to notice her body
freeze, muscles clenching as if for an attack, at the same time.
He checked his movement but didn't drop his hands for a
long moment, eyes roving over her face like he was trying to
find some kind of alternative meaning to what she was
saying in her features.

They stared at each other for a long moment, and the
tears in Maggie's eyes finally overflowed. She wiped them
roughly on the sleeve of her dress, and the moment broke.

"I should go," Jeremy said. Something in him seemed to
have hardened in the moments she spent wiping her eyes,
some distance he was pushing into place between them. He
stood up jerkily, the sound of the chair pushing backwards
heinously loud in the silence.

"I really am sorry," Maggie said. "You have to know that.
If I knew how to fix it, I would."

"Maybe when it's fixed, you'll come back to me," he said,

turning to look at her, holding her gaze with his own. Something flickered in his eyes, something she couldn't identify. Something dark. An unfamiliar expression flitted across his face, a ghost of a sneer. "And maybe when you do, you'll realise I'm not the kind of man you let go."

As the door swung closed behind him, she wondered what he'd seen in her face.

Chapter 8

MAGGIE TRIED TO BE GOOD, to be respectful of the fact that her relationship had just ended, but in the end, the draw she felt pulling her towards Raj would not be overcome. She called him three days after what she was thinking of as The Jeremy Evening.

He answered the phone on the second ring. "Hi."

"Hi," Maggie said, suddenly tongue-tied. "It's Maggie."

"I know, Magnolia, I have your number saved. Caller ID is a thing."

"Oh, right." There was a pause. "Is this a bad time?"

"Seeing as I'm sitting outside the library eating lunch in the sun, I'd say it couldn't be a better time, actually." Raj's voice sounded utterly contented. "What's up?"

She'd been so ready for him to say yes, it was, and could she call back later, that his response stunned her into silence. She froze, panicking. Had this been a terrible idea?

"Maggie?" Raj prompted her.

"I was just wondering," she started, the words coming out hesitantly, "if you wanted to get another coffee sometime."

The last part of her sentence flooded out in a rush of syllables. This was so stupid, putting herself out there like this. What if he thought she was talking about their kiss and asking for more of that, even though she hadn't had a chance yet to mention that she was no longer with Jeremy? What if he thought she was some kind of cheater?

"Sure, that sounds great," he said, effectively dissipating the torrent of anxiety that had just flowed through her brain in the space of half a breath.

"What?" Maggie asked, struck to stupidity.

"Sure, that sounds great. Let me know your shift roster and we'll find an afternoon we're both free. I'm assuming, working mostly nights, you won't be up for a morning catch-up."

"Only if you want to speak to me while I'm borderline comatose," Maggie said, her caught breath leaving in a rush of laughter. "I'm not exactly a morning person, especially with my timetable."

"Me, either, unless forced into it by the unreasonable demands of my job, so I get where you're coming from." How was it possible that just *hearing* this man smile was enough to make warmth glow beneath her skin? "Afternoon works perfectly for me," he continued. "Do you want to go back to Café Luci, or is there somewhere else you'd rather go?"

"No, Café Luci is good. I actually don't live all that far away from it."

"Della might've mentioned you live right near the Pack's territory line in that area," Raj said, and she could just picture his cheeky grin. "It's a great café. I'm there all the time since it's so close to work, but I did pick it because I thought it might be easy for you to get to."

"That's really thoughtful," Maggie said, wondering why it

was hitting her so much that he'd thought about her convenience. *Jeremy never did that,* said a little voice in the back of her head. *He just decided he wanted to go to extravagant places and expected you to be available.* She shoved the thought away and focused on Raj.

"It was nothing. Does it look like you'll have an afternoon off this week, or should I languish in desperate wait for your presence until next week?"

Maggie didn't even try to smother her giggle at his dramatics. "You wouldn't know languishing if it bit you in the ass, Rajesh Lewis."

"Best not make me try it, then." He laughed, the sound a great boom that warmed Maggie from top to toe.

"How about Friday?" she said once she'd overcome the strange sensation of second-hand happiness. "I finish early that morning, so I'll be all right by mid-afternoon, and I'm not working that night. One of the other nurses needs the overtime, and I can sacrifice a shift or two here and there, so I let her have my Friday."

"That's a kind thing to do, Maggie," Raj said after a beat.

"She needed it more than I did," Maggie said.

"Still a kind thing," Raj said.

Uncomfortable with the praise, Maggie bit her lip and said, "So, Friday? Just text me what time works for you if the day's all right."

"The day works fine. And I promise not to make it before mid-afternoon, so it doesn't count as an early morning in your wacky sleep cycle." She could hear that he was grinning again.

"That would be much appreciated." Maggie laughed. "And bring your A-game on the book recommendations, please, because I've just finished rereading *Lord of the Rings* and I'm floundering for something to follow it."

"I'll see what I can do," Raj said, "And if we have it, I

can tell the library to hold whatever takes your fancy until you get in there to pick it up."

"That would be fantastic," Maggie said. "I've got to go in anyway when I get a chance and return my latest bunch. And pay the fines on them, because they are, once again, a few days late and I'm disorganised."

"As if Emily will let anyone charge you fines," Raj retorted. "That woman adores you."

"Good thing, too, or I'd be the one picking up extra shifts," Maggie said.

"You could always just return your books on time," Raj suggested.

"Let's not be ridiculous," Maggie retorted.

"All right, fair enough." Raj was laughing, and the sound made something in her chest feel like it was glowing. "I'll just get through a couple of days of the languishing, then, and see you on Friday?"

"Sounds good," Maggie said, knowing he would hear her smiling. "Good practice for you, the whole languishing thing."

"Oh, you're planning on making me languish again in future?"

"Absolutely," Maggie said, making her voice snooty. "It's good for your constitution."

"What happened to 'first, do no harm'?" Raj demanded, still chuckling. "All right, I'll message you a time for Friday. It's one of my Beta Jobs days, so I'll see how much I have to get done that morning and text you when I'll be finished by. And no earlier than, let's say three. Sound good?"

"Yeah," Maggie said softly, "I'm good."

"Perfect," Raj said. "Now, a large group of uni students is approaching the front door and Emily is signalling me, so I'd better finish this sandwich and head inside. I'll talk to you later?"

"Looking forward to it," Maggie said, a little surprised that she was purely, entirely, telling the truth. In the space of one short conversation, all her nervousness had somehow been eliminated. All it took was a few minutes of joking with Raj, and her concern about her attraction to him all but dissolved. It should have been unthinkable, but somehow, it wasn't. She felt none of the pressure or weirdness she'd worried would be between them after that kiss. This was Raj —how could she have thought he'd be anything but a gentleman? Sure, he had another side she'd seen in the Ring, but she was no longer thinking of it as a dangerous attacker; somehow, in the back of her mind, that thought had been converted to a kind of appreciation for his skill and comfort in knowing that if trouble ever struck, he'd be able to defend himself. The side that he kept showing her—not the *savage*, as Jeremy had described werewolves, but this gentlemanly, book-loving, joke-cracking side—was one of the nicest people she'd ever met, plus or minus a few awkward moments. Why did it still come as a surprise every time he was nice to her?

And stranger still, why did such a simple thing make her want him even more? Just hearing him laugh, listening to his gentle teasing that made her feel like part of the joke instead of the butt of it—why did something so simple, so *normal* have her blood heating like he was stroking his fingers over her skin? Why did making a time to chat about books with him leave her feeling like she'd done something so *right?* Like the universe had aligned to put them in the same place, and this was exactly what she was meant to be doing?

Something in that thought triggered some remnant of a memory in the back of her mind, but when she reached for it, it disappeared. Maggie shivered and put her phone away. All that was left was to get through the remaining days until Friday.

And it kind of felt like, in the interim, she'd be doing some languishing of her own.

She'd thought she might be able to avoid Jeremy since their shifts rarely overlapped, but she hadn't taken his nights on call into account. Or that he might seek her out.

She was finishing her observations round, checking on a sleeping patient whose blood pressure seemed to have been slowly rising for half an hour, when she heard a throat-clearing sound from outside the room. She knew who it would be even before she caught sight of his livid expression.

"Why didn't you page me when Mr Farid needed attention?" Jeremy demanded, gesturing towards the sleeping patient. His voice was hushed, since most of the patients were asleep, but she could still hear the venom in his voice.

"Because you're a senior doctor?" Maggie said, her tone unintentionally making her comment sound like a sarcastic question. "He's just having arrhythmias. He's admitted under cardio. Why would I call you?"

Jeremy's expression switched to a smile as another of the nurses walked past, finishing up her own obs round. When he looked back at Maggie, the grin disappeared, replaced by fury once more. "I would have thought you, of all people, would realise that Mr Farid has been my patient for *some time*." He made a face like those words should have some special meaning for her, and suddenly, she realised why the patient's face had looked slightly familiar. He was one of the fighters from the Ring. She hadn't recognised him without the bruises, but if she imagined one of the battered faces Jeremy had healed that night... yes, the werewolf in the bed could definitely have been one of the fighters. And now that she thought about it, hadn't there been some others among the influx of werewolf patients the cardio ward had received recently who had looked familiar? Were the Ring fighters being injured so significantly that their hearts were giving out?

"Did he do something to his heart *the other night?*" Maggie demanded. She whispered the final words, just on the off chance someone was close enough to hear. "Is that why I've seen some of *the others?*"

"Of course not," Jeremy snapped. "I heal them before they leave. If nothing else, surely, you know I'm a good doctor." He looked down his nose at her for a moment, as though considering her inferiority, before explaining, "It's because they're all on drugs, these werewolves. They cook them in their pack territories and take them to make themselves more vicious when they fight. There must just be a bad batch doing the rounds of *that place*. I've admitted a few of them and listed myself as the doctor to call with issues, but I thought you'd at least be smart enough to recognise them and call me first, even if I wasn't listed."

"What do we do?" Maggie asked. "Is there some way to inform the organisers? And they can make sure the bad batch isn't... doing the rounds anymore?"

Jeremy huffed out a nearly silent laugh. "They wouldn't care. None of the wolves and criminals who run that place give a shit who they hurt. They'll just leave it for better people to deal with." He lowered his voice. "Surely, you didn't think they'd pay us that much if the job ended the moment we walked out the door."

"I signed up for one night only," Maggie protested, fighting to keep her voice from rising. "If all these werewolves coming to us are drug reactions, I want someone held responsible. I won't be your accomplice in keeping something like that quiet."

Jeremy considered her for a long moment before sighing. "I'll see what I can do. And in future, call *me* for these cases—anyone you even think you might recognise from *the other right.* Otherwise, it'll turn into a law enforcement issue, and the last thing I want is for you to get tangled up in something like that."

She felt some of the wind go out of her defensive sails. "Okay. Thank you, I guess."

"I'll always try to protect you, Maggie," he said, and before she could reply, he was gone.

Chapter 9

RAJ WAS, to put it gently, something of a nervous wreck. Even after the way their last coffee not-a-date had ended, Maggie still wanted to see him again. She'd specified that she was after book recommendations, which he figured was probably a subtle way of saying that she'd liked spending time with him, but what had happened between them wasn't going to get a repeat. And he was just going to have to be able to live with that, to live with the knowledge that his mate didn't even want to kiss him again.

Yet, contributed a hopeful voice in his mind.

He hesitated over even thinking the single syllable, not wanting to jinx his chances. He just had to follow Em and Leo's advice and become her friend for now, and then, hopefully, her attraction to him would blossom the way Della's had to Leo even though Della wasn't a wolf. And *then* she'd realise that they were meant to be together, fall desperately in love with him and finally, *finally* let him lay his hands on the gorgeous body that had been haunting his dreams, along with a significant chunk of his waking moments. If he kept having to hide out in the stacks to wait for his aching erection to go down after remembering the taste of her lips and the feel of her body against his, he was going to start getting into trouble at work. But no matter that he'd been jerking off —over the same memory, like he was a pup again who couldn't keep his cool around females for more than a few seconds—so much that he was at risk of a sprained wrist, just the memory of the way she'd kissed him had him hard as a fucking rock. And he didn't seem to be able to stop himself from reliving that memory, what felt like every ten seconds.

Suffice to say, it was damned fortunate that his job meant he could have a book in his lap without raising any questions.

And there you go, he was starting to get hard just thinking about all the orgasms he'd wrung out of his cock in Maggie's honour since the last time he saw her. This time, it was happening while he was standing outside Café Luci waiting for her to arrive. On the street. In the middle of a Friday afternoon. Gods, this was messed up. How the hell was he supposed to play the part of platonic book club buddy when just the memory of her scent made him stiff?

"Hey, Raj. You okay there?"

Gods, he'd been so caught up in trying to stop himself from getting hard, he hadn't noticed Maggie approach. Some apex predator he was. "Oh, hi. Yeah, I'm good. Just, um, wool-gathering." *And imagining how your pussy will taste when I finally get between those thighs.* He shook off the thought. "How are you? You look…" His vocabulary failed him. *Stunning. Gorgeous. Edible.* "…nice," he finished lamely, and mentally kicked himself. She didn't just look nice, with all that dark hair framing her face and the frayed hem of her denim skirt tickling her upper thighs. She looked like he imagined a feast would look to a starving man, and he wanted to dig in.

"Thanks," Maggie said, tucking her hair behind her ear in what looked like self-consciousness. Shit, had he said the wrong thing and embarrassed her? Weren't women supposed to like compliments? That was what all the books said!

"Do you want to go inside?" he added lamely in the hopes of covering up the potential mistake. "I didn't want us to get stuck like last time, so I figured I'd wait outside. Less chance of me missing you."

"I'd have a hard time missing you," she said, then bit her lip in a way that was so enticing he completely forgot what she'd said. "Actually, I'm dying for a coffee," she added.

"Lay on, MacDuff," Raj said, gesturing for her to precede him through the door. Luckily, his goofiness got a giggle from her, and the sound ran through him like electricity in his veins as he fought to keep his eyes off the way her cute little skirt cupped her pert little ass. She preceded him through the café all the way to the same table where they'd sat last time, and as soon as they'd sunk into their seats, Lucille appeared. She patted Raj's cheek like he was a child and asked, "Coffee or tea for you today?"

"I'd love a coffee. Thanks, Lucille."

"And you've brought your friend again! Same as last time for you?" she asked Maggie.

Raj didn't even hear Maggie's response—he was too caught up in the way the afternoon sunlight struck her hair, highlighting all the different shades.

"Won't be long," Lucille assured them before expertly wending her way through the sea of chairs and tables.

"I wouldn't have picked you for a Shakespeare buff," Maggie said, and it took him a moment to realise she meant his comment by the door. "But then," she added, eyes roving over him with a slight frown, "I wouldn't exactly have picked you for a librarian, either." She met his eyes again and a cheeky grin spread over her face, and the urge to lean across the table and kiss it right off her mouth was so strong, it was almost painful.

"I think all librarians are Shakespeare buffs," Raj managed to reply. "It's practically a job requirement."

"Do you have a favourite, of his plays?" Maggie asked, then admitted, "I specify plays because I'm not so good with the sonnets."

"It's all right, you're not a librarian. No one will kick you out of the club for not knowing the sonnets." He winked at her, and did he imagine it, or did her breath catch just slightly? He decided it had probably been a product of his desperately overactive imagination where she was concerned and tried to pick up the conversation again. "It'd have to be one of the comedies. No one does comedy like Shakespeare."

"Nobody?" Maggie asked with a laugh. "Nothing else can compare? *The Office? Seinfeld? Austin Powers? Deadpool? Arrested Development?* Okay, I'm running out of comedies I can think of off the top of my head."

"Look," Raj said, feeling himself grinning, "listing my favourite shows and movies is not going to make me change my mind. No one beats Shakespeare. I mean, *Twelfth Night? Much Ado About Nothing?* You can't top that."

"Even *The Hangover?*"

"Even *The Hangover.*"

"*Schitt's Creek?*"

"Now you're just listing off titles. Have you even watched all of these?"

"Irrelevant," Maggie brushed off the comment with a flick of her hand. "Am I getting anywhere? Because, with a moment's preparation, I can come up with a long list of these." Gods, was that smile-and-head-tilt combination supposed to be so sexy?

"You can keep going all afternoon, but you're not going to break me."

She laughed again, and again, the sound ran through

him like quicksilver. "All right, fair enough. Do you have a favourite Shakespeare quote?"

Raj barely had to consider. "Okay, you might laugh at me for it, but it's just about the subtlest high-class burn in literary history. I've gone through so many Shakespearean insults, and this one, in my opinion, is the most perfectly succinct and perfectly savage while, at the same time, you know it would take someone a minute to realise they'd been insulted. And it's not quite Old English, so it doesn't immediately come across as a Shakespeare insult."

"Lay on," Maggie said, echoing his *Macbeth* quote from earlier. "You've talked it up now. My expectations are high."

"In *As You Like It*, Orlando comes out with the line, 'I do desire we may be better strangers,' and I've been wanting for years to say that to someone I want nothing to do with."

Maggie laughed. "I would've thought you'd go for one of the dirty jokes."

"No way. Shakespearean sick burns all the way. 'I'll beat thee, but I would infect my hands'? 'You are as a candle, the better burnt out'? Comedy gold."

"The only Shakespearean burn I can remember off the top of my head is 'Villain, I have done thy mother'," Maggie admitted.

"*Titus Andronicus*." Raj nodded. "Good pick."

"I've got another one, actually, but it's not Shakespeare."

"Out with it," Raj said, grinning. "I'll see if I can guess where it's from."

"Okay." She straightened up, striking a pose as if she was about to read a soliloquy from the Bard himself. "'May your genitals sprout wings and fly away'."

"Weirdly, I'm pretty sure I do know that one," Raj said. "I remember it's Terry Pratchett. Give me a second, and I'll come up with the book. *A Hat Full of Sky*?"

"Nope."

"Wait, *Small Gods*?"

"It's like you have a library indexed in your brain," Maggie said, shaking her head. "That was seriously impressive."

"Just a good memory for pithy insults I've recently wanted the opportunity to use," Raj said. "How about this one: 'He would make a lovely corpse.'"

Maggie's face scrunched up as she thought, and Raj wondered if anything in the universe had ever been so cute.

"No, all right, you got me," she said. "I've heard it before, but I can't remember where."

"It's Dickens. *Martin Chuzzlewit*. Maybe getting slightly too deep into the indexed library of literary insults."

"No, give me another one," Maggie said. "It doesn't have to be an insult. I need to prove myself now."

"All right," he agreed easily, and before he could stop himself, he found himself quoting, "'Whatever our souls are made of, his and mine are the same.'" Gods, could he be any less subtle? Surely, she'd notice how he spoke the words directly to her, as if he could somehow imprint them on her soul the way she was imprinted on his.

Maggie blinked several times, as if she was trying to clear spots from her vision. "Oh, I think I do know that one. It's by one of the Brontë sisters. *Jane Eyre*?"

"Close. It's from *Wuthering Heights*."

"Dammit, so close." She leaned forwards to take a sip of her coffee, the coffee he hadn't even noticed arriving, he'd been so wrapped up in her. Book talk with his gorgeous universe-chosen mate? What could possibly drag his attention away from that?

"I think I may have to concede that you have something of an advantage over me here," Maggie said with a sigh.

"Come on, I know you're not giving up that easily. How about this one? It's one of my favourites." He cleared his throat and adopted as dramatic a pose as he could in the deep-seated armchair. "'In the beginning, the Universe was created. This has made a lot of people very angry and been widely regarded as a bad move.'"

"Oh, I know this!" Maggie crowed, her eyes lighting up. "Give me a second, give me a second... Douglas Adams, right? *Hitchhiker's Guide to the Galaxy?*"

"So close. It's from the sequel, *The Restaurant at The End of The Universe.* It's one of my favourite books."

"Thinking of getting that one tattooed on you too?" Maggie asked teasingly. Oh, but he loved that she would tease him. It made him ache to tease her back, but in a very different way...

"It wouldn't really be in theme with the rest of the tats," he managed to reply, his throat as dry as sand.

"Really? What's the theme?"

"I..." He found himself pausing, considering his words. "You know, now I think about it, I've never really tried to put it into words before," he said slowly. "Books. Life. How to live better. How to love better. Reminders of things that have meant something to me. That kind of thing." He looked down, a little embarrassed, and was shocked to see one of her small hands cover one of his, her pale skin stark against his own. Her touch sent electricity shooting through him.

"That's really beautiful," she said quietly, and he looked up to see that her face had gone a kind of soft he'd never seen on her before.

Foolishly, he shrugged off the compliment. "Maggie, I'm six and a half feet tall. Men like me aren't beautiful."

"I thought there were no men like you," she teased again, withdrawing her hand. A buzz went through him at the realisation that she was referencing their last conversation. Did she remember that meeting with the same crystal clarity that he did?

"All right, genius, point taken." He laughed. "Come on, give me another one. It's your turn."

"My turn? All right, let me think…" Her face scrunched up adorably, then broke into an equally adorable smile. "Okay, I've got one. 'Somewhere inside all of us is the power to change the world.'"

"Roald Dahl," Raj said immediately. "*Matilda.*"

"That was fast!"

"We read it at storybook hour a few weeks back," Raj admitted. "Otherwise, there's no way I would have remembered. If we're doing kids' books, though, I'll give you an easy one, 'Oh the thinks you can think up if only you try!'"

"Too easy," Maggie said, "since you already told me about your other tattoo. Dr Seuss, right?"

"You got me," Raj said. "*Oh, The Places You'll Go.*"

"This is easier for you," Maggie said with a self-deprecating grin. "You must have a million quotes to whip out at the drop of a hat. I'm just working from books I've read recently."

"You've read Roald Dahl recently?"

"Okay, maybe not that one," Maggie conceded, then brightened. "But this one, yes, 'It is a far, far better thing that I do than I have ever done; it is a far, far better rest I go to, than I have ever known.'"

"Dickens again," Raj said, smiling. "*A Tale of Two Cities.* Though, I'll admit," he added, leaning closer and lowering his voice, "I did get a hint from scanning in your last round of returns."

Maggie laughed. "I knew you were cheating somehow!"

"Just with that last one. It's a little dark, though."

"Kind of describes how I feel when I finally get to drop into a coma-sleep at the end of night shift," Maggie said. Her smile faded slightly. "The first part used to be how I felt about my job, too."

"Used to be?" Raj asked, trying not to do anything that could make her stop sharing.

"I got into nursing because I wanted to help people," Maggie said. "I could have tried for medicine, trained as a doctor, but I thought nurses had a better relationship with their patients. More consistent, more present, while the doctors kind of flit in once a day and make the big decisions, then leave us to do the work to put them into practice." She cracked a smile. "Not that I'm biased or anything. And all of that is true, but I guess I've started to feel a little disillusioned with it lately. So many of the patients we have coming in at the moment, especially with all these werewolves appearing, come into Emergency for something small, usually minor trauma like a broken bone or a deep cut they need closed, and then their hearts just... give out. They last maybe a day or two before they crash. Some recover, but not all of them. And I just hate that it might be..." She paused and bit her lip, then continued. "Anyway. Add that to the normal cast of characters of cardiac patients, and so many of our patients are either getting sent back to ICU or their hearts are slowly getting worse and worse, and there doesn't seem to be anything I can do to stop it. And losing so many is starting to get to me, I guess." She shook her head as if trying to shake off the thoughts. "Sorry to get all deep and morbid on you."

"No need to apologise," Raj said. In truth, he was fighting the—in this case useless—urge to kick the shit out of anything or anyone causing his mate distress. "Would it be worth trying to be moved to a different ward if this one is causing you so much grief? Or something that might make it a bit easier? Day shifts, instead of overnight ones? I think it was you who told me that lots of patients, um, let go at night."

"You can say 'die', Raj, I'm not going to fall to pieces over it," Maggie said with a ghost of a grin, then sighed. "Maybe you're right. Maybe once this current wave dies down. They're so understaffed at the moment, it wouldn't be fair to do it now. But maybe that much of a change will give me the kick in the pants I need to stop feeling like this. To start enjoying it again." She sighed. "All I know is I'm too young to be feeling this burnt out."

"I can imagine. It sounds like it's really weighing on you."

"I know I have to do something about it," Maggie said, her voice soft. "I can't just keep chugging along under this much frustration, this much loss. I can't just lie here under the weight of it."

Entirely unbidden, and entirely inappropriately, Raj's brain supplied him with the image of Maggie under *his* weight, of how his muscles would tense to keep the bulk of his body from crushing her beneath him, of the way he'd relish the eventual burn in service of her. He tried to inhale while drinking and, instead, choked violently on the dregs of his coffee.

"Gods, are you okay?" Maggie asked, half-rising from her seat.

"Fine," Raj croaked, which set off another coughing fit.

"I'm not sure I can Heimlich someone your size," Maggie said once the coughing had passed. "I'd give it a go, of course, if you needed me to, but it's not like I have werewolf strength. I'm just a puny human—I think it'd be beyond me."

"Hey," Raj said, his voice rough from the coughing. "You're not *just* anything, Magnolia. Why would you say that?"

"I didn't mean anything by it—" Maggie started, looking nonplussed, but Raj was already on a roll.

"Just because you couldn't lift me off the ground, doesn't mean you're anything *less* than a werewolf, Maggie." He heard his own anger in his voice, that she might think that of herself, that someone might have made her think that, and the bonded male roared to life. *Protect her*, his wolf seemed to howl. *Any way you can. Even from herself.*

"I can't do lots of things, Raj," Maggie said, her voice becoming heated. "I can't heal people with some herbs and a flick of my fingers. I can't clean an entire ward full of beds in the time it takes to blink. But I came to terms with that a long time ago, because that's how life is."

"Is that warlock boyfriend of yours making you feel bad because you can't do magic like him?" Raj snapped, his blood heating further as he considered the option. The doc was so goddamn unworthy of her, and the fact that he might make her feel that way... Raj felt his eyes complete the shift to silver that he'd been fighting since the he caught her scent outside.

"Jeremy? No, he's not—"

"He'd better not be," Raj heard himself growl.

"No, he's—" She caught sight of his silver eyes and her own widened. "Okay, calm down."

"I am calm."

"You're bloody not, and I don't need you shifting in the middle of a café. All right?" She paused and took a breath, then another. "Look, Raj. I appreciate that you're getting all worked up over this in my defence, but you don't have to. I don't need you to protect me from the concept of species differences, and I definitely don't need you to reassure me that I'm still worth something even though I'm human. And I do appreciate where you're coming from, that you're trying to be nice, but to be honest, it's kind of patronising that you'd immediately make this assumption."

Raj blinked at her as she, rather pointedly, took a sip of her own coffee. He had never so acutely understood the phrase "biting his tongue". Okay, yes, what she was saying was definitely true, and he'd kind of been an idiot, assuming she needed his assurances, but then again, she didn't know he was repressing his instinct as a bonded male to protect her from even the most minor threats to her happiness.

With an effort, he reined in the part of himself that wanted to shower her in assurances, since she'd made it clear that would not help his case. The wolf inside him, still growling at any potential threat to his mate, quieted under force, though he was pretty sure his eyes remained fully silver. Maggie looked at him over the rim of her cup, her gaze as steady as her hands. Why did he get the sense that she was giving him time to process her words, when some part of him felt like it should be the other way around?

"I'm sorry," Raj managed eventually. He went with the first quote that fit the situation. "'I've been an inexplicable fool.'"

The moment drew out as she paused, and he wondered if she was just going to get up and leave. Instead, she cracked a smile that grew like a flower blossoming and rolled her eyes. "How dare you manipulate me by using the words of my one true love, Mr Fitzwilliam Darcy of *Pride and Prejudice*?"

"I saw it in your returns pile," Raj admitted. He steeled himself. "Look, I'm sorry. I didn't mean to go full man-splain about your own intrinsic value. Wait, that's not right. Wolf-splain?"

"Raj-splain," Maggie corrected him with another generous smile. "Just do me a favour and don't do it again, okay? I know I'm a human surrounded by supernaturals, and I'm okay with being the one with the least magic in my veins, but I don't necessarily want to be reminded of it more than necessary."

"I'll do my best," Raj said. "But as stated, my inexplicable foolishness does come out on occasion, so please forgive me if it takes a minute to take effect. And I really am sorry."

"I'll keep that in mind," Maggie said. "What were we talking about before, um, that?"

"Your job, I think," Raj said. "And whether there's anything I can do to help you in your quest to fall back in love with it." *Ideally,* said a voice in his head, *paralleling my quest to make you fall in love with me?* "Short of getting a 'Maggie is the best nurse ever' tattoo, but only because it wouldn't be in theme, not because I don't believe it."

Maggie gasped in exaggerated shock. "I can't believe you're refusing to do that for me. So selfish." He noted her eyes catching on the tats on the back of his hands and extended them so she could look.

"They're not all quotes," she said, pointing to the old American-style compass, surrounded by roses.

"No, I've also made space for some classic clichés," Raj said with a laugh. "The ones on my body are mostly quotes. The compass is so I can always find my way back to where I'm meant to be. It doesn't have a needle, so it's also a reminder that it's up to me to decide where that direction actually is."

"And I don't have to ask about the crescent moon, Mr Blue Crescent," Maggie said, gesturing to his other hand.

"The pack has been everything to me for a long time," Raj said. "Back when tradition was everything, every wolf in the pack would have a blue crescent tattooed somewhere on their body. Some people even got them in absurd places, like in the middle of the forehead, just to show how deep their tie to the Pack ran. I decided on the back of the hand, because there's a motion they used to do in some of the older cere-monies where you'd strike your chest over your heart with a closed fist, then extend an open hand. The really old rituals are hardly ever used these days, but I like the tradition of it, the meaning behind the movement. So, I have the crescent on the hand I'd use for it."

"That's... really powerful," Maggie said, and for a moment, their eyes met and held, and Raj almost forgot how to breathe, she was so lovely.

"What others do you have that I can't see?" she asked, looking down.

"You didn't see them at the Ring?" Raj asked. "I was shirtless on your gurney."

"I was a little preoccupied," she said softly, and then before he could read too much into her words, added, "let me guess, angel wings on your shoulders?"

"Am I that much of a cliché?" Raj asked, only half-pretending his horror.

Her eyes flicked to the roses surrounding the compass, and she raised her eyebrows.

He laughed. "All right, I'll give you that one. No, most of my back is covered by an open book, actually. There's a poem written on the pages, from a book called *The Prophet*, by Khalil Gibran. He's one of the only poets I've ever really resonated with—don't tell Shakespeare, but I was never much of a sonnets guy—and this one is all about how to love well. It's one of my favourite things I've ever read, so I got it inked on me."

"Wow," Maggie said, looking stunned. "I would not have guessed that."

"A couple more on the front of my chest," Raj went on, suddenly wanting her to know every piece he'd had preserved on his skin, wishing he could show her, wishing she was running her fingertips over every last one as he described them. "A few quotes, some more pictures that mean something to me."

"Which is your favourite?"

Raj laughed. "I think of them like children. You don't have a favourite, you love them all equally, just in different ways."

"And you have a whole brood of tattoo-children," Maggie said, a smile curving up one side of her mouth.

"Actually, don't tell any of them, but my favourite is probably one I don't have yet," Raj said, wondering why he was sharing this detail.

"It's always about the next one?" Maggie asked.

"No, actually," Raj said. "When I started getting inked, I decided to leave the space over my heart clean until I found my mate, so I could put something of her there. Em and Leo thought I was being ridiculous when I told them—they didn't believe mates were real, called it a myth right up until it happened to them. But I've always believed it was true, or at least hoped it was true, and I wanted to keep the space to honour my mate when I found her." Carefully, he didn't allow himself to stare at Maggie as he spoke, feigning embarrassment when what he really wanted to do was ask, *so do you want to come with me when I have them write your name there?*

"Raj," Maggie said, and when he looked up, her face was as soft and open as he'd ever seen it. "That's beautiful. You're a secret romantic under all that big-man bluster, aren't you?"

"Nothing secret about it," Raj said with a laugh, knowing he was breaking the fragile moment, but also knowing he had to if he was going to avoid announcing to the entire room that his mate was *right there*, enthralling him further with her, every moment, and she didn't even know it. "I've always believed there was truth to the stories about mates, or else why would there be so many of them? Or maybe "hoped" is a better word —hoped that the universe would manage to make someone just right for me, meant for me, as much as I was made to be theirs. Someone who would love me as much as I loved her."

There was a long silence, a deep silence, and Raj realised he might have alienated Maggie with that statement—with her not knowing that every part of him craved her—rather than making her want to lean more into the mating thing, maybe to learn more about it.

He crooked her a smile. "But I'm having fun in the meantime." No, wait, that wasn't the right thing to say. That implied that he was fucking around while he waited for her. That was a terrible thing to have said—

"It's the only way to do it," Maggie said. "If the universe has a special man for me, I'm yet to find him."

It's me, Raj wanted to shout, but he didn't. He was still trying to let her get used to him, he reminded the mated wolf crawling beneath his skin that wanted nothing more than to immediately steal her and overcome any reservations she might have, using the power of his body. And his mouth. And his tongue...

"So, if you were going to get a tattoo," he heard himself say in an attempt to draw his mind away from that train of thought, "what would you get?"

"Oh, I have one," Maggie said, inadvertently, igniting his desire to know every inch of her body. "It's small, but I have one on my left arm, just a line down the bicep."

Raj realised in that moment that he'd never seen her in a short-sleeved shirt, and on one level, he mourned not having this knowledge of her, but on another, he was glad that he was getting to have this little secret exposed and explained to him on her terms.

"It's not fancy," Maggie said, "just typewriter script. 'I have not come this far, to only come this far'. Two lines of words."

"That's beautiful," Raj said.

"Oh, you can call my tattoo beautiful, but the minute I try to say it about yours, you're suddenly too manly for it to count?"

"Darling, when you're seeing my tats bare and in person,

you can call them beautiful. Until then, it's just the story you're complimenting."

His voice had come out rough and low, and was it his imagination, or did his words have her catching her breath as she stared at him? Was she imagining the scene he'd just described, just as he was? At the very least, she seemed lost for words and, fortunately, was saved by the bell by Lucille popping her head into their little bubble of closeness. "Sorry to bother you," she trilled, "just wanted to let you know we'll be closing shortly. I don't have any extra carrot cake for you today, Raj, but I've wrapped you up a few of the blueberry muffins, and you'll be back soon at any rate, so there'll be more."

"Back soon. Of course." Raj knew his voice sounded a little false, but it was jarring to be brought out of the one-on-one bubble he and Maggie had been in, insulated from even the thought of other people by the background hum of the café's other patrons. "Thanks, Lucille."

"And I packed up a few for your young lady as well," Lucille said cheerfully, producing the two parcels, brown paper bags stamped with the songbird emblem of Café Luci. She dropped one in each of their surprised laps, then collected their cups and whisked away, wending her way sinuously through the many clustered armchairs.

"I haven't been called a young lady in years," Maggie said under her breath with a giggle.

"Well, Lucille is about a hundred and ten by my reckoning, so we all count as young to her, I think," Raj said. "Shall we head off?"

They both managed to manoeuvre their way through the now mostly empty café, leaving with a wave to Lucille, and for a moment, they lingered on the doorstep.

"Which way are you going?" Raj asked.

"Just down here," Maggie said, gesturing left.

"Same as me," Raj said, though he would probably have said that if she said she was going straight upwards, just to spend more time with her. They turned left and, for a moment, walked together in silence. "I remember you saying you lived quite close, have I got that right?"

"It's about a twenty-five-minute walk, according to my GPS," Maggie said. "I'm actually only a few streets over from the corner of Blue Crescent territory. I partly moved there because it's fairly close to Della's old place—Avalon coven's territory is only a ten-minute drive."

"I thought you didn't drive."

"Will it alarm you if I remind you that taxis exist?" Maggie asked with a laugh.

Raj grinned. "Fair point. How long does it take you to get home from work if you're not driving?"

"It's about a forty-five, fifty-minute walk."

"You're not walking for an hour in the middle of the night!" Raj protested.

"I usually get one of the late buses that drops me off a block from my house," Maggie said. "Sometimes the walk is therapeutic, though. Being on the ward right now, is a little stressful. It can be useful to decompress."

"I'd rather you weren't doing that in the early hours of the morning, alone, through streets that might not be safe."

"I hate to tell you this, Raj," Maggie said pointedly, "but it's kind of none of your business what I do in the early hours of the morning."

He looked down at her and realised that they had stopped just outside the entry to the alleyway where they'd so fiercely kissed last time. And he couldn't stop the growl from entering his voice as he replied, "And what if I want it to be?"

He was certain this time that he saw her pupils dilate, as

certain as he was that her mouth dropped slightly open, taking in a quick breath in surprise at his words.

"Maggie——" he said, but she interrupted.

"Raj." She sounded slightly breathless. "Raj, I have to tell you something."

There was a pause, and even that slight waiting was too much for him. "Whatever you say, just know it's not going to change anything."

"I broke up with Jeremy," she said, and it changed everything.

Her words seemed to pass into and through his body like an X-ray pulse, leaving everything inside him visible for all to see. She was free, she wanted to spend time with him, her eyes were flicking between his mouth and the entry to the alleyway beside them, her scent was intoxicating him, and everything in him was begging him to take her in his arms and kiss her until she forgot the doc's name, until the only thing she was repeating was his.

"Maggie——" he said again, but she was on a roll.

"I didn't… I couldn't…" She took a breath, looking slightly frantic, slightly desperate. "I couldn't let him touch me anymore. Not when I was thinking of someone else."

"Magnolia," Raj said. "Tell me it's me you were thinking of, or I might die right here."

Instead, she launched forward and kissed him.

He caught her in his arms, knowing she'd trusted him to do just that when she jumped up to wrap her arms around his neck. Her scent was in his lungs, every part of him clamouring that this was exactly the thing he was meant to be doing, just *this*, right now, so perfectly that one of the carefully scripted scenes in his books couldn't have done any better. She was perfect, her hands bunching in his hair, her tongue meeting his, the *taste* of her, the intoxicating taste that he knew he would never stop craving. She was perfect, his Magnolia, her legs wrapping around his waist just as they had the last time they did this, only, this time, there was none of the sense of wrongness about it, because she was free, and she was *his* and she'd been thinking of *him* just as he'd been craving her every moment since he'd met her. His hands came up her thighs, cupped her ass, squeezed even as his tongue traced over hers, memorising the taste of her. She gasped against his lips, her hands grasping at his hair, this little queen demanding everything he had to give, tilting his head so she could sink her tongue deeper into his mouth, stealing his soul. He'd already been certain that she was his, but now, he truly felt what it meant to know that he was hers, that every part of him belonged to her, that he would fight and kill and die to protect her, to protect what was his.

His body was still shaking with the intensity of that realisation when they separated, and he felt a visceral satisfaction at the knowledge that she was breathing like she'd just run a marathon.

"Wow," Maggie said and then looked down, like she hadn't meant to say it out loud.

"You got that right," Raj said, unable to stop the grin that was spreading over his face. This was *it*, the moment he'd be able to look back on all the years of their lives, the moment that she came to him completely free and his for the taking, and he held her as his own for the first time.

"You can put me down," she said, "if I'm too heavy."

"Baby, I bench press more than you," Raj said, pressing her close against him, letting her weight rest against the rock hardness of his cock pushing up between her spread legs. "I wouldn't let you get any farther away than this if there was a train bearing down on us."

She tilted her head. "Not sure mutual suicide is where I was expecting this conversation to go." But she was smiling, her face soft and sweet and entirely focused on him, like he was the entirety of her universe in that moment.

His own smile felt like it couldn't possibly get any bigger. Was this what love felt like, separate to the mate bond, and yet entwined with it in every way? That every moment with her in his arms was like someone had given him everything he'd ever dreamed of, wrapped up in a bow? "I didn't say I wouldn't jump out of the way of the train, just that I wouldn't let you go even if I was in the process of saving our lives. I like you right where you are."

"I like it here too," Maggie said. "Thank you for saving me from the theoretical train."

"Any time," Raj said, lowering his head and kissing her again.

"Do you mind?" someone close by demanded, and Raj was suddenly reminded that they were standing still half-on the footpath, though he'd taken a step back into the mouth of the alleyway when she'd launched herself at him for that first kiss. He pulled back from the intoxication of Maggie's mouth to see a short, very round man wearing an apron, holding a chair in each hand.

"I'm trying to set up for dinner here," he said acerbically. "Mind getting a room?"

Immediately, Maggie loosened her grip on Raj's waist and slid down his body to the ground—an act which in and of itself raised his internal temperature even further—but he kept her in front of him with a hand on her shoulder.

"We'll get going," Raj said. The man set up his chairs, pushing one so close to Maggie, it was practically in her lap, then went back inside. When Maggie looked up at him, he added, "Magnolia. You can't imagine I'm in any shape to be walking down the street right now. I'll take someone's eye out."

Her smile when she realised what he was saying was a

unique flavour of wicked. "I'd say I'm sorry," she said, "but I'm really not."

"I wouldn't believe you if you did. I can literally see your delight right now."

She giggled. "So, what's your plan? Hide out in the alleyway until things, um, calm down?"

Raj took a step backwards, pulling her with him. "Right now, my plan is to work out whether your place or mine is closer, followed by getting there as soon as possible, taking the phone off the hook, and seeing how interesting I can make your three-day weekend."

"Oh," was all Maggie said, her eyes wide, lips parting in surprise as she stared at his mouth. She blinked, twice, apparently collecting herself. "And do I get a choice in my participation in this plan?"

"Always," Raj said, "but judging from the way you were just grinding on my dick, I'm going to assume that you'll say yes."

"That would be... a fair assumption," Maggie said with another cheeky grin and reached up to trace a fingertip over his mouth.

"You're not helping with the whole calming-down thing."

"I'm not aiming to."

"The longer we have to stay here for me to be suitable for public view, the longer it will be before I get you on your back in my bed and show you all the things I've been dreaming of doing," Raj said. He knew his eyes, obviously fully silver, would be glinting in the dim light of their surroundings.

She immediately withdrew her touch. "Well, far be it from me to prevent that from happening."

"That's what I thought," Raj said, grinning freely. He took a deep breath. "All right, talk to me about something completely non-sexual, before I have to start this process all over again."

"Um... how's the whole Beta thing going?"

"Oh, that," Raj said. He took a deep breath, trying to form his sex-scattered thoughts into words and then sentences. "Well, the Pack elders are finally coming around to the three of us as leaders. Which is saying a fair bit, because we used to be the ones they routinely had to punish for breaking rules and getting into fights all the time. I think they're starting to see us as adults rather than those idiot teenagers—it only took them ten years—and they're coming around to the whole two-Beta thing slowly. Leo's rationale was that, as Beta, he was so busy, he didn't get to have much else in his life, no career, barely enough time to chase Della down. He figured it made sense to make it a part-time job for two people, rather than have it take over the life of one. Because the role of Beta is hereditary in our Pack unless a new one is actively chosen by the Alpha, if Emmett or I have a kid, they'll move into the position when we die or retire, whichever comes first."

"Wait, how come being Beta is inherited, but you have to challenge to be the Alpha?"

"Well, for the more traditional packs, the role of Beta is not supposed to need to be the backup Alpha, or the enforcer of the Alpha's will. The Alpha is supposed to be able to do that themselves. The Beta is more like the Brains Trust to provide intelligent support to the Alpha, who makes the final decisions and is capable of enforcing them. From the reading I've done, I think, ideally, the Beta is older and the Alpha is the younger, stronger one. Then, when the Alpha has grown past their fighting prime, they move into the role of Beta, and the child of the Beta, who has grown up and is entering their own fighting prime, has the opportunity to become the new Alpha if they can win the challenge, which often isn't a difficult fight. For some of the super-traditional packs, the challenge for Alpha is effectively ceremonial, because they follow that blueprint almost to the letter. It backfires, of course, when you get an Alpha like James, who wouldn't even hear of stepping down, even after he was completely relying on Leo to do most of his job. Anyway, choosing two Betas, especially two who are the same age as the Alpha, is kind of diverging from the traditional ways. Obviously, the elders aren't too fond of that, but the fact that things are running so much more smoothly since Leo took over from James has really helped with gaining their approval."

"I actually didn't know any of that," Maggie said. "I thought I knew quite a lot about supernatural cultures, but I didn't know that."

"It's not exactly surface-level info, from what I've been able to tell. I had to do a bit of research to even be able to put together what the original ethos was. Even the packs that still follow it closely don't exactly talk about the reasons behind it, and given that they're usually the most conservative ones, they don't always share a huge amount with the outside world, even other packs."

"Have we taken care of your... problem?" she asked, and he could have sworn he saw an actual twinkle in her eyes.

Raj realised he'd been so involved in what he was talking about, he'd managed to redirect at least some of the blood that had been swelling his cock back to his brain. "Taken care of it enough. So, is your place or mine closer, do you think?"

"Twenty-five to mine," she reminded him.

"Then it's mine. Can I take you home, Magnolia?"

A wicked smile spread across that perfect mouth as she said, "Yes."

Chapter 10

IN THE END, it took them well more than twenty-five minutes to get to Raj's house, because they couldn't keep their hands off each other. Maggie had never been so passionately kissed, so many times, in such a small space of time. And she gave as good as she got, repeatedly finding herself shoving her hands up under the hem of his shirt to stroke over his bare skin, revelling in the feeling of his abs clenching under her touch. Minutes could have stretched into hours for all she knew before they turned down a quiet suburban street and Raj guided her up a path through a well-kept front garden.

"This is your place?" she asked in surprise.

Raj paused and looked around the organised yard, as if he was taking in the white-picket-fenced area for the first time. "Were you expecting something different?"

"I mean, I wasn't expecting you to live in a dirty bachelor pad full of cockroaches and rats, because that wouldn't be good for the books."

"Oh, that's the only reason you weren't expecting that?"

"Of course not. I just didn't expect something so... homey."

"Homey?"

"Well, it looks like somewhere a Stepford Wife would live. Like there should be an apple pie cooling on the windowsill. It looks like you cut your grass with a ruler. Do you have a golden retriever as well?"

For a moment, he looked slightly sheepish. "I've been thinking about it."

"*You're* the Stepford Wife!" Maggie exclaimed. "Where's your floral apron?"

"I'll cook you breakfast in just that in the morning," Raj said, steering her towards the front door once more. "But I've been waiting a long time to get you into my bed, Magnolia. Don't make me wait any longer just because you need to overcome your horror at how nice my house is."

"It's not horror," Maggie said, but then Raj was dragging her through the front door and into a space that she had no time to register because, within half a second, he had her pressed up against the back of the door and was kissing her again, lifting her easily into the air so her mouth was even with his and her legs were so easily wrapping around his waist, like this was the exact place she'd been designed to end up. Like she was always meant to be right here.

His mouth broke away from hers long enough to press kisses to her neck, to her collarbones exposed by her shirt, his tongue tracing patterns on her skin, and she moaned, the noise loud in the dim interior. Then his lips were on hers again and she found herself dragging the fabric of his own shirt up his back, pulling it over his head, and he turned the two of them and walked deeper into the house, passing through doorways she barely registered because she was so focused on his mouth. On *him*. He tasted sweet and perfect, like the most addictive drug she could imagine, his mouth claiming her own over and over.

Finally, his grip on her ass loosened slightly and she opened her eyes to find that they were standing in a dim bedroom dominated by an enormous carved wooden four-poster bed. Maggie released the grip of her legs around his waist and slid down the front of Raj's body to find her feet. There were several windows covered by curtains, just enough light seeping in around their edges to show that almost every inch of clear wall space was covered in bookshelves. She turned in a circle, taking in every detail from the bedside table stacked with more books to the dark wood dresser the same colour as the bedframe. The sound of their breathing was loud in the dim space. She could almost hear her own heartbeat, could certainly feel it pulsing through her body. She went to grab the hem of her shirt to pull it over her head, but Raj's hands stilled hers.

"I've been dreaming of this. Let me do it."

His words seemed to touch her with physical weight, stroking over her skin to settle in the most private places of her body. He pushed her backwards until she was against the bed, then pressed her shoulders down so she sat on it. It was so high, her feet were almost dangling off the ground. He knelt before her, removing her sandals, then sat back on his heels, trailing his hands up her shins, gripping her knees and pressing them apart, his eyes hungry on her skin.

"Did you choose this skirt to torment me?" he asked.

"Torment you?"

"I've been stopping myself from staring at your legs all afternoon. The way you had them crossed in the café... if the hem had ridden up any higher, I would've needed to protect you from public indecency." He grinned wolfishly. "But I don't think the public would have liked the way I covered you up any better."

"Did you have a plan, then?" Maggie asked.

"Yes," Raj said, his voice sounding deeper than ever. He traced one hand up the inside of her thigh until it met the line of her underwear, then cupped her sex in a smooth motion. "My mouth, right here. It's been on my mind since the moment I saw you. Now, let me take off this fuckin' skirt and give it to me."

She had no breath left in her body to argue, and even if she had, why would she have wanted to? Not letting her gaze fall from his, she leaned back until she was resting on her elbows on the bed's firm surface and spread her legs as far as the skirt would allow. "You're welcome."

Before she could blink, he was shoving her skirt out of the way, his mouth sealing over the wet fabric of her panties, the pressure of his tongue through the cotton almost more than she could bear. Then he was tearing them down her legs, and his fingertips were tracing her, stroking her slick skin, and then his mouth. He licked at her like he was starving, like her taste was the ambrosia of eternal life. Like he never wanted to lift his tongue from where it moved against the most sensitive part of her. Like he'd be happy doing nothing but this, forever.

And based on how good it felt, hell—she might well take him up on the offer.

The orgasm came out of nowhere, spearing through her with sudden violence as he pressed a single finger inside her. She felt more than heard his combination growl-groan against her skin, as though he was the one receiving pleasure, rather than giving it. Gratification rolled through her like an arriving tropical storm, and the cries that left her mouth sounded like they'd come from someone else. Not possibly her, sensible Magnolia Gawler, making those wild noises. It couldn't be her arching her back and tilting her hips so he could push deeper inside her, so she was angled better for the endless strokes of his tongue, in between the waves of pleasure still making her arch and cry out. Not her hands wrapping in his hair so hard, it must have hurt him, but he didn't make a sound of protest, just more of those low growls that reverberated through her flesh.

The pleasure peaked again, and she barely had time to gasp out, "*Raj*," before her legs were flexing around his face like she was trying to hold him to her core with every stroke of his fingers, every pass of his tongue. The noises that came from her mouth were incoherent, just jumbled combinations of strange, disjointed syllables, clustered around endless repetitions of his name. Part of her brain fought to stay sensible, to maintain her awareness, but the pleasure overwhelmed her until there were no thoughts in her mind, nothing but the pleasure and *him*. This mountain of a man, who could snap her like a twig without thinking twice, on his knees before her, worshipping her like his own personal goddess.

She went to pull away, thinking to bring him the same pleasure he was giving her, but his free arm wrapped around her thigh and held her to him, immobilising her without a hint of effort. He pinned her to the bed, and then one of her hands had released its death grip on his hair and was gripping his hand like he was the life raft keeping her afloat in this sea of ecstasy.

"No," she cried as the pleasure began to build in her again, and instantly, he froze, then pulled back gently.

"Are you okay?" he asked into the sudden silence. "Did I hurt you?"

Maggie nodded, breath heaving in and out of her lungs like she'd just run a marathon. "Fine," she managed. "Please... let me..." She was barely getting words out through her gasping breaths.

"Did I hurt you?" he asked again, his voice soft as the

fragments of light pushing past the edges of the curtains, barely lighting the room.

"No," Maggie said. "I just… it can't just be me." Her breaths were slowing now, enough that she could speak. "I want to make you feel good, too."

"You think this doesn't make me feel good?" The tone of his voice changed, even deeper now, somehow both darker, more erotic, but also still containing the humour that was so definitively *him*. "You think I'm down here just for your pleasure, Magnolia? That I'm not getting off on it every time you say my name, every time you lock down so tight on me?"

Maggie bit her lip. "Well, when you put it like that—"

"I think I'll put it however I want," Raj said, his wicked grin appearing. "And you'll let me, won't you?"

Mutely, slowly, not quite believing she was acquiescing in this way, but knowing deep within her that it was *right*, Maggie nodded.

"I'll tell you when I've made you come enough times for me to be satisfied. And then I'm going to come up there and fuck you until the *only* thing you can say is my name. Do you understand me?"

"Yes," Maggie managed.

"Good. Then stop interrupting me while I'm eating." And before she could say anything about *that* particular phrase, he bent his head to her again, slid his fingers back inside her, and proceeded to blow her ever-loving mind.

A while later—an hour? A week? She felt him pull back from her. Her limbs, already shaking, went to liquid at the sight of him rising over her like some kind of demon freed from beneath the earth, his form barely marked in light and shadow in the dim light. He reached for the hem of her shirt and dragged it upwards, leaning down to press kisses to the skin he revealed. She managed to coordinate the movement of her arms enough to help him pull it off over her head, then looked down at her plain black bra.

"Sorry. I didn't dress for the afternoon to end this way."

"For what? You look... perfect." He hesitated before settling on a descriptor.

"I'd rather you saw me looking nice."

"I doubt it could ever make me want you more than I do now." He bent his head and kissed the place where her neck met her shoulder, then bit it gently. She felt every imprint of his teeth, every place where his skin touched hers. Without realising she'd moved, her arms were wrapped around his head, relishing the pleasure-pain of the bite.

He released her and kissed the place his teeth had been. "I might have marked you. I'm sorry. I should have asked first. I can't control myself around you."

"I don't mind," she said, and he must have felt how little she minded because his body was pressed against hers from navel down, and her thighs had jolted together at the sensation of him biting down. "Do it again," she heard herself say. "Please."

"Where?"

"Anywhere."

Her bra was gone before she had a conscious thought, torn away and thrown aside, and then he was licking at her nipples, sucking, then biting down—so gently, so careful—on her sensitive skin, causing gasps and moans to spill from her mouth. Her skirt was still around her waist, but he bypassed it in an instant, pressing his fingers into her once more.

"My beautiful girl," he murmured as his touch had her writhing beneath him. "I never would have guessed that a few bites would have you so gods-damned wet."

"The bites are nothing," Maggie said, some combination of sass and honesty driving her. "It's just you."

His fingers exploring her were gone before she could take

a breath, her skirt stripped down her legs so she was fully naked, and then he was standing over her, his big hands slowly stripping his belt away, then shedding his trousers until he was as naked as she was, rolling on a condom, then standing over her in the semi-darkness like some kind of beautiful demon there to corrupt her. And she was longing to be depraved.

He saw her glancing over at the belt where he'd discarded it, with undisguised arousal. "Really, Magnolia?"

"Really, what?"

"Really, you're looking at that belt like you're interested in it for more than just dress sense?"

"It's a nice belt," she said faux-innocently, the sassiness rising up in her, refusing to admit what they both now knew to be true.

"See if you're still saying that when it's laying marks across your ass," he growled, shifting back on to the bed and repositioning her so her head was on the pillows. "Not right now. I need you too much. Sometime tonight… I'll introduce you to my belt."

A shiver went through Maggie from the tips of her toes right to the top of her head, her core clenching. "I'd like that."

"Now, though…" He knelt over her, surveying her body like a kingdom to be pillaged. "Now, I'm making you mine."

His hands were firm, pushing her legs apart, his movements sure as he moved forwards between them, covered her body with his own and reached down to position himself at her entrance.

"Are you sure you want this?" Raj asked.

"Yes," Maggie said, breathless with anticipation.

His mouth came down on hers as he pressed inside her. His movements were slow, measured, and she wrapped her legs around the back of him to pull him closer, deeper, faster.

His growl reverberated against her lips. "Maggie." Her name sounded like a warning.

"Please," she pleaded.

"When you're on top, you can decide how fast you fuck me. I'm in charge right now, and I say, this time, we go slow."

She made a noise that was awfully close to a whine in desperation, feeling him pressing and retreating so smoothly, a little farther each time. "Maggie, I'm a big man. You're tight as hell when it's just my fingers and I'm a hell of a lot bigger than that. When we know you can take me, I'll fuck you like a toy. Right now, let me do this right."

A rush of warmth went through her at the realisation that he was trying to protect her, even from himself. "I thought you were teasing me," she said breathlessly.

"It doesn't hurt that I like you squirming underneath me," Raj said, a laugh in his voice as he pressed and retreated, pressed and retreated, entering her more deeply with each sure stroke. "I've waited a long time for this, baby, I'm not letting it go fast."

That warmth coalesced into heat right where he pressed inside her, and she reached up to pull his mouth down to hers as he finally entered her with his entire length, his pelvis flush against hers. She could have sworn he touched somewhere she hadn't even known existed inside herself, and when he started to move, smooth strokes that somehow slid across every single sensitised place she had, she moaned into his mouth repeatedly, sharing his breath, her legs wrapped behind him, urging him deeper, deeper, faster.

A growl from him reverberating into her body had her pulling away for just long enough to ask, "Is this the part where you fuck me like a toy?"

"Hold on and find out."

It had felt incredible, perfect, even when he was going slowly, but when Raj began to speed up, gripping her hips, his body thrusting into hers, tightness immediately began to coil in her pelvis. They were breathing the same air, panting into each other's mouths, begging noises leaving her lips for him to never slow, never stop. His body was so big and so hard and so warm where it covered hers, and Maggie felt herself climbing towards pleasure. Her body clenched down, preparing for what was coming, and again, Raj growled, pressed himself deep and ground his hips against hers, and release exploded behind her eyelids.

Her back arched and she was barely cognisant of his mouth again coming down on the place where her neck met her shoulder, his teeth pressing on her skin as she convulsed in pleasure that seemed never-ending, a river that dragged her along in its inescapable current, Raj growling against her skin as he found his own pleasure in three hard, jagged thrusts.

He went to pull out of her, roll to the side, but she held him close with her legs wrapped around his back.

"Maggie, let me go."

"No," she panted.

"I'll squash you."

"I like it."

A sound from him that she hadn't heard before, something like a "huh" but with undertones she was too post-orgasm-blissed-out to decipher. "Can I roll you?"

"What?" Maggie asked.

"If I roll, you'll be on top. Then I don't have to worry about crushing you."

"But then you won't be on top of me."

"Yes, Magnolia, that's kind of the point."

"To the side," Maggie conceded, realising that he was probably doing a plank to avoid putting his full weight on her, and that even with all those muscles making ridges and valleys on his body that she wanted to explore with her tongue, it probably wasn't fun to do that for very long. He rolled to the side, pulling out of her in the process, and tucked her in to his side, so most of her body was actually resting on top of him.

"View's good from up here," she said with a smile, admiring the bold lines of his face in the dimness.

He grinned unreservedly. "You want to ride me, Magnolia, you're welcome to stay up there as long as you want."

"In a minute," Maggie said, assessing the delicious tenderness between her legs, already starting to ache for his touch once more. "Maybe I'll just lie here for a bit first. Catch my breath."

"Oh, did I wear you out?" Raj teased. When she looked up at him to roll her eyes, he smiled gently and added, "You can do that for as long as you want, too."

Raj had never been so happy to do an evening of nothing. They tried leaving the bed several times—to shower, to cook dinner—but never lasted more than a few minutes before they were sneaking touches once more, skin grazing heated skin, until he found himself leaning back against the shower wall as she sucked him deep into her mouth, stroking what she couldn't reach with desperate hands, her moans of pleasure vibrating through his skin as the wild sounds that left his own mouth echoed off the walls. Until he was forced to boost her on to the kitchen table and tear the t-shirt of his that she was wearing in half, just so he could suck on her sweet nipples before he made his way down to her pussy. He'd dreamed of fucking Maggie on just about every flat surface in his house, and by the time they were lazing on the couch in front of the random movie she'd chosen, takeaway containers littering the coffee table—they'd tried to make dinner, but wound up getting distracted and burning it, almost setting off his smoke alarms—he'd made a pretty good attempt at most of them. He'd never be able to be in these rooms without remembering how she'd tasted, how she'd felt, the way she gave and gave just as she took everything he had, her nails scoring lines up and down his back, her cries and moans and snarls echoing through his head. He never *wanted* to be here again without her.

He needed to tell her she was his mate. It was deceptive not to. But not tonight, not in the aftermath of the half-dozen times they'd made love in the past few hours. It wouldn't fit with the story, he decided, stroking his fingers through her hair as she lay atop him on the couch. It would be incongruous to drop that bomb now, and she was probably as exhausted as he was, so it wouldn't be fair to throw something that big on her at the end of the day. Tomorrow morning, maybe. He could take her out for a nice breakfast and tell her when she was awake enough to be able to rationally deal with it. She might be upset that he hadn't said something earlier, but surely, she'd understand why he'd made the choices he had. She'd realise he was so desperate not to drive her away that he couldn't. And she'd understand that part of him needed to know she'd choose him, even if she didn't know about the bond between them.

Maggie was a reasonable person. She'd understand.

The movie wound to a close, the main characters fell in love, and the credits rolled.

"I am so full of Pad Thai," Maggie said, "I'm about to turn into a noodle. I'm probably about 50% noodle by weight already."

"You're a very good-looking noodle," Raj said, sitting the two of them up.

Maggie tugged at the hem of his t-shirt where it ended around her knees. "I should probably put my clothes on."

"Why?"

"What do you mean, why?"

"Why would you put your clothes on?"

"Well," she looked at him, a crease forming between her eyebrows, "I'm not exactly getting in a cab in this." She gestured towards the fabric engulfing her small frame.

"Why would you be getting in a cab?"

"To go home?"

"Maggie, it's almost midnight and you're on top of me, in my shirt. What part of that sounds like I want you to go home?"

"You want me to stay the night?" she asked.

"You're getting it," Raj said, a smile forming on his face.

"Isn't that a little… fast?"

Raj pulled her onto his lap and kissed her soundly. "I've been waiting weeks to have you right here. Why the hell would I want you to leave?"

Her cheeks were beginning to blush. "I don't have a toothbrush."

"I have spares."

"I don't have spare underwear."

"You really think you're going to be wearing underwear while you're here?" He stroked a hand up her bare thigh in reminder. "That's unlikely."

That had her grinning, but still, she looked hesitant. "I talk in my sleep sometimes."

"I'll write it all down and tease you about it in the morning."

There was a beat of silence. "You really have an answer for everything, don't you?"

Raj's felt his grin get even wider. "If it means I get you in my bed, I get to wake up to you, then, yes. Absolutely."

She sighed, but he could feel her smile where she tucked her head under his chin. "You got me. I'll stay."

Raj held her body against his for a moment that felt far too short. He could have held her in his arms forever. "Let's find you that toothbrush, then," he said, before his desires let the silence stretch for too long. "I'm wiped. Someone wore me out."

"Lucky someone," Maggie said, letting him help her to her feet before he stood and stretched.

He led her to the bedroom and provided the spare toothbrush before she had a chance to ask for it. "So prepared," she purred, and he immediately had to stop himself from stripping her naked and feasting on her sweet pussy once more. Would he ever have his fill of this woman? It felt like every time he touched her, his hunger for her only grew. He was desperate for her, every moment they spent together. Surely, this level of intensity would decrease over time... right? And if it didn't... Raj had a sudden burst of empathy for Emmett, who had been late to just about every appointment they'd made since he found his mate. If the need between them was anywhere near what Raj felt for Maggie, it was a wonder Em and Petra ever left the house.

There was something almost painfully domestic about brushing their teeth together in the bathroom, and after the constant meeting of eyes, followed by laughing around their mouths full of toothpaste, over and over, he swept her up in his arms and carried her to the bed, turning off lights as they went until the only illumination in the room was the bedside lamp.

Once he set her down in the sheets, she rolled to the place he was already thinking of as "her side", his t-shirt sliding up her thighs. He tried not to stare at the place between her legs he was so quickly coming to worship, and clearly failed dismally, because she dragged a hand up her leg, tugging the shirt with it.

"Didn't you say something about showing me the belt a

little later?" She bit her lip, and he wanted nothing so much as to bite it himself. "Well, it's later now…"

"You want to be introduced to my belt, Magnolia?" A rush went through him, something primal coming to the fore at her words. It was almost like the feeling of changing into his wolf form, except the person he became could be described with a single word.

Hers.

"I might," Maggie said with a cheeky smile.

"You'll have to ask a little more nicely if that's what you want," Raj said, embracing the sense of wicked purpose filling him. The need for control, for dominance, for power over her. He needed her to give it over to him. He needed her permission, to become someone who did not ask for permission, who did what he wanted with her. Took her, claimed her, used her. He needed her to ask him to become that person for her, and when she did…

"Please," Maggie said, her eyes now wide and entirely focused on his. The force of her complete focus was intoxicating. "Please, Raj."

He pulled her towards him, flipping her over so she was on her knees at the edge of the bed, her bare feet over the edge. He drew a hand down her spine, and she arched at his touch.

"Take the shirt off," he ordered. She knelt up slowly, pulling the t-shirt off over her head and tossing it off the edge of the bed. He couldn't see her eyes, so he watched her body, her breathing, the way she slid her hands down her thighs as she sat back up, waiting for his instruction. He pressed close to her, his back against her front, wrapping his arms around her.

"Tell me you want this," he said, and his voice was harsh because what he really meant was, *tell me you want me. Tell me you want all of me, even the greedy, depraved parts. Tell me you want this as much as I do. Tell me you want me as much I want you.* He tried to shove the mate-bond-desperation thoughts from his mind and added into the silence, "You want me to... introduce this perfect ass to my belt. It will hurt, and it might mark your skin, and I'll take care of you every minute. But if you want to stop right now, I'll be just as happy to curl up and go to sleep if that's what you want." His inner voice tried to tell him that that was a lie, that he was dying for her to accept every part of him, even this part that he rarely had the freedom to bring out. That he was desperate for the knowledge that when the gods and the universe had selected him for her, they had chosen them to be aligned in all things, even the depraved ones.

"Yes," Maggie said, and something in him that he had never even realised was tense relaxed. "I want it. I want all of it with you." She glanced over her shoulder, and something told him that if she'd been a wolf, her eyes would have been as silver as his. "This isn't my first time. You don't have to go easy on me."

The wolf within him howled.

Raj grabbed her, pulled her face to his to share a searing kiss that felt like it branded her name on his soul. Then, all gentleness removed, he pressed his hand to the back of her neck and shoved her down onto her hands and knees on the bed. Her ass, every perfect inch of it, was exposed to his eyes, to his hands, to his mouth. He peppered the skin with gentle spanks, revelling in her brief intakes of breath, warming her up for the true assault. She squirmed, muscles clenching, gasping a few times as he slowly increased the intensity of his blows. The sounds falling from her lips as her skin began to redden were like the music of the gods to his ears. He could have listened all night, alternating between spanking her ass and running his hands over her bare back, massaging her muscles, reintroducing all of her to his touch.

Eventually, he wrapped a hand in her hair and tugged to indicate she should shift back to kneeling upright. The brief intake of breath when her reddened ass met her calves sent Raj's wolf all but howling. He pressed in close against her once more, turned her head sideways with a light touch on her chin, and turned himself so he could meet her eyes.

"Do you like that?" he asked roughly, suddenly needing her to say the words.

"Oh, yes," Maggie breathed. Her face was flushed, her breathing almost ragged.

"And the belt?"

"Yes, please," she moaned.

All it took was the lightest of touches, to send her back down on to her hands and knees, that perfect ass presented beautifully for him in the dim light. Her skin was glowing with red warmth, and for a moment, he was struck by the beauty offered up to him.

Then he laid the first strike of the belt across it.

Maggie hissed through her teeth, then moaned, arching her back. "More."

"You want more? You'll get it." Another strike, another. Stripes of red began to appear on her flesh as he set the belt aside and stroked up the skin of her back, her body moving with the deep breaths she was taking, then moved his touch back down, massaging the muscles along her spine. He cupped the heated skin of her ass and squeezed with both hands, digging his thumbs in, and revelled in her harsh intake of breath and the soft moan that followed. He rubbed over the skin, tracing the marks of the three blows he'd already given her, then collected the belt again, making sure he did it loudly enough that she knew what was coming. She arched her back once more in presentation, and he took that as his cue.

Another strike. Another. Another. By the sixth, she was

rocking away and then back towards him with each strike as she mastered the pain, moaning each time. The perfect pinkness displayed between her legs was shining with her arousal.

"Last one," Raj said, "and then I'm going to fuck you so hard, you feel me for a week."

"Do your worst," Maggie replied, her voice dripping pure seduction, and so Raj swung a little harder for his final blow. Her cry when the belt met her flesh had his cock harder than it'd ever been in his life, and he dropped to his knees behind her position on the bed and feasted on her wet pussy. Her orgasm rocketed through her as soon as he pressed his fingers inside, and he revelled in the evidence that she'd enjoyed her beating just as much as he had. Moments later, he was on his feet behind her, rolling on the condom before thrusting deep in one long stroke, his skin registering the heat radiating from her ass. This time, he took her slowly, with deep, rough thrusts, before the animal in him took over and his pace increased, relishing every wordless cry that dropped from her lips as his grip on her hips had him as deep as he could go with every thrust. His own orgasm built within him, but he shoved it away until the moment he felt Maggie tighten up around him, then let his release take him just as she found hers.

He caught himself before he could collapse on top of her, his body curving over hers where she had fallen bonelessly on the bed. For a long moment, he just listened to the harmony of both their ragged breathing, the heat radiating between them from their spent bodies. Then he forced himself to pull away from her and run his hands, featherlight, over the bright red marks that now striped her ass. Her breath caught at his touch. He moved to cupping her ass, his skin barely touching hers over the sensitive marks, then stroked outwards, massaging the tight muscles of her back and shoulders, her hips and legs. Finally, he knelt behind her, his own breath still coming ragged, and pressed his lips to the belt marks, first on one side, then the other.

"Magnolia," he said softly, "how are you feeling?"

"*Goooood.*" Her still-breathless reply floated back to him. "Oh, you've got wicked hands," she added after a moment. "And a *wicked* swing."

"Can I hold you?" Raj asked, his hands resting low on her hips.

"Absolutely," Maggie said, and he fancied he could hear the smile in her voice. He rose to sit on the edge of the bed and gathered her carefully into his lap, relishing every touch and every smile she sent his way. She seemed softened, this Maggie, cuddling into him, looking up at him with a smile every time she gasped at contact on her beaten ass, as if knowing he needed the reassurance that she'd enjoyed it.

"I didn't even know I'd been needing that," she said eventually, tracing a lazy fingertip in random patterns on his arm where it wrapped around her.

"Me, either," Raj said, holding back the words he wanted to add. *I just knew I'd been needing you.* "But I can take care of it for you regularly if you like. No more long wait times."

"Just dial 1-800-BEAT-MY-ASS?" she asked, shooting a cheeky grin up at him? "Raj on demand?"

"I offer excellent service," he said, tracing his fingertips over the visible edges of the lines he'd belted into her skin in reminder.

"If I'm a good girl, do I get cuddles after too?"

"Of course," Raj said. Gently, he shifted her to her side of the bed, then slid in beside her. When she snuggled in against his side, settling her head on his chest, something inside him that he had never realised was tightly coiled relaxed in a rush of endorphins. This was *right*, his wolf was howling to the moon. This was exactly where he was supposed to be—where *both of them* were supposed to be.

"I think I'll be dialling that number pretty often," Maggie said. "You okay with that?"

"Definitely," Raj said, with the world's biggest grin stretching his face.

They lay in the dim light of the single lamp for a long moment, both catching their breaths. Eventually, she pressed a kiss to his chest, then looked down, tracing her fingers over the lines on his skin. "This is the first time I've really looked at you without a shirt. You have so many tattoos."

"I did warn you."

"Does it weird you out if I look at them?"

Raj tucked his free arm behind his head. "Have at it."

Maggie looked down at him, tracing her fingers over the lines of writing and small images that marked his skin. "What does this one say? The one with the... is that a heart?"

"Most of them are instructions, or images that mean something. How to live, how to love. The words with the anatomical heart are from a Rupi Kaur poem. 'And here you are living, despite it all.' To remind me that strength is in persisting despite the setbacks. I have another of her quotes, actually."

"Where?"

"You're on the arm it's on."

"Maybe just tell me about it, then. I don't feel like moving."

"I like you just where you are," Raj said with a grin, squeezing her closer. "It says, 'Do not look for healing at the feet of those who broke you'."

"Powerful," she said. "And high praise, to have not one but two of her quotes inked on you."

"She's a brilliant writer."

"I agree. What's the lighthouse for?" She traced her finger over the tattoo on his ribs.

"When I was younger, my parents took me on holidays in Tirawi City one week each summer. I loved being by the beach there, and I thought the lighthouse was the coolest thing in the world. It's one of the tallest ones in the world. I'd test myself by seeing if I could sprint up and down every step in the building in one go, multiple times as I got older."

"That's such a man thing to do. 'Here's this beautiful structure, let's use it as an exercise test.'"

He laughed. "O ye of little faith. I did it because I remembered the moment, after you've ground your way up all those stairs, when you burst into the highest room and the whole ocean, the whole world is out there in front of you. It's beautiful."

Maggie bit her lip. "All right, I may have judged a little fast without hearing the whole story."

"I think I'll forgive you."

"The flowers here?" She traced the lines of the inter-woven flowers, covering his left shoulder and reaching down towards his pectoral muscle.

"I liked the kind of mandala-style of the petals, and the flowers themselves have different meanings. Roses for love, the iris means faith or wisdom, and the one called a gladiolus means hope."

"Did you get all of your tattoos at the same time?"

"No, it's been an ongoing project since I was old enough to get inked. Why?"

"There are lots of individual ones, but they all look like they fit together, like they're part of a bigger picture. Do you choose them or plan them that way?"

"No, I just have an excellent tattoo artist who makes them all cohesive. She charges me through the nose for it, but given that I'm going to keep her work forever, I'm happy to pay."

Maggie sat up and surveyed the expanse of his chest,

noticing for the first time that her head had been pressed against what looked like the only significant blank space on his torso. "And here?" She touched her fingertips to the skin on his left pec.

There was a long pause, and she looked up to find Raj's eyes on her. He looked down at where her hand lay against his skin. "For when I find my mate. Her name goes there."

―――――

As his words dissolved into the air around them, the reminder of something he'd said on one of their coffee dates, Maggie could physically feel something in her shrivelling at the thought of him with another woman. She went to pull away, but he held her close, staring at her with something she couldn't translate in his dark eyes. She blinked up at him, words failing her.

"We should sleep," he said after a long moment.

"Raj―" she started, but didn't know what to say. This was their first night together. How could she rationally explain that there was something in her that cried that what they had was more than that, and that the idea of him with someone else made her feel like she was breathing acid?

"Maggie," he said after a moment. "Sleep. We're both exhausted. We'll talk about it in the morning."

"In the morning?"

"I promise."

Maggie held her breath for a moment before conceding. "Okay."

He reached over and switched the light off, pulling her tight against his body so her head rested on his chest. She listened to his heartbeat, slow and steady, for a long moment, before saying into the darkness, "Raj?"

"Yeah?"

"I think your tats are beautiful."

There was a moment of silence, then a low, huffed laugh. "Thank you, I guess."

"You guess?"

"Didn't I tell you men like me don't get called beautiful very often?" She could hear the smile in his voice.

It was a moment before she said softly, "I don't think there are any men like you."

His arm around her tightened, but he said nothing more, and she pressed herself as close as she could get and slowly slipped into sleep.

Chapter 11

MAGGIE ROSE from sleep like she was gently surfacing from a cool pool of water, softly shifting towards the light of wakefulness. She registered Raj's quiet, rumbling snore from his position behind her—apparently, he wasn't big on personal space while sleeping, because he'd curled his body around hers and wrapped an arm over her to hold her close.

Then she heard the knocking on the door. "Yoohoo!" called a female voice from down the hallway.

Not sure what else to do, she tried to pull away from Raj's embrace. Sleepily, he growled and held her tighter.

"Raj!" Maggie hissed.

He mumbled something indecipherable.

"Raj!" she said again, slightly louder, shaking his arm where it wrapped around her. "Raj, someone is here!"

"Hmm?" he muttered sleepily, clearly still not fully conscious.

"Raj!" the female voice called again, closer this time. "We brought bagels!"

Raj rocketed into consciousness faster than Maggie had ever known someone to awaken. One moment, he was wrapped around her like a pair of nested question marks, the next, he was shoving himself in front of her, just barely managing to yank the blanket over both of them before the door opened just a touch and a woman's head peeked around, calling out,

"Are you still in bed, sweetie?" Maggie saw her eyes widen in the millisecond before she jolted back behind the door, which yawned open slowly like something out of a horror movie, revealing two women in the doorway.

The one who had peeked around had her hands clamped over her eyes, and the other just managed to ask, "What's wrong?" before the opening door revealed Maggie and Raj in bed together, and slapping a hand over her mouth.

There was a long, awkward moment where none of them moved.

"Magnolia," Raj said tightly, "these are my mums. Whom I have *repeatedly* asked not to let themselves in without warning."

"We knocked!" the one with her hands over her eyes protested, without uncovering her face.

"But did you wait for an answer?" Raj asked exasperatedly, but there was a smile in his voice, and she realised that she would have predicted he was a man unable to stay mad at the people he loved. Even if they'd just startled him in bed with his... whatever she was now.

The one who'd covered her mouth took a step forward to grab the handle and close the door, pushing the one covering her eyes behind her. "We'll wait for you in the kitchen," she said. There was a smile in her voice too, and in a flash, Maggie could see so much of how Raj had become the man he was now.

She met his eyes. "So those are your parents," she said. "I guess we got the introducing-me-to-the-family thing out of the way pretty early."

"I can ask them to leave," Raj said.

"I don't want to get in the way," Maggie said. "I can go."

"You want to abandon me to their endless questioning on my *own*?" Raj asked, pretending horror. "I'm not sneaking you out the back. You'll have to walk past them."

"Whose side are you on?" Maggie demanded.

"My side," Raj said, gathering her in close. "The side of introducing you to them now so I don't have to answer forty thousand questions about who the beautiful woman in my bed was, solo. I mean, you were always going to meet them eventually."

He stopped moving for the briefest of moments, as though he'd been caught doing something he shouldn't. For a moment, her mind flashed to the space on his chest where his mate's name would someday be written. Sure, they could put off the meeting-the-parents awkwardness for another day, but that would just mean having a conversation about her place in his life, her own knowledge that she could lose him at any moment to the person he was meant to be with forever. And after the intimacy of the night they'd just shared, Maggie didn't know if she was up for that conversation right now.

"Do you think they'll wait long enough for me to get dressed?" she asked eventually.

She could actually feel the tension go out of his body. "I'll keep them occupied if you want to take a minute." Raj kissed the bare skin of her shoulder, then released her to go in search of his clothes. He tossed hers onto the bed from where he'd discarded them onto the floor.

Maggie lifted her arms to rake her fingers through her hair, stopping when they almost instantly got caught on the tangles. "Gods, you did a number on me. I probably look like I've been dragged through a hedge backwards."

"Nah," Raj said easily, without pausing in his dressing.

"Still beautiful." Before she had a chance to process that, he was pulling her forwards to press a kiss to her forehead then heading out the door. "Just come when you're ready. I'll get started on coffee."

Slowly, Maggie pulled herself out of bed, part of her revelling in all the places her body was tender. She pulled on her clothes from yesterday, uncertainty overtaking her when she remembered Raj's comment about how short the skirt was, but chose to put it out of her mind due to the fact that she had no alternative, and she wasn't about to meet Raj's parents wearing just one of his big t-shirts. She checked her hair in the bathroom mirror, saw that it was at full Einstein levels of insanity, and pulled it back into a tight ponytail, then splashed water on her face and took a deep breath, holding on to the edge of the sink to keep herself grounded. *You can do this,* she told herself firmly. *These are just Raj's parents, and there's no way they can be bad-tempered enough to require sedation, like some patients you have dealt with. Ergo, you have faced worse. You can do this.*

Taking another deep breath, she went out to meet her new lover's family.

When she emerged into the kitchen, it was to find that only one of Raj's mothers was there—the one who had covered her mouth rather than her eyes when they burst in on the two of them in bed—sipping from a mug while shelving books from the large pile on Raj's enormous wooden table, while the man himself was pouring his own coffee.

She had been a little too distracted last night to fully take in the large open space that took up most of the front of Raj's house, combining kitchen—separated from the rest of the space by a large island bench—with both living and dining rooms. Unsurprisingly, the walls were lined with more bookshelves, apart from the area down the far end that held the massive television, but there were also large windows on each wall that lit the space with natural light, highlighting the rich dark colour of the bookshelves—the same wood as the floor, it appeared—and preventing it from feeling gloomy. A large L-shaped sofa where they'd collapsed last night, as well as a reclining chair, grouped around a rug of dark greens and browns, faced the television, and a huge dining table filled almost half of the space. Raj's mother was standing by the large pile of books at one end of the table, examining each before finding it its place among the enormous collection lining the walls.

"I don't understand why you can't just put these back when you're finished reading them," she was saying. "Your *job* is to put books back on shelves at the library. How can you be so bad at doing it at home?"

"You don't have to do it," Raj said. "Sit down and drink your coffee. I'll do the books later."

"You say that every time, but then I come back the next week and there are still piles of books everywhere," his mother retorted.

"They're new piles," Raj said. "I've put the old ones away, and new ones have accumulated."

His mother brandished a book. "Don't you lie to me, Rajesh. You and I both know this copy of *Les Misérables* hasn't seen a shelf in six months, at least."

Raj noticed Maggie loitering in the doorway and strode over to her, tucking her under his arm and steering her towards the kitchen. "Mum, this is Magnolia. This is my mum, Andrea."

"Lovely to meet you, Magnolia," Andrea said, smiling.

"Most people call me Maggie," Maggie said. "Only Raj and my grandparents really use my full name."

"I have to apologise for our unorthodox entry this morning," Andrea said, visibly straightening her shoulders for the pressure of diving into the embarrassing conversation. "Raj can sleep through almost anything, including the loudest possible knocking on the door, so when we come for breakfast, we usually just let ourselves in and wake him up as part of the process. We never would have barged in if we knew he had company."

"Mum's so embarrassed, she's run away to get you a bagel," Raj said, taking a sip from his coffee. Now that none of them were naked save for a blanket, he seemed completely unaffected by the awkwardness. "She'll be back once she's calmed herself down."

"Belinda can be a little dramatic," Andrea said, not even trying to hide the fond smile that lit her face. "Do be prepared for an extravagant apology. Though the extra bagel was a necessary excursion—we always bring four, but Rajesh will be claiming starvation in half an hour if he only gets one."

"I appreciate you making room for me," Maggie said.

"Do you work at the library as well?" Andrea asked, turning to shelve the book in her hand slightly too slowly to hide her inquisitory expression.

"No, I'm a nurse. Raj and I met through some friends. They thought we'd get along because we both love books." Maggie glanced at Raj, who sent her a grin and a nod in approval of her story.

"And do you think books belong on their shelves, filed appropriately?" Andrea asked pointedly. "Or do you keep all your books in piles all over the place?"

"I'm taking the fifth," Maggie said, taking a hearty sip of coffee.

Andrea laughed. "A good decision. I hope you like cream cheese and salmon on your bagel, by the way. That's what we all usually have, so I assume it's what Belinda will be getting."

"Do we have to wait until she gets back to eat?" Raj asked. "I only have so much coffee to tide you over."

Andrea eyed her son. "I would think you'd know better than to ask that." She glanced over at Maggie. "I promise I have worked hard to civilise this boy, but somehow it never quite seems to stick." She couldn't quite hide her loving smile as she spoke, and suddenly, Maggie could see how Raj must have grown up, with people who so clearly loved him. Still, it was a little strange to hear this woman, so much smaller than her son, referring to him as 'this boy'. Not to mention the fact that the boy himself had done every dark deed under the sun with Maggie herself only hours previously.

"I'm perfectly civilised," Raj said, interrupting her thoughts, "I'm just hungry, and you've put food on my bench, but you're not letting me touch it."

"Not until your mum is back," Andrea said firmly.

"This is just like when I was a teenager, and we'd get in the endless cycles of 'ask your mother'," Raj said, grinning mischievously as he dramatically rolled his eyes. "Seriously, Maggie, I've spent hours of my life running back and forwards between the two of them. 'Ask your mother, ask your mother'."

"Well, I see you've inherited her talent for histrionics," Andrea said with her own smile.

"What's this about histrionics?" asked Raj's other mother as she appeared through the door, paper bag and cardboard tray of coffee cups in hand. Seeing Raj open his mouth, she shot a finger in his direction. "Don't you say a word, Rajesh I would have knocked this time too if I didn't already know you'd be right here."

Raj spread his hands out wide in surrender. "And I appreciate that."

Belinda looked over at Maggie and her face immediately flushed red. Raj's other mother was tall and willowy, with red hair and very pale skin that starkly showed her embarrassment.

"Mum, this is Magnolia," Raj said.

"Maggie," she corrected.

"I'm very happy to meet you, Maggie," Belinda said, apparently intending to ignore her deep blush. "I'm sorry it was under such… unexpected circumstances." She bit her lip, apparently tongue-tied, then blurted, "Do you like salmon on your bagels?"

"It's how I always make them myself," Maggie said with a smile.

"These are the best ones in pack territory," Andrea interjected firmly. "I've tried them all, and these take the cake."

"Don't give her such high expectations," Belinda said, walking over to deposit the extra paper bag with the other bagels already on the bench. "We don't want her to be disappointed."

"As if she could be disappointed by these bagels!" Andrea said. Raj put down a pile of plates in front of his mothers and they quickly separated the bagels on to them, putting two on one plate for Raj.

"I wasn't sure how you take your coffee, Maggie, so I got a white one but without sugar, in case you don't have it with any. I am assuming," she added pointedly to Raj, "that our son has sugar in his house."

"I do," Raj said with an air of outraged superiority. "And if she's not happy, she's already drinking the coffee that I made, the same way I make it every time, so you do not need to buy takeaway coffees." On the back of that spiel, he reached out to take Maggie's hand and drew her over to the full-length cupboards that opened to reveal a somewhat sparsely filled pantry. "I only bought sugar for these breakfasts," he muttered to Maggie. "She always orders hers without sugar, but watch how many she puts in." He handed her the container, then leaned down to press a kiss to her cheek and she distantly heard a pair of sighs from behind them.

"I don't usually have it with sugar," Maggie said, fully aware that she was now the one blushing furiously, and placed the container on the bench in front of Raj's parents just in case he was telling the truth. "Thank you for thinking of it, though."

"This'll be your coffee, then," Belinda said, passing her a takeaway cup without even acknowledging Raj's protests that she need not have bought them. "Come on, let's make use of this enormous table, shall we?"

"Mum didn't think I needed a table this size," Raj said, picking up his plate as well as one of the single-bagel plates. He set them down next to each other and Maggie gratefully slid into the seat beside him.

"All I said was, you could do a lot with this space if so much of it wasn't a huge table and a thousand bookshelves," Belinda said, gesturing around the room.

"Mum, the room is massive," Raj said, with the air of one who had had this argument many times before. "It needs the shelves and the table, or it'd feel like you were standing in a basketball stadium. Besides, Leo made it for me. It would have been rude to turn down the gift just because it was bigger than I expected."

"He told me you sent him specifications," Andrea interjected.

"That traitor," Raj said good-naturedly. "Anyway, you have as many bookshelves as I do."

"But ours are white," Belinda said in exasperation, "not this dark wood that makes the whole space feel smaller."

"It's my house," Raj said, "and I say, why would there be walls in it if they weren't meant to be covered by book-shelves?" He took a big bite of bagel, as though signaling that he wouldn't argue it further, but Maggie could see the smile he couldn't quite hide. His mothers looked at each other and both rolled their eyes, clearly recognising an unwinnable fight.

"So, Maggie, how did you two meet?" Belinda asked.

"They were introduced by friends," Andrea said.

"You have friends in the pack?" Belinda looked uncertain, and Maggie was reminded that until recently, Blue Crescent had been ruled by an Alpha who tried to keep anyone who wasn't in his pack away from their territory.

"My best friend is Della Greenbranch," Maggie explained.

"Now, she is one hell of a witch," Andrea said in clear approval. "Leo needed someone who can keep him in check. We've known him for as long as we've had Raj."

"And he was a forceful character even then," Belinda added with a laugh.

"I absolutely agree," Maggie said. "And Della would never have been happy with someone who didn't challenge her. Most people would be cowed by someone as powerful as she is, but he's never seemed to worry about it."

"Then he's finally met his match," Belinda said with an air of great satisfaction. "And just when half the young members of the pack were convinced that mates were a myth. And now look at you three boys!"

Even his mothers can see that I'm just a placeholder for Raj's mate. The thought shot into Maggie's mind, unbidden, and for a second, she felt like all the air had been sucked out of the room. There was silence as they all registered what had been said, and out of the corner of her eye, Maggie could see Raj frantically shaking his head at his mother. Belinda's eyes went wide as she flushed red once more. "I—"

"So, you're a nurse, Maggie?" Andrea cut her off, clearly

signalling to her partner that no further discussion of the topic was needed.

"Yes, I work at St Philippa's. Cardiac ward, at the moment, but I originally trained as an emergency nurse."

"Now, that's got to be a stressful job," Belinda said with forced cheerfulness, her cheeks still bright red.

"It can be. In the cardiac ward, most of the time, everyone is doing fine right up until they're not. So, there can be stretches with a baseline low level of activity, but then, suddenly, it's interrupted by someone needing immediate resuscitation. Or, more often, several people at the same time. Most of our patients aren't like that, though," she added quickly, seeing Raj's parents' matching expressions of concern. "Sometimes it's intense, but the best part is just seeing people get better."

"That part must very rewarding," Andrea ventured.

"It's a great privilege to be part of someone's recovery," Maggie said, repeating the words she must have said a hundred times before. They didn't ring as true as they once had, though, and she wondered when she had stopped loving her job the way she used to. Was it just an effect of all the extra patients—the recent influx of suddenly acutely ill werewolves, and Jeremy's implication that it was drug-related—that they'd been unable to save?

"I guess emergency training would stand you in good stead for the high-stress moments," Belinda said. "That sounds like a super stressful job."

"The only way you can really get through it is to have good people by your side," Maggie said. "If there's a good team, you can rely on each other's expertise and keep morale up, even when you're dog-tired. That's the real secret of surviving nursing—have good nurses around you."

"Is St Philippa's a good hospital?" Belinda asked.

"Give her a minute to eat while you're interrogating her,

Mum," Raj said, looking pointedly at Maggie's untouched food. Maggie looked up at him gratefully as she took a bite of her bagel, and her eyes widened.

"This is delicious," she exclaimed once her mouth was empty. "What spell have they put on this, to make it so good?"

"They make their own bagels, obviously, but they also pickle their own capers," Andrea said, with the air of a detective giving away details of how they solved a complex mystery, "And I swear there's something addictive in them, because I can copy the ingredients and proportions exactly, but if it's not from this bakery, it won't be as good."

"I spoke to Cameron, who runs the bakery, just a few days ago, and he says he's seeing a lot more of other supernaturals coming into the territory, especially in the last few weeks. Even some humans." Belinda glanced over at Maggie. "Which is a good thing, obviously."

"I think people are finally getting the message that Blue Crescent territory is no longer its own city-state," Andrea said happily.

"Our Alpha is mated to a witch," Raj said with a laugh. "Surely, it can't be any clearer than that."

"Change takes time," Belinda said.

"It's been months," Raj protested.

"More time than that," his mother said. "You can only do as much as you're doing, Raj. Change will happen, but it will be slow. Don't doubt the efficacy of all the work you're putting in."

The three werewolves discussed how the pack was changing under Leo, Emmett and Raj's lead.

"Who would have thought these three reprobates would become the leaders of our pack one day?" Belinda asked, smiling at her son proudly as they ate their delicious bagels, and then they were interrupted by the noise of Raj's phone ringing. He excused himself from the table and went to answer it, leaving Maggie with his mothers.

"So, you're a reader as well, Maggie?" Belinda asked.

"It was one of the reasons our friends thought we'd get along," Maggie said, trying not to look guilty at the half-truth. "And one of the first things we bonded over."

"I teach literature at the university," Andrea said. "When we got Raj, he was already a voracious reader, but I definitely encouraged it. Who would have known that it would become such a big part of his life?"

"I take credit for his appreciation of ancient texts," Belinda interjected. "I teach ancient history, so, of course, I was going to point him towards Homer, Aristotle, Aeschylus... the list goes on."

"I can imagine," Maggie said. "We'd met briefly through our friends, but I think the first time I had a proper conversation with him was when I was returning books at the library. The job he moved to is at my local one, and I'm there so often, it was inevitable that we'd run into each other eventually."

"And have you been seeing each other long?" Belinda asked with a carefully casual expression that didn't quite hide her excitement.

"A few weeks," Maggie said and was saved from further questioning by Raj returning. He placed a hand on the back of her chair, fingers grazing her back.

"We might have to wrap this up, unfortunately," he said. "Leo broke Emmett's ankle sparring, and they've asked if I'll cover his training sessions today."

"I thought wolves could heal like lightning," Maggie said, then had to work to shove away the reminder of the wolves who had been arriving in her ward, clearly disproving that statement.

"It'll be fine for his classes next week," Raj explained,

"but he's in plaster for a few days, so he won't quite be trustworthy for today and tomorrow."

"We'll let you two say goodbye, then," Andrea said, placing her hand over Belinda's. "Thank you for having us for breakfast, Rajesh, and Maggie, it was lovely to meet you."

"I could just clean up if you like," Belinda offered.

"Mum, it's a few plates and a few cups. I promise to put them all through the dishwasher before I go to training. You don't have to do it."

Belinda looked slightly pained but managed to take it in stride. "All right, as long as you promise."

Raj's mothers both hugged him, and when Andrea went to the front door, Belinda unexpectedly hugged Maggie too. "Lovely to finally meet you, Magnolia," she said quietly and followed Andrea out the door.

Raj pulled Maggie to him almost before they'd heard the car drive away, holding her close. One of his hands wove into the hair at the back of her head, holding her cheek gently against his chest.

"Sorry about that," he said. "They can be a bit intense. I didn't know they were coming, or I would have warned you ahead of time. And, you know, given you time to get dressed."

"It was fine," Maggie said. "They just wanted to see their son."

Raj let her go, and the brief glimpse of his expression that she caught as he turned away made Maggie wonder if she'd made him uncomfortable. "It took them a long time to get through the adoption process," he said slowly, collecting the crockery from the end of the table. He was still facing away from her. "Back then, you were only considered to adopt a child of your own species, and very few werewolf pups go into the public system—the packs tend to take care of their own, rather than letting a child go into outside care."

"How come you were in outside care?" Maggie asked. "I thought you'd been in Blue Crescent your whole life."

"Most of it," Raj said. "From what I've been able to find out, my birth mother was a human having a werewolf child whom she didn't want to raise, so she stuck around long enough to name me, but not long enough to find a pack that would accept me. I came to my parents when I was almost seven. There were very few werewolves in the foster system, so they were dealing with that complication, plus, they were a same-sex couple trying to get approved to foster a child. It was years before they got me, and sometimes I think they still feel like if they don't keep a close eye on me, I'll disappear."

"You're very precious to them," Maggie said. "I can't imagine I'd be less worried about a child of mine."

He looked at her for a long moment, then nodded. "Still, I'm sorry they ambushed you."

"I can handle a little ambush," Maggie said, holding his gaze.

"Good to know." Raj turned to open the dishwasher and load the plates in. "Because let's be realistic, they let themselves in all the time. It will almost definitely happen again. '

Maggie laughed. "Do you want a hand cleaning up?"

"It's just plates and cups," Raj said. "Do you want to grab your stuff? I'll drive you home before I head to the training centre."

"I can just call a cab," Maggie offered. "I don't want to put you out or make you late."

Raj straightened, turning to frown at her. "Baby, I'm losing out on two nights of you in my bed. The absolute least I'm going to do is get you home safe in the meantime."

"Two nights?" Maggie asked, realising she'd half-expected him to ask if he could collect her again after training, so they could spend the night together again, after he'd promised to help her *make the most* of her weekend. Realising that she'd been looking forward to it, too, looking forward to spending the evening breaking in every room in his house before falling asleep wrapped in the strength of his arms. She'd sort of presumed he was unusually driven to spend as much time with her as possible, in the same way that she was. Maybe that assumption had been a mistake.

"Leo wants to have a 'serious discussion' after I finish with Em's classes," Raj said, looking as frustrated as she felt. "He was with Emmett when they called." He put his hands on her waist, pulling her body flush against his. "I tried to get out of it, but it's something important. He doesn't often pull rank, but something's stressing him out, enough that he wants to talk about it as soon as possible, and I have the feeling it'll run long. I don't know what time that'll finish. Then I have to cover Emmett's training sessions tomorrow, and a pack meeting tomorrow night, but if you're not doing overnight shifts, maybe I could catch you on Monday?"

"That sounds nice," Maggie said, fighting to avoid letting her disappointment show on her face. "I'm on day shifts for the first half of next week, so I could come here after work." She felt like an addict whose high was receding, desperate for another fix at just the suggestion that her current one was fading.

Or maybe, she told herself, she was just horny, and now *finally* knew how good he was with that gorgeous body, not to mention his perfect mouth. Even though he'd been inside her for what must have been a combined total of *hours* last night, she was already craving that physical connection once more.

"I'll cook if you like," Raj offered, returning to finish loading the dishwasher.

"I could help?" Maggie suggested, letting the end of the sentence tip up into a question.

He paused, looking awkward. "I'm not big on cooking with other people," Raj admitted. "Someone always ends up standing in front of the exact cupboard you need to get things out of."

She laughed. "You won't get an argument from me if you want to be my chef for the night. I'll just drink wine and smile prettily?"

"I don't know, I think I might like a Magnolia with a few glasses of wine in her," Raj said, his expression turning lazily sexy.

Just the way he raked his eyes over her, made her skin tingle. "Maybe I'll just spend the time finding ways to distract you," she threatened, knowing she was failing to hide her smile.

"You want me to burn the house down?" Raj laughed. "Wouldn't take much to distract me, with you in that skirt."

"What if it's me in just the skirt?" Maggie asked boldly, sensuality unfurling in her like an opening flower.

Raj slid the dishwasher closed and stalked towards her. Even though he looked every inch a predator as he approached, she couldn't find in herself a single iota of desire to move away. She stood her ground until he stopped in front of her, lifted her into his arms and sealed his mouth over hers. Automatically, Maggie's legs slid around his waist, her skirt sliding up her thighs. Raj's hands slid with them.

"You see what I mean about this skirt?" he said against her lips. "It's going to drive me crazy thinking about how easily I can get my hands on your sweet ass."

"Careful, or we're going to make you late for your class," Maggie said, giving the lie to her words by weaving her fingers into his thick hair.

Raj growled low in his throat, boosting her up on the surface of the bench and shoving her skirt up around her waist, then hooking his fingers into her panties and dragging them down her legs. He knelt before her, pressing her thighs apart to accommodate the width of his shoulders. He set his hands on her inner thighs, framing her pussy for his avid gaze. Maggie's breath was coming shallow, loud in her ears as she watched him stare at her centre like there was no more beautiful sight in the world.

"They can wait," he growled and went to work.

Knowing it wasn't the right time but unable to resist his mate's draw, Raj set his mouth to her, revelling in the taste of her, in the sounds that almost immediately began to fill the air around them. Some part of him knew that this was wrong, that he was taking advantage of her by deepening their relationship before telling her that she was his mate, but what was he supposed to do? Interrupt his mothers' visit to tell Maggie what was undeniably the biggest news of his life? Or drop it on her now when she was still reeling from their unexpected comments over breakfast? No... it wasn't the right time. In the books, there was always a *right time* to break news like this, news that could change a relationship entirely. It needed to be at the *right time*, so she didn't immediately freak out and flee at such a massive, life-changing piece of information.

There would be time, he told himself, to set things up properly, to deliver this massive announcement in a way that wasn't too shocking to her. The heroes in the books he'd read would set it up nicely, so she was comfortable and not in the slightly befuddled state of being immediately pre- or post-orgasm, the way she almost always was if he had anything to do with it.

He'd cook her dinner on Monday, set it up with candles and roses, just like one of the romance heroes would do. Then he'd find a way to ease her into the knowledge that they were destined to be together—oh, and of course, also, that if she didn't choose to be with him, he was likely to go insane with the challenge of repressing his side of the bond. This wasn't a conversation that was meant to be had lightly or in the heat of the moment, he reminded himself as he pressed his fingers inside her, glorying in her moans of pleasure, in the way she gasped out his name. He couldn't whisper this news in the seconds before he made her come, or spring it on her in the moments after. When the heroes in his books had a secret to tell, it always went badly if it occurred in the heat of the moment. Maggie would understand that he'd been trying to do things right by waiting until a time when she felt comfortable enough to get life-changing news like this.

Of course, in the books, mostly the heroes' secrets were spilled at an inopportune moment no matter how carefully they planned their revelation. But Raj wasn't thinking about that as he set all his attention to the task at hand—feeling his mate come.

Chapter 12

MAGGIE RANG Della in the middle of the day on Sunday, once she'd finally run out of jobs to do around the house and had to find something else to occupy her mind around the massive space that was just dedicated to missing Raj. How could she be missing someone *this much* whom she'd only spent one night with? Every second thought that passed through her mind revolved around him, something she wanted to tell him, or wanted his opinion on, or else—more often than she cared to admit—she found herself remembering the way their bodies had fit so perfectly together, the pleasure he'd brought her. Even the pure joy that she felt when she saw the faint marks his belt had left on her ass, she wanted to share with him. Followed, ideally, by repeating the process a few times. Every twinge in her body from their hard, beautiful coupling sent her straight back to thinking of him. More than once, she'd come back to her senses to find that she'd been staring into space, reliving their intimacy, for long minutes at a time.

Della picked up on the third ring. "Mags?" There was a loud clatter and the sound of someone swearing distantly, then her friend's voice returned. "Sorry. Dropped the phone. My muscles are atrophying from lack of use because all I'm doing is bloody paperwork, twenty-four/seven."

"Hi, Dells," Maggie said. "I was going to ask how your day's going, but I think I already know the answer."

"I'm drowning in paperwork for the Witches' Council," Della said. "Ever since the Alpha fight, the slimiest excuses for witches have been sucking up to me because they've realised I'm powerful. And all the time I'm wasting on these little complaints and queries being directed straight to me means that I barely have time to do any siphoning off of power other than encouraging the bloody garden, so everything is overgrown, and I'm magicking everything within my reach just to get a bit of relief from the build-up of magic..." She finished her tirade with a long groan. "I've changed the colour of every wall in this house twice in the past week just to take the edge off. And Leo won't let me just magic the garden back into order, which would at least be a decent use of power, because he has this bull-headed Alpha wolf approach to manual labour being done by magic." She paused and heaved in a breath. "Please tell me you're calling with an excuse for me to stop chasing my tail in circles like this."

"I can provide one if that's what you want." Maggie grinned. "I figured it was about time for you to renew the protection spells, which would help with getting rid of a little magic too, I'm thinking."

"That would be *perfect*," Della said, sounding pathetically grateful. "A nice, slow ritual that I can pour all this excess power into, and then the spells should last you a bit longer, too, if I focus the magic right." She gave a deep sigh, then added, slightly reproachfully, "I didn't know you had this weekend off. I've been trying to pin you down to get something to eat and redo these spells for weeks! I feel like I've hardly seen you since the party. When did this weekend become free?"

"It was a late-notice shift change," Maggie said, unsure how much she should reveal.

"Don't you try to hide things from me," Della said in a warning tone. "We've been friends for too long. I can hear it in your voice."

"You can *hear it* because all that excess magic is making you too perceptive for your own good," Maggie said glumly. Of course, Della would immediately realise something was up. "I'll tell you in person. When do you want me?"

"Is it okay if I come to you?" Della asked. "I can bring all the supplies for the ritual. It would do me good to be somewhere other than my house or the office for a little while, I think."

"No problem," Maggie said. "I'll make coffee. When will you be free from the paperwork?"

"There's probably another half-hour to do before I can dig myself out from underneath it," Della said. "And then I'll have to find the right supplies. Is about an hour, hour and a half okay?"

"I'll have the coffee on standby," Maggie said.

"I'll bring one of Grandmother Elise's teas, too," Della said. "It'll work in concert with the spells." She heaved another sigh. "Somehow, just knowing that there is a light at the end of this tunnel has made the rest of this paperwork not nearly as unappealing. Thank you!"

"You focus on getting it done," Maggie said. "I'm here all afternoon. My garden probably needs as much care as yours does, even with no magical encouragement. If I don't answer the door, it'll mean I'm out the back pulling weeds. Just come round through the gate."

Once she got into the endless work of maintaining a garden she'd been ignoring, even a small one, Maggie found that the time flew. Before she knew what was happening, Della appeared around the side of the house with a big canvas bag full of supplies.

"You have let it get a little wild," she commented with a grin, taking in the untrimmed bushes and piles of leaves Maggie had only just raked up. "You know, for someone who keeps their house so scrupulously clean, I am always amazed by how little of a shit you give about the garden."

"I have twelve-foot-high hedges surrounding it," Maggie said, standing up and wiping sweat off her forehead. "No one sees it but me. And these damn things never stop dropping leaves," she gestured to the two massive trees that took up most of the space behind the house, "so I get bored of raking them up and leave it for too long, until someone reminds me it needs doing."

"I'm not criticising," Della said with a warm smile, ignoring Maggie's sweaty, dirt-streaked form and pulling her into a hug. "You know I think gardens look better when they're not all perfectly manicured."

"Well, this one is far from manicured," Maggie laughed. "Careful, I'll get you all sweaty."

"As long as it's not blood you're wiping on me, I'm good with it," Della said. "I've missed you."

"You too," Maggie said, giving her friend a squeeze. "You know, if you want to siphon off more magic, you can always help me get all these leaves into their bags for composting."

"That's a great idea, actually. I'll do it after the ritual. More importantly, though, I didn't realise you had this weekend off," Della added. "If I had, I would have kicked Leo out for the night so we could do dinner and rom coms again."

"You know, if it's easier, we can just do them here," Maggie offered. "Don't have to kick anyone out for the night."

Della looked slightly guilty. "Don't tell him I admitted it, but his TV is better. Hard not to be, when it's the size of a cinema screen and takes up an entire wall."

"That's true enough," Maggie said. "Come on in. I'll make us that coffee."

"Good plan," Della said, "and you can tell me why your energy feels so super-charged today. You know I don't normally pick up on that stuff, so it must be pretty intense for me to feel it."

Maggie busied herself with preparing coffee, knowing Della was just waiting to have an opportunity to pounce on the source of the apparent change in Maggie's energy. Finally, they sat down at Maggie's small dining table.

"You can't tell Leo," she said without preamble.

"I won't lie to him," Della said, looking a little concerned.

"I know that, and I wouldn't ask you to. But just... don't volunteer the information," Maggie insisted.

"That, I can promise." Della lifted her cup to take a sip.

"I slept with Raj," Maggie said, and Della's mouth fell open as she dropped the cup back on to the table, where it shattered. Coffee sprayed across the table.

"You did *what?*" Della exclaimed after a moment of stunned silence. "I thought you didn't even *like* him!"

"Let me get a tea towel," Maggie said.

"Oh, no, you don't," Della said, putting the cup back together with a wave of her hand. She didn't even need to glance down as the coffee collected itself back into the repaired cup. "You're not running away that easily. How did this happen?"

"Well, he works at the library near me now," Maggie said, then bit her lip, unsure how to continue.

"What about Jeremy?" Della demanded.

"Oh," Maggie said, a little ruefully. "Well, we broke up."

"*When?*"

"Before I started things with Raj, of course."

"And why didn't you *tell* me?"

"I tried!' Maggie protested. "I called you three times that week, but you were running to get to a Council meeting, and then there was Leo's thing you couldn't be late for, and then you were doing dinner with his mum."

"You could have mentioned you had something this big to tell me," Della said, but her intensity had reduced a little. "I would have made time."

"Dells, your life is already more complicated than you know what to do with, or have *time* to do anything with. I figured it wouldn't be the end of the world if I waited until you actually had a free moment before springing something like this on you."

"Mags," Della said, looking slightly pained, "none of that stuff is more important to me than you. I know I've been less… available since Leo and I got together, but you're still a priority to me, not an afterthought to slot in when there's a gap in other things. I will *always* make time for you."

Maggie bit her lip, trying not to let herself get emotional. "Well, you know now. And I'm sorry you didn't know earlier. Next time I break up with someone, I'll be sure to interrupt whatever you're doing to tell you immediately." She reached out and laid her hand over Della's, and they held on for a minute.

"So, let's take a step back," Della said. "You broke up with Jeremy, and now you've slept with Raj. You do mean *Leo's* Raj, yes?"

"Yes," Maggie confirmed a little sheepishly, feeling her skin growing pink under her friend's scrutiny.

"Do you maybe want to fill in a few of the steps between those two things?" Della asked. "Last I saw, you were glaring daggers at him at our party."

"Well, he works at my local library now," Maggie said.

"We met again when I was returning some books, and we started talking. We had coffee a few times, mostly to talk about books, but—come on, Dells. You can't pretend you haven't noticed he's stupidly attractive. I was... attracted. The Jeremy thing had ended, and the opportunity was there, and then last night, we kind of... took the opportunity."

"So, what is it, some kind of rebound thing?"

"I don't think so," Maggie said slowly. "I mean, he said he'd been thinking of me that way for a while, and we have so much in common—I was attracted to him from the start, obviously, but I think we were honestly getting to be friends before we, you know..."

"*Took the opportunity?*" Della suggested with a smile, raising one eyebrow. "I won't pretend I'm not relieved it's not just a hook up, because obviously, we're such close friends with both of you."

"Dells, I have more sense than to pick one of your boyfriend's Betas for a random hook up," Maggie said. She took a deep breath. "Honestly, I don't know what it is, but this... attraction... was kind of the reason I had to break up with Jeremy. I couldn't get Raj out of my head. I didn't want Jeremy touching me anymore, because it felt like he was the wrong person to have his hands on me."

"Hmm," Della said, a crease forming on her forehead as she frowned.

"So, Raj and I had organised to have coffee and talk books again on Friday, and I mentioned that I wasn't seeing Jeremy anymore, and things just kind of... happened. I spent the night at his place. And then his *mothers* showed up the next morning—"

"His mums showed up?" Della gasped.

"I was as surprised as you," Maggie said. "They came in without knocking and found us in bed together. Covered by a sheet and doing nothing but sleeping, fortunately," she added at Della's look of horror. "We got dressed, everyone apologised, we had breakfast, they left."

"I can't believe you met his parents like that." Della laughed. "I would have been *so* embarrassed."

"I was probably blushing tomato-red the whole time," Maggie admitted.

"Was it weird, meeting them so early? I mean, he wasn't calling you his girlfriend after one night, was he? That's more of an Emmett thing to do, from what Leo's said, or rather it used to be."

"That's where it gets a little weird," Maggie said. "Raj and I were talking about his tats last night, and he told me he's kept the space on his chest over his heart clear for when he meets his mate, so her name can go there. He *really* believes his mate is out there, Dells. Like, he's totally convinced. One of his mums made a comment about it at breakfast and I could see him just shaking his head at her, trying to get her to shut up. And I really like him—I can't seem to get him out of my head, even when we're not together—but..." She paused and took a deep breath. "I know I'll never be able to take the place of his mate. So, I'm kind of scared to even think about getting more invested, no matter how much I want to, because what if he meets her someday and I lose him, just like that? I wouldn't even be able to be angry with him because it's not like he'd be choosing someone else over me. I just... wouldn't be able to compete with the choice of the universe." Just the thought of it had tears springing to her eyes, and she swiped them away furiously. "And I'm so mad, Dells, because after all the fuckups, I finally meet this amazing guy, and as far as the universe is concerned, he's already promised to this other woman."

"You don't know that he'd ever even meet her," Della said. "What if she's in, like, Nepal?"

"And what if she's walking down the street in Mystic City right now, and he finds her tomorrow? And I'm just left behind?"

"You don't know that that's going to happen," Della said.

"But I'll never be able to be sure that it *won't*," Maggie said. "You know Leo was meant for you, Della. Supernatural magic, that's what you told me—magic beyond even the kind that you can control, that's what brought you together. But I don't think I can even consider being in a relationship with someone where I constantly have to be watching over my shoulder and waiting for him to find the person he's actually supposed to be with." She could hear the tears in her own voice as she spoke the last few words.

Della slid around the table into the chair next to Maggie and wrapped her arms around her. "It'll be okay," she said softly.

"I can be the human in the department who can't save people's lives with magic," Maggie said against her friend's shoulder. "I can be the friendly little colleague who takes the night shifts no one wants, so everyone else can have *their* lives. But I can't be second-best for someone it would be *so easy* to fall in love with."

"It kind of sounds like you're already halfway there, honey," Della said gently.

"He's so... he's so silly, and so funny, and so kind," Maggie said. "And I already don't want to lose him. I don't even want to think about losing him. Just the idea of it hurts so much."

For a few gentle moments, Maggie let the tears fall to soak the shoulder of Della's shirt, and Della rubbed comforting circles on her back.

"Why don't you finish up your coffee, then jump in the shower?" Della suggested. "You'll want to be fresh and clean for the ritual. We'll go outside and get the spells cast, and then we'll have a cup of tea, and *then* we can talk about where to go with this. Okay? It's not a problem that needs to be solved right at this minute. Let's put it on the backburner for an hour, and come back to it with fresh eyes."

"Good plan," Maggie said, then went to clean the dirt and sweat off herself. At least in the shower, she could pretend the wetness on her cheeks was just the falling water.

They'd performed the ritual to cast the protection spells easily two dozen times over the years—basically, since Maggie had started taking night shifts and Della got worried about her safety getting home. Maggie had assented to her friend's wishes but had never thought the spells were particularly necessary; she could take care of herself well enough, even without magic. Today, though, the repeated actions that she could now do with her eyes closed—grinding the herbs, casting the circle of protection, lighting the candles, mixing the oils, repeating the mantras—combined with the warmth of sitting in the sunlight of the garden, in the glow of Della's magic, was as comforting as cuddling up with a hot chocolate and a good book would have been. With her usual sensitivity to magic, Maggie felt the spells as they passed over and around her, like a gentle stroke of kind hands. They finished the spell as the sun was slipping down behind the high hedges that edged her garden, and Della released the circle of protection with a deep exhale. "Time for tea?"

"Time for tea," Maggie said, standing up and dusting herself off. Though she'd admitted after a while that the spells were probably useful, she still usually kept up the pretence of enduring them for Della's sake. Today, though, she couldn't help but feel fiercely grateful that she'd had the ritual to complete, just for a chance to focus on something other than her brain's preferred constant litany of *Raj, Raj, Raj*. It was as if she could feel the power Della had settled on her like a warm blanket, perfectly protecting her from the perils of the world outside her little garden, outside this small, safe moment of oneness with the power of the world.

"What type of tea do we have this time?" Maggie asked as they collected the ritual materials back into Della's bag.

"I had a couple to choose from," Della said, leading the way inside. She knew from experience where to look for a cloth for each of them to wipe the oils off their hands and faces and handed one to Maggie. "Grandmother Elise is being startlingly generous with them, now she thinks I've fully embraced my power. She keeps dropping around unannounced with different teas, but I realised a few days ago that all of them subtly contain herbs for fertility. I think she might be trying to organise a great-grandchild now I'm settled with someone she approves of. Or at least, doesn't openly disapprove of." She fished out the jar of mixed herbs from the bottom of her bag. "This one doesn't have anything in it to encourage the next generation of Greenbranches, or Gawlers, I promise. Clear-sightedness, this one is, but I mostly brought it because it tastes nice."

Maggie filled up the kettle and put it on to boil. "So, your grandmother must actually kind of like Leo. I don't think I've ever seen her *not* openly disapprove of... anyone. I didn't realise she could turn it off."

"She likes you well enough," Della said, measuring out the tea into their cups.

"Last time I saw her, she asked me if it was difficult being so short that I only come up to the navels of, and this is a quote, 'more evolved individuals'." Maggie made air quotes around the old witch's words.

Della laughed. "Okay, I'll admit that is pretty rude. She's got past the dog jokes with Leo, though, so I think he might be making some headway in charming her."

"Leo could charm the scales off a fish."

"True enough." Della laughed and poured boiling water

over their tea leaves. "It must make it easier to be an Alpha, though."

They settled in position on opposite sides of the kitchen table. "Has transitioning to Alpha been much more work than what Leo was doing as Beta?" Maggie asked. "It sounded like the old Alpha was making Leo do most of his job too."

Della looked down at her hands. "He says it doesn't take up too many more hours than he was putting in previously, but I know he wishes he had more time for his carpentry and working in the garden. We've both been pretty busy these last few months."

"It certainly sounds like it. Do you ever think about reducing your commitments, so you could have a little less on your plate?"

"If things keep going the way they are at the moment, I might have to reduce the hours I'm doing at work. I'm just drowning in Council work at the moment, and I don't think my boss would mind. It could just be for a little while, until the hubbub about me fighting in a werewolf war dies down and the Council stops throwing so much stuff at me."

"It's been months, Dells. I'm not sure that's ever going to happen."

"Well, I have a couple of projects that are coming to fruition soon, and then they'll need less hours. I can keep working on the afterschool integration programs as my primary focus, and keep to basic oversight of the others. I don't think the department would have any issue with it. They'd probably be happy to have someone who keeps winding up in newspaper headlines a little less closely associated with the department."

"You've been in the newspapers three times, and one of them was for preventing an all-out territory war. I can't believe they would want to be less associated with the woman who stopped the werewolf infighting from escalating to war all by herself."

"It wasn't just me," Della protested.

"Oh, I'm sorry," Maggie grinned, "was there someone else there burning up the energy of a full-grown werewolf, using her own lifeforce, in order to stop a crazy mob boss Alpha?"

"It sounds insane when you say it like that."

"It was insane! Your life is insane! Just a few months ago, you were fighting an underground coven of evil vampires!"

"Maggie—" Della started.

"I read books that are less exciting than your life, Dells."

"It's not like I go looking for it," Della objected.

"Did you, or did you not, volunteer to hunt down the evil vampires?" Maggie demanded.

"It's not like I could say, 'No, I'm not interested'!" Della protested. "They needed me. Even Raj isn't as strong in a fight as I am with my full powers." She seemed to realise that she'd mentioned the elephant in the room at the same moment that Maggie did, and her face fell. "Shit, Mags, I'm sorry. Here I am trying to distract you and I bring him straight into it."

"We were going to get there eventually," Maggie said in resignation. "I can't seem to keep him out of my head for more than about ten seconds anyway. It's like there's some-thing in me that just keeps reaching out for him, wanting him close. Which is especially ridiculous because we've been on *two* coffee dates, if you can even call them dates, and spent *one* night together. It's insane that I'm this worked up over the guy, after so little time. I mean, Jeremy and I were seeing each other for *months*, and the second Raj came on to the scene, it was like no one else could even hold my attention, you know?" She dropped her head into her hands. "Have you ever felt anything this ridiculous?"

There was a pause. "Actually... yes," Della said slowly. "That's exactly what it felt like when I first met Leo."

It took Maggie a moment to realise what her friend was saying, and then she felt her eyes go wide. "Are you saying what I think you're saying?"

"Mags," Della said, "Has Raj ever actually said you're *not* his mate?"

"That's crazy," Maggie said. "You know that's crazy, right?"

"Is it?" Della asked. "From this angle, things kind of seem to line up."

"I'm not a werewolf," Maggie said, the words pouring out of her. "I'm just a human. We don't mate like wolves—why would his mate bond affect me like this?"

"I'm not a werewolf, either, and it affected me," Della said. "Remember, I even did that spell to test whether someone was manipulating my feelings magically?"

"Do it on me," Maggie said, grabbing Della's hands. "What do you need? Check it for me. Right now."

"The spell checks whether there's any magic cast on you," Della said. "I just cast half a dozen protection spells over you, Mags. It will definitely show up positive for those spells whether or not you're Raj's mate."

"Don't say it like that," Maggie said, feeling her shoulders curl forwards like she'd just taken a blow to the gut.

"What are you so scared of?" Della asked. "That you're not his mate, or that you are?"

"Both!" Maggie cried. "Because if I'm not, I'll never be able to be with him in case he finds her. And if I am..." She trailed off. "If I am, h-he let me fuck around with the Jeremy situation, then spent hours talking with me in that coffee shop, kissed me in the alleyway, pretended it was nothing, then took me home and *slept* with me, all without telling me."

"Maybe he just didn't think it was the right time," Della said.

"The *right time* would have been before he *fucked* me, Dells. God, I feel like an idiot." She dropped her face into her hands. "I can't believe this."

"Believe what?" Della asked, and her voice was unexpectedly fierce. "That he didn't want to make you feel like you had to break up with your boyfriend just because he said so? Or that you didn't get a choice whether or not to be with him? Or that he was trying to avoid you feeling like the only reason he wanted you was because the universe decided you were a good fit? In what part of that are you the one who's been screwed over here? Because it sounds to me like he's been trying to make this as easy for you as possible."

"I had a right to know," Maggie insisted. "It's not just his life he's messing with; it's *mine* too."

"He's not the one messing things around here, Mags. That's the supernatural magic doing that." She reached over and laid a hand over one of Maggie's. "Look, Raj is a good man. He must care about you, or he wouldn't have done the taking-home part of it, or introduced you to his parents. If he didn't care about how you'd feel about it, he would have just announced it and let you deal with the fallout. It sounds strange, I know, but maybe he didn't tell you *because* he cares about you."

Maggie took several deep breaths. "Maybe we're getting a little ahead of ourselves. I still don't even know if it's true." *And it will break my heart all over again if it's not,* added the voice in her head. *It will hurt me even worse to have this sudden hope and then have it taken away.*

"Now, that is a conversation I'm leaving to you two," Della said. "Drink your tea first, then I'll drop you over at Raj's house."

"I won't see him until tomorrow," Maggie said. "He told

me he had a pack meeting tonight."

"Not with Leo and Emmett. They've pre-emptively kicked me out of the living room for the evening so they can watch some international sports game. Maybe you misheard him—normally, pack meetings are around full moon nights, when everyone's at their werewolf-iest, and then they can shift and go running out in the forest afterwards. It's a new moon tonight."

"I must have misheard," Maggie said, wondering why the moon thing sounded significant. Now that she was—maybe —the mate of a werewolf, would she start developing wolfy traits like sensitivity to the moon's phases? Surely not.

They finished their tea, and though Della offered to stay, Maggie knew she needed space to think through their conversation and the ramifications of both whether she *was* or *wasn't*, looking at being mated to a werewolf. She needed to *think*, and when that happened, her first instinct was to do something productive, and she couldn't do that with her friend sitting there. She hugged Della goodbye, promised to call her as soon as she knew more, and set about the house with a vengeance. She'd already done a fairly comprehensive clean in the time between Raj dropping her off yesterday and calling Della today, but this level of thinking meant a *deep* clean was in order.

She was halfway through scrubbing the grout in the shower with a toothbrush when she realised why the night of the new moon had sounded familiar.

Tonight, might just be fight night at the Ring.

Maggie's first instinct was to ring Della and beg for her to come back so they could work out a plan. What human wouldn't want one of the most powerful witches of her generation at her back when entering a den of iniquity, where suffering was the object of sport? Her mind flashed back to the conversation she'd had with Jeremy when he first told her about the Ring, though, and the comments he'd made about needing to get exceptions to the secrecy spells to even be able to tell her about what he did when the moon was dark. Maggie wouldn't be *able* to tell Della about the Ring—she'd come up against secrecy spells before, though, admittedly, not since she was a teenager. But if there was one thing a good witch knew how to do, it was keep the lips of her allies and her enemies closed tight when it came to her secrets. If she was seriously considering charging into the Ring and accosting Raj about whether she was his mate, Maggie knew she was going to have to do it alone.

Some sensible part of Maggie's brain clamoured for her to be reasonable, to not charge into unknown and illegal territory just to get her answer from the man she maybe, just a little, ever so slightly, might just be seriously developing feelings for. But she had to *know*. There was a drive in her to get close to him that would not let up, and Maggie knew, somehow *knew* deep inside herself, that she needed to do this. She needed to see him. She wouldn't get close to him before his fight, wouldn't break his concentration, but the *nanosecond* Raj was out of the Ring, he had some gods-damned explaining to do. She needed these answers like she needed her breath, and there would be hell to pay if she didn't get some information.

And if Raj said that her suspicions were wrong and she wasn't his mate? Well… she'd deal with that when she had to. She couldn't think about it now, or she started feeling sick.

Now, she only had to face one issue about getting to the warehouse in the industrial area of Mystic City where the Ring was held; she was going to have to do it via public transport.

Chapter 13

RAJ HAD NEVER BEEN SO INTENSELY chock full of whirling testosterone, while also being completely uninterested in fighting. He was going to have to picture his opponent—a werewolf male from a pack on the other side of Mystic City, with hair so blond, it was almost white, that gave him his Ring name (the Swede)—as a male coming to hit on his mate in a bar, to be able to motivate himself to throw a single punch. Of all the nights for the Ring to be on, it had to be one of the few he could spend with Maggie between her night-time shifts. And he'd had thoughts of his mate on his mind since he'd dropped her off at her house, images of their night together, memories of the sensation of her body on his, the way she tasted, the sounds she made when he gave her pleasure. He'd been fighting an erection for forty-eight hours without cease, and all he could think about was getting to his mate, pinning her under his body and making her come until the only words she could remember were his name and those of the gods. He had no passion for this fight, none of the rush of impending violence in his veins that usually brought him that sick, addictive anticipation of pain.

He just wanted to get back to Maggie. If there hadn't been a seriously large prize for this one night, he would have called in sick and left it to the bastards who ran the joint to find someone to stand in for his fight. If he could have just rid himself of the vague sense of honour among thieves—or in this case, illegal brawlers—he might have been able to spend this night relishing his mate's touch, rather than the blows of a random male followed by the careful touch of Doc.

Raj was trying not to think about Doc. He had the satisfaction of knowing that the man—*Jeremy*—was no longer permitted anywhere near Maggie, but knowing that his hands had been on her, that he'd slept beside her, known her body... it was enough to have the wolf beneath his skin growling for the chance to rip the man's hands off.

Maybe he should go and eyeball Doc just before the fight started, so he could channel that aggression into the fight with the Swede, and hopefully get the match over as soon as possible. Get it finished, get his wounds healed—he'd accept having all his injuries taken care of this time, rather than just the visible ones, so that he'd be in perfect physical condition to take full advantage of his mate tomorrow night. He didn't need bruised ribs and sore muscles when he intended to spend the whole night worshipping Maggie's body. He needed to be at his best for her, so that once they finished the candlelit dinner part of the night, and she, hopefully, heard that she was his mate with bright-eyed enthusiasm, he could finally claim her with no secrets between them.

Well, maybe one secret. Automatically, used to the effects of the spells that kept the Ring's existence a secret, he'd lied about what he was doing tonight. Not because he didn't want to tell her, although he expected she'd be less than supportive of his returning to the fighting club that she so clearly did *not* enjoy. Just because he wasn't used to being *able* to tell anyone about it, because the spelled secrecy had guarded his tongue with everyone for so long, that it didn't even occur to him that he *could* have told her the truth until he was driving away.

He was working the kinks out of his shoulders when Doc stuck his head around the door of the changeroom. Seeing Raj, he came inside and closed the door behind himself, leaning against it. "How are things? Any pre-emptive injuries you need me to take care of?"

"Feeling good," Raj said, keeping his answer short, to reduce the risk of saying something he shouldn't, something that would give away that he was now irrevocably tied to Doc's ex-girlfriend. Trying to stop himself from wanting to rip the man's head off while no one was around to see. "You?"

"Busy night," the other man said. "Your lot are fighting hard tonight."

"Always keen to put on a good show," Raj said, wondering what response the doc wanted from him.

"That's what they pay you for, right?" Doc asked with a grin that looked forced. "A good show."

"Gotta give the audience what they want," Raj replied unemotionally.

"I think we'll do that tonight," the man said with a smirk. "No doubt about that. You're fighting the Swede, right?"

"Yeah," Raj said.

"He prefers his right. Tries not to, but when he gets tired, it's visible. And I healed up some fractures on his left side last time, so he'll probably be trying to protect them."

"Thanks for the tip," Raj said, choosing not to mention that he'd studied the Swede's fighting patterns before and knew pretty much everything Doc could tell him, except perhaps the part about recently broken ribs.

"I look forward to you taking the stage tonight," Doc said, turning back to open the door. As he slid out through it, he added, "I'm sure it'll be a hell of a show. Just give me a signal when you want me to snap his neck." He winked as he left and closed the door behind himself before Raj could question the strange offer.

Raj went to sit ringside for a few matches before his own, watching the fighters and cataloguing their moves as he always did, in case one of them was his next opponent. He searched for the fire that usually burned in his blood in the lead-up to the fight but couldn't find more than a few sparks. The Professor had clearly been demoted to a lower fighting grade—he easily beat his opponent even though he looked like he'd lost a chunk of weight since Raj fought him. Often people who lost in the high-level fights didn't return after their loss and were never spoken of again. Not all of the lower-grade fighters were people Raj had bested, but since he'd become one of the Big Guys in their little fight club, he'd got to know most of them. The Blacksmith, Hard Hit Harry, even Raj's old competitor Running Robert all made an appearance. Some of his former opponents, like Robert and the Professor, seemed to be performing at much lower rankings than Raj would have expected. Maybe they'd decided to forego the higher prize money of the more difficult fights and stick to ones they could more easily win. Running Robert, though, looked like he'd lost even more weight than the Professor—he was practically wasting away. Every one of his wiry muscles was outlined starkly through his pale skin. No wonder the man had needed to drop down a few grades—he looked like he was in the process of starving to death. And a couple of Raj's other former competitors looked to be in pretty bad health, too. Maybe they were fighting for drug money, then—some of the spelled pills and powders made by unscrupulous witches could be so strongly addictive that the person taking them forgot all about food. He shouldn't be surprised that some of the strong-willed men he'd come up against in the Ring had dodgy reasons for being there—it was hard to take the ethical high ground when you were illegally fighting for money.

The crowd became bigger and more excited as the night continued, time ticking down towards Raj's own fight, and finally, their enthusiasm began to infect his own body, filling his veins with a power and energy that surely no drug could ever properly match. Here was the savagery he loved, the primitive nature of man versus man, beast versus beast, fighter versus fighter. Part of him wondered how Maggie would feel if he continued fighting in the Ring. Maybe not every time it was held, but every so often; there was something in it that he couldn't deny he loved. He rolled his shoulders as the energy continued to both tense and relax him, somehow all at once. He felt like his body was settling into its proper shape, preparing for the moment when it would just be him and the Swede in the Ring, and nothing would matter but strength and skill and pain.

When there were only a few fights left before his own, Raj went back to the preparation area, finishing his stretching and warmup and vaguely exchanging greetings with some of the other guys. The Professor was cleaning blood off his knuckles but waved Raj down. Up close, the man looked even worse than he had at a distance.

"Librarian." He grinned at Raj. "I hear you're the last fight of the night again. The Swede is one tough motherfucker. Give him hell."

"I plan to," Raj said. "Hey, man, are you all right? You don't look great."

"Heart condition, apparently," the Professor grunted. "Went into the ER with a broken nose a few weeks back, and they found the defect. The hospital where the doc works, actually—he took care of me in a real hospital for once.

Turns out he's a fuckin' surgeon." He tapped his own chest. "Apparently, it could stop ticking at any moment." He barked out a laugh.

"Should you be fighting?" Raj asked.

"Pills don't pay for themselves," the Professor grinned wolfishly. "I won't be in your league anymore, though—they can't risk me dropping dead in the biggest fight of the night. Small ones are fine, apparently."

"Do the organisers know?"

"Doc told them. We had a chat. Apparently, there've been a bunch of guys who've come through here with a similar problem. It's been cropping up in werewolves especially. Doc looks after 'em all. So now, I have my favourite illegal doctor taking care of it legally." The roar of the crowd intensified suddenly, signalling the end of the fight, and the Professor finished cleaning his hands then clapped Raj on the shoulder. "Good luck tonight, man. My money's on you. Don't lose it for me."

Raj had no team ushering him out into the Ring, no cameras he could shadow-box at to demonstrate his readiness. He stepped out into the walkway that linked the warmup area to the Ring and saw the Swede was already in position on the other side. The Ring's two organisers were standing in the centre of the Ring as they always did before the night's biggest fight, flanking the small man who was the usual announcer. Doc was standing on the other side of the ring, sweating like he was the one who'd been in the last fight. He grinned savagely at Raj, his face oddly flushed, and Raj had a moment to wonder whether perhaps the doc was sampling some of his own wares—or perhaps, someone else's. Maybe he wouldn't let Doc heal him tonight, even if he had visible bruises. He wasn't sure he wanted a warlock on drugs magically messing around with his insides.

"Introducing," the announcer yelled, "tonight's challenger, the Swede!"

The crowd went insane. Cheers and jeers in equal measure roared down from the tiers of seats lining every wall of the massive space. The blond werewolf climbed into the Ring and stood in the corner, calmly surveying Raj and the rest of the room as though his victory was already a certainty.

"And ladies and gentlemen, your champion, the Librarian!"

The screams that followed Raj's introduction made his ears ring. Part of him was deeply satisfied that he'd managed to become such a personality in this place, such a threat to other fighters. He had the adoration of this crowd, even as they were baying for his blood and betting on him to lose, and balled his hands into fists then threw his arms in the air, playing for their cheers.

Raj expected the two organisers to leave the Ring as they usually did, prepared to give the big-time criminals the nod of respect that they required when they left the announcer to call the beginning of the match, but instead, all three of them were standing almost uncannily still even as the crowd's cheering died, as though they had suddenly turned to stone. There was silence, and then a faint hum of confusion in the crowd, and then, suddenly, the heads of all three men exploded.

Complete silence reigned in the moment after the blood and gore spattered across Raj's exposed skin, and then the screaming began. But even that halted after barely long enough for the noise to register, a few seconds at most, and complete stillness held every member of the crowd. Raj went to step forwards as the three headless bodies collapsed to the ground but found that he couldn't move. Not his legs, not his arms, not even, when he tried to speak, his mouth or tongue.

His body would not respond to the directives of his brain. He could still move his eyes, but that was it.

The entire screaming episode had lasted only long enough to cover the sound of the headless bodies hitting the ground. Silence now reigned, the kind of pregnant silence that could only exist in a room packed with people not making a sound. Fear had the most microscopic chance to coil inside Raj before Doc stepped through the spreading pool of blood to the centre of the Ring and raised his hands as though he was greeting an adoring crowd. The watchers remained silent, mouths open in soundless screams.

"Well, thank you all very much for coming," he said, pausing as though waiting for a laugh in response. His eyes, sweeping the crowd over the top of Raj's head where he was frozen motionless, were bright with enthusiasm. He spoke as though he was greeting a small group of friends he'd invited around for a meal. "As you can see, we are undergoing some changes in management. As of this evening, this operation belongs to me.

"We've had some difficulties, as the Ring has grown in size and infamy. Difficulties with the confidentiality spells. Too many people trying to tell our secrets. And the owners and I had a difference of opinion as to the importance of confidentiality." He stepped out of the pool of blood, beginning a circle of the rope boundaries of the Ring, and his expensive shoes left crimson footprints on the scuffed floor. "As I'm sure you all know, Rod and Abram are career criminals—or should I say, *were*. This particular operation is only one of the many games they were running. In the grand scheme of things, if the Ring was to continue to become more popular, it would make them enough money each night that it would be well worth it even if the secrecy spells should prove incomplete, and the operation was shut down in as little as a few more months. Their involvement is legally untraceable. Only evidence from attendees or fighters could connect them with the Ring, and they were positive that none of you good-hearted people could be convinced, gently or otherwise, to give them up."

He halted at the edge of the Ring, resting his hands on the uppermost ropes. "But I'm somewhat more... sceptical of the reliability of you who attend this event. And I have far more to lose. And none of you fear reprisals from me nearly as much as you do from the likes of Abram and Rod. Consequently, of course, I suggested investing more in the Ring's magical protection. Our esteemed owners..." he glanced down at the corpses in the centre of the Ring, "...disagreed. So, I'm sure you understand, I had to take matters into my own hands. And here we are."

Not a sound had been uttered in the enormous space for the entire time Doc had spoken. Raj was fairly sure they were all breathing, since he was still able to, but otherwise, the room had been completely silent. Everyone stood as still as the corpses on the floor, no sounds of clothing rustling or feet shuffling on the floor. Their facial expressions were frozen in fear, some of them halfway through cut-off screams. The doc held every single one of them frozen with his spell.

"This has been a long time coming," Doc continued, now running his fingers over the fibres of the ropes before him. "I've been waiting for the right time to officially stake my claim over this place. There's nothing I like more than seeing a couple of savage dogs beat each other bloody." The smile that spread over his face looked halfway to a sneer.

"You're a doctor!" someone screamed from the crowd, clearly having broken from the stillness spell. "You can t kill all of us!"

"Yes, I am a doctor," Jeremy said, making movements with his fingers. "But I've seen the kind of money you can make on nights like these, and frankly, the hospital doesn't pay me enough. And to answer your other point, yes, I *can* kill all of you, and with very little effort. But that would be rather a waste, wouldn't it? To have put on this great display for you tonight, only to have no one walk out of here alive?" He walked over to where the Swede was standing, frozen, in the opposite corner of the Ring to Raj. He kicked the side of the blond werewolf's knee, and the crack reverberated through the space. The Swede toppled over like a broken mannequin, his posture unmoving. Doc stood over him. "So, why don't I give you a brief demonstration of what will happen if you decide to stand against me. Get up," he barked at the Swede, making a gesture in his direction. The Swede stood slowly, his magically forced movements not allowing him to favour his injured leg, and Raj could see how his eyes widened with pain, tears spilling, as he put weight on that side. Doc was making no allowances, and the man would not be able to stand evenly weighted for long without collapsing, no matter how powerful the magic holding him up was.

"I'd like you to see what I've built into this system that allows me to control every last one of you," Doc said, then called out, more loudly, "Fighters!"

A line of the men from the warm-up area and change-rooms walked out from behind Raj. He couldn't see them until they were halfway across the room, with his head unable to move, but who else would be coming out of there? Doc wasn't controlling their movements; their steps were cautious, out of time, some of them limping from injuries earlier in the night. Almost every single one was a man Raj had fought in the past, and all of them were looking worse for wear since he'd faced them in the Ring. Not just from the battering most of them had taken tonight; more than that. Weight lost, muscles faded, skin sagging with age. They looked decades older than the men he'd fought months and years before. They stood around the raised platform of the Ring, facing out towards the audience, like wooden soldiers guarding a castle.

"You see these men?" Doc asked, still performing as though the silent crowd was going to respond. "Every one of their hearts is controlled by me. All I have to do is *think* that they should stop beating, and every one of them dies. I'm very good with hearts. I've been studying them for a long time. And I've been practicing. All the fighters who left here and never came back—what did you think happened to them? Heart failure, just because they looked at me wrong. It's a very clever spell, one of my own devising. It takes a while to cast, but all I needed to do was leave them sick enough after a fight that they'd come to my hospital, and I had all the time in the world. You need something to keep dogs in check, I find, and with fighters like these as a risk to my health, it seemed smarter to have some insurance.

"So, here's what you need to know, my friends. Every man you've seen smash someone's face in at these nights is my insurance. In a moment, I'm going to leave a magical mark on each of you here tonight, so I can learn anything about any of you without doing more than casting the simplest of spells. I will know where you live. I will know who you love. And I have a large group of very angry, very dangerous fighters who will kill any one of you the moment I ask it, because their lives belong to me."

Raj took in as much of the Ring as he could see in his frozen position. How many people was Doc holding under his spell? If he had to hold it much longer, would he get tired —and then maybe Raj could break from the enchantment and take him out, while he was distracted? He looked fit, but he was a doctor—that didn't always lend itself to extreme fitness. Though, then again, that was what people usually thought about a librarian, and look how false that was.

He had to be prepared for the man to be a fighter—and to be able to use his magic, which gave him a considerable advantage. Raj couldn't hope to stand against a warlock strong enough to hold hundreds of people frozen in place, at least not in his human form. The wolf was his strongest form, but the shift took long moments, and he couldn't guarantee that he'd get long enough to complete it fully—couldn't guarantee he'd have any time at all, but if he managed it, then he'd have to use every nanosecond carefully. Half-shifted, then. Teeth and claws. While Doc was distracted, he'd tear him to shreds.

"Leave us alone!" someone screamed from up in the crowd. Perhaps Doc wasn't as powerful as Raj had estimated if people kept breaking out of his immobilisation spell. Still strong enough to stop a single werewolf's heart, though, if such a person were foolish enough not to kill him instantly.

"You don't want to follow my plan, is that it?" Doc made the same gesture up at the crowds, and the screaming did not return. There was, of course, no response to his question. "Very well. I'll assume you're all in agreement, then. Let's see how much these fighters want to live."

The men standing around the bottom of the Ring's platform sent concerned looks up to the doc, eyes going wide. The blood from the headless bodies of the organisers and announcer had covered the entire Ring surface and was starting to drip down to where the fighters stood around it.

"Each of you can pick one person in this crowd and kill them," he said, his voice becoming enthusiastic, like he'd just come up with the idea. "The first one can take out the Swede. I'll even hold him still for you. And once you've killed someone, I'll let you leave. For now. Prove your worth to me, or I'll stop your heart where you stand."

"I won't do it." The words came from the Professor, standing just near where Raj was frozen. Raj simultaneously wanted to hug the man for his bravery and punch him in the face for drawing the doc's attention in their direction. "Kill me if you want," he went on. "I won't murder an innocent."

"You think the people who come to your little fight club are innocent?" Doc asked incredulously.

"They didn't come here to fight," the Professor said. "That makes them innocent in my books."

"Well, that's your choice then," Doc said with a smile, his eyes shining in the dim light, and made a gesture towards the Professor.

For a second, nothing happened, and then the man's eyes went wide. He seemed to be trying to keep quiet, muffling sounds that would have indicated pain, as though he didn't want this death to affect anyone else in the room. As though his silent passing might lessen the power this move showed Jeremy to have. The Professor collapsed, still keeping quiet, but from his position close to the man, Raj could hear every gasping breath. And hear when they stopped.

"That's a good demonstration, then," Doc said loudly into the silent room. "Anyone else feel like making a sacrifice, they're more than welcome. Either I'll stop your heart, or my man here will make your death hurt a whole lot more."

With his head in this position, unable to see farther than the distance he could roll his eyes, it took Raj a moment to search his peripheries for the doc's man coming forward to deliver judgment.

And another to realise that the warlock was gesturing towards him.

"Stand up here with me where you belong," Doc ordered, and Raj realised suddenly that the spell on him— and apparently him alone—had lifted. He could move. He had a single, infinitesimally brief impulse to sprint from the room and leave the others to their fates, but it died as fast as it appeared. He couldn't leave all these people unprotected.

And if the doc thought Raj was on his side, he was clearly as mad as that insane gleam in his eye was making him look.

"Now," the doc ordered, and Raj rose to his feet. Rather than moving around to the position of support behind this new would-be Godfather, though, he stepped in front of him.

"I'm not your attack dog," Raj said. "I don't know who you think you are, or I am, but I'm not going to hurt people for you. Kill me if you have to, but I won't do that."

"Don't be ridiculous," the doc said, suddenly focused on their conversation as though there was no one else in the room, as though it didn't feel to him like some kind of macabre performance being put on for the benefit of the ensnared watchers. The doc still had a ghost of a smile on his face, like he was just waiting for Raj to stop joking around and fit to his plans. "Of course, you are. Why do you think I've been saving your life all this time, every time you had a brain bleed that could have killed you, or a pneumothorax? Who do you think kept making your body stronger than everyone else here? Are you telling me you didn't *notice* that I was saving your ass all these nights?" His cool calm was shifting. "I have *created you*, and you will do whatever the *fuck* I tell you to do, or I swear to all the gods, I'll turn your blood to acid and watch you die screaming." By the end of the rant, Doc's previous relatively calm manner had slipped into a kind of mad intensity that seemed like it should have him all but foaming at the mouth, like the eggshell covering his fanaticism had cracked, and insanity was starting to leak out. His words were still clipped and controlled, his tone as educated as it was unstable.

"Try it," Raj snarled, "and we'll see who dies first." And he lunged for the warlock's throat.

The doc flicked him away with a wall of air that had Raj slamming back against the blood-spattered ropes of the Ring and bouncing forwards to land on the floor. The spell that had continued to hold all the others immobile had already locked into place around him again, and he had no way to cushion his fall. His head slammed into the ground. He felt something crunch in his side and one of his knees. The first coherent thought he had after the impact of his head on the floor was that he didn't want to die on the ground, unable to defend himself. What had all those years of fighting and training been worth if he was going to die unable to fight back?

"Oh, you fucking traitor," the warlock spat, and then pain worse than a thousand bone-breaking blows slammed into Raj. If he could have moved, he would have screamed. The wave receded after an immeasurable amount of time. A minute? A year? And there was Doc, standing over him, grinning luridly down. "Magical deaths are usually quick," he drawled. "A few seconds of pain, a few minutes. But I'm a doctor, Mr Librarian. I'm a fucking expert on filthy scum werewolf bodies like yours. And that means I know how to make the death part happen slowly."

Movement out of the corner of Raj's eye, had his gaze flicking to the side, his eyes once again the only part of his body that could still move. He could barely see anything, only a slight shifting through the crowd on that side, but there was someone there. Desperately, he wished it might be his friends, maybe a Blue Crescent army come to save him the way they'd rescued Petra from the vampires. He wished it might be the cops because he'd take however long they gave him in prison over another wave of that pain. Maybe it could even be some friends of the owners, who somehow knew their enterprise was being stolen and a new criminal overlord had to be taken down to restore the correct order of things.

But then the bond spinning out from his chest tightened, and he knew it was none of those groups.

Maggie.

Chapter 14

MAGGIE HAD SPRINTED what felt like miles, from the bus stop to the entry to the Ring building, and told the intimidatingly large security guard that she was the nurse assisting Doc that evening. Clearly employed specifically for the physical threat he posed, rather than any semblance of intelligence, the guard had barely even looked her over before allowing her past. Maybe her knowledge of the workings of the Ring, the fact that she'd clearly been made an exemption to the spells of silence that protected it, was enough to prove that she was allowed to enter. She didn't care, though, just sprinted through the halls until she arrived in the massive space that housed the Ring itself.

From her position at the top of the tiers of seating, she could see Jeremy was standing in the Ring. Raj lay against the ropes on the opposite side of the space. And three dead bodies, which looked like their *heads* had exploded, also lay inside the ropes, the gore of bone and brain making lumps in the coat of blood that all but covered the floor of the arena.

She hadn't realised she was close to the huge fighting space, mostly because she hadn't been able to hear the raucous noise of the crowd that had left her ears ringing the last time she was here. The whole room was all but silent, and as she felt the flicker of magic running over her skin, she realised that someone—*Jeremy*—had frozen every member of the crowd in their places.

The magic hissed over her skin, seeming to recoil from her, and she praised every god she could think of that Della had cast the protection spells today. It must be that the magic couldn't get through them, and, she hoped, if she was lucky, it might protect her from Jeremy's attention too. She shoved her way through the tiers of seating, packed with hundreds of people, trying to find her way down to the Ring itself. She had no idea what she would do once she got down to the platform itself, but she knew she had to get closer, to understand what was going on. And Raj—something she couldn't understand, didn't have the time to consider, was dragging her towards Raj.

The only sound was Jeremy's voice, not quite loud enough for her to hear at this distance, but he sounded incensed. She had no idea what was going on, no concept of what she would do once she made it down to the fighting level, but something in her was screaming at her to get to Raj and make sure he was all right. Make sure he was *alive*. Certainly, all this must be some kind of misunderstanding. Surely, if everyone just calmed down for a minute, they'd be able to come to a reasonable conclusion where everyone was safe and no one else's head exploded, and Jeremy stopped yelling down at Raj's unmoving body.

The moment he felt Maggie in the room, every protective instinct Raj had went into overdrive. *She's here. I have to keep her safe.* He wanted to scream at her to run, he wanted to tear Doc into shreds with his bare hands. More than anything, he wanted her *safe* and as far away from here as possible.

The doc saw his eyes move, though, and then the warlock's own gaze was flicking over to where his mate must be visible as the only movement in the crowd.

"Maggie," Doc said, as though she was some kind of ghostly apparition that he couldn't quite believe he was seeing. "You came back. You came back to me."

There was a pause, as though Maggie was collecting her thoughts, and then she spoke. "Not to you," she said coldly. "Jeremy, what the hell is going on?"

"If not for me, then why would you be here?" he asked jovially, as though she might be waiting to reveal the punch-line of a joke. "You said you'd never come back to this place. What else could have made you change your mind? You don't have to be coy, Maggie. I've always known you want me."

Maggie paused, and every muscle in Raj's body strained against the spell, begging to be set free so he could protect his mate. "I'm here for him," she said finally, and out of the corner of his eye, Raj could just see it as she raised her hand to point at his own crumpled body.

The change in Jeremy's mood over the next few silent seconds was so sudden, it could have been from the flick of a switch. It was as though he'd been keeping his madness on a steady boil, restraining it, and then it had violently, savagely boiled over.

"*Him*," he said to Maggie, his voice now growing unsteady. "You're here for the fucking *dog*?" He paused, and comprehension lit his eyes. "He's the reason you... you—"

"Yes," Maggie said. Raj could just barely see as she spread her hands out towards him, open-palmed, calm, beseeching. "I think I might be his mate."

"He's an animal," Jeremy said, then gave a derisive laugh. "I know I improved him, but Maggie, he's not like us."

"I love him," Maggie said simply, but before Raj could even process her words, Jeremy was wildly denying them.

"No, no, no. You can't love him. You love *me*. He's an animal. He's a fucking *animal!*"

"Jeremy—" Maggie entreated, but the warlock was already turning back to Raj, and he felt the massive wave of pain break through his body once more, his lungs begging to release the screams trapped in his immobile body. Raj wondered distantly, abstractly, through the agony, how long it would take before Jeremy killed him.

"You were the one I spared!" Jeremy was screaming down over Raj's twitching body. It seemed whatever magic Jeremy was putting him through was enough to just slightly break the immobility spell. "You fucking *savage*. You were supposed to be the *different* one of your gods-forsaken species. You were supposed to be *better!* I made you *better* so you could help me protect what's *mine*." He roared the last word like a man possessed. "But now, I see you for what you really are. Nothing better than one of the dogs, sniffing around what's mine, trying to take her from me." He brought his hand up, muttering an incantation, and squeezed it into a fist. Maggie *felt* the way that Raj faltered at that moment, his body returning to stillness as though it was scared to move.

"You feel that, dog?" Jeremy taunted him. "I have my hand around your fucking *heart*. Just like I did every *single one* of those opponents you should never have beaten. Brought you fame and glory, didn't I? Made you the hardest man in the Ring, the man no one could beat? Because I thought you were *better*. You were trying to make yourself *better* than the gods-damned *scum* of Blue Crescent. An intellectual born out of a doghouse, full of fucking animals!" He gave a self-depre-cating laugh. He was starting to shake—Maggie could see from this distance—from the effort of keeping so many people frozen in place? Or was this just the extent of Jere-my's extremism, that he was fully overtaken by his wild emotions? After a moment, Maggie realised he was contin-uing to laugh, the silent shaking turning into a high and hysterical sound. "You pretend you're better than the rest of us, just because you can fight like beasts. Well, I have more power in my *little fucking finger* than you've ever felt with your demonic shifting and your moonlight orgies! I can stop your heart, I can stop everyone's heart in this fucking room, because I bothered to *learn*. I honed my craft to become the most deadly warlock anyone has ever seen, because I know your animal bodies and I know *exactly* what it takes to kill you."

Someone broke from the spell, several rows in front of Maggie, a strangled scream bursting from his freed throat, and from her place up amongst the spectators, she had a full view of Jeremy shooting one arm out towards him, not even looking away from Raj to do it, and a wave of power approached.

The man's body exploded, showering those around him in blood and gore. The worst part, though, strangely, wasn't the shower of liquefied intestines and fragments of bone that spattered those around him. It was the complete silence, the powerful magic that held everyone stock-still and completely silent.

Almost everyone. There was someone else moving now too, a few rows into the audience, trying to crawl past people's frozen feet to make it to the exit. Maggie wouldn't even have noticed, except that his scrambling knocked down one of the standing audience members, creating a domino effect as several frozen bodies toppled.

"Oh, you want to play?" Jeremy drawled from his position at the centre of the room, turning away from Raj to focus his attention on the person scrambling past a forest of unmoving legs in an attempt to escape. "You want to play hide and seek, you little fucking *worm*? All right. Let's play."

It was the splitting of his attention that did it. He raised his hand up, bringing the crawling man out of the crowd, lifting him above their heads where he screamed, high and shrill.

"You think you can hide from me?" Jeremy demanded. "I am more than you will ever be. I control more magic with one hand than you've ever seen in your gods-damned *life*—"

He was interrupted by Raj slamming into him. Maybe he had felt the loosening of Jeremy's power while he was focused on the crawling man; maybe he had just taken advantage of his distraction. But in the moments that followed, he was moving almost too fast for Maggie to see more than the impacts as he slammed fist after fist into Jeremy's face and torso. The warlock writhed and yelled, and the crawling man was dropped on to the unforgiving bodies of those unfortunate enough to be standing below him.

It didn't take long for it to come to an end. Raj was thrown backwards by a huge surge of power, bouncing off the ropes circling the Ring and slamming into the blood-spattered floor.

"You want to play?" Jeremy repeated, dragging himself to his feet. He spat out something that looked like a tooth, or maybe several teeth, and began dragging himself, clearly with significant pain, towards where Raj was scrambling back to his feet. "Mr Librarian, I've been playing with werewolf bodies like yours for years. I know your anatomy like the back of my hand. I could stop your heart without blinking. But you know what I'm going to do instead?" He brought both his hands up this time, performing intricate movements with his fingers so quickly that Maggie could barely follow them, pushing them towards Raj like he was forcing unwilling magic out of his body. Raj was immediately slammed backwards like he'd taken a blow to the chest with the strength of ten men, and Maggie heard bones crack.

Jeremy must have heard them too, because a slow smile spread across his face, and his next words came with the slow, precise dictation of someone who thinks they are in absolute control. "You know what I'm going to do, werewolf? I'm going to make your blood into acid. Didn't I warn you? And I'll do it slowly, bit by bit, because you deserve to fucking suffer as you die. Let's see how long your superpower were-wolf healing can save you as you slowly die, on the floor in the dirt where you belong. Let's see how long it takes you to start begging."

Maggie was moving before she realised she was able to, bursting through the last of the rows of spectators and screaming out his name, and then it was too late to come up with a better plan. "Jeremy!"

He turned to look at her, and none of the effervescent fanaticism was removed from his features. This was the Jeremy she had never known, she realised, the one who had been hiding behind that suave mask all this time.

For a moment that felt like an eternity, time was frozen as neither of them moved.

"Maggie," he said softly, his eyes raking over her features like he wanted to memorise them. "Maggie, don't worry. I'll save you from him. You don't have to do anything you don't want to do. He can't force you again."

"He never forced me," Maggie said. "Jeremy, he never made me do anything I didn't want to do."

"I knew you were different," Jeremy said, ignoring her

words. His voice was soft, gentle, a voice she remembered from sleepless nights and slow mornings. He sounded entranced. "A human who can hide from my spells? I knew you couldn't just be a worthless mortal. You have a magical aura around you, like you've been blessed, so I knew there was power in you. So, you're mine, and I'll protect you from dogs like this. Even this one, that I thought I could save from his roots. I'll kill him for you. Just for you. You don't have to do anything for him. You don't have to be his mate just to save him from the madness. You can be mine, and he will never hurt you again."

"He didn't hurt me," Maggie said, shoving down the fear that was rising in her like an inexorable tide. Was it insanity to try to talk him out of his madness? Or maybe, if she took up enough of his attention, some of his spells would weaken, and people would be able to escape? She took a deep breath and tried to put their story into words. "He... he took me out to coffee and talked to me about books, Jeremy. Remember all the times I wanted to talk to you about what I was reading, and you were too busy?"

"He's the Librarian," the warlock said scathingly. "Of course, that's how he'd trap you."

"He didn't trap me," Maggie said, trying to hold back tears. "He didn't even tell me I was his mate. He... he let me fall for him without any of the mate stuff getting in the way."

"Doing what?" Jeremy snapped. "Talking about books? That's not enough to fall in love. He spelled you, the sacred magic of the universe violated in their twisted werewolf games, *making* you fall in love with him."

"I would have fallen in love with him anyway," Maggie said, now ignoring the tears dripping down her cheeks. "Maybe it would have taken a little longer without the magic, but I would have fallen in love with him anyway. Please, Jeremy, don't take him away from me."

"You won't need him, once he's gone," Jeremy said, and in that soothing voice was the strangely discordant feeling of having been once soothed by it and now knowing that it meant nothing. "The spell will be broken. Maggie, you won't need him. This magic dragging you two together, we'll be away from it once he's dead. It won't be able to take you from me. We'll be able to be together again, with nothing of him. Just us. You and me. Forever."

"Over my dead body," Raj said as he ripped his claws across the man's throat.

The action spun Jeremy on his feet as he screamed. For a fraction of a second, he stood facing Raj, blood fountaining out of his wound. He raised a hand towards Raj—*how was he still standing*—and Maggie heard the words boom through the space psychically more than she heard his mouth shape them.

"*So be it.*"

At the same moment, he thrust out one hand at Raj, and Maggie instinctively braced for another explosion of power. Instead, smiling even as he choked on his own blood, Jeremy clenched his hand into a fist.

Raj's entire body changed shape as the bones in his arms and legs cracked, so loudly Maggie felt the sound in her soul.

Unable to stay still, Maggie sprinted down the rows and ducked under the ropes, hauling herself on the blood-sheened platform of the Ring. She threw herself at Jeremy, knocking him forwards on to his knees and breaking his sight line with Raj. The warlock was wheezing now, inhaling through the torn mess of his throat as much as he was through his mouth and nose, choking and coughing. He rolled onto his back slowly, torturously, and met Maggie's eyes as she stood.

I knew you loved me. He mouthed the words silently.

"Not a fucking chance," Maggie spat and kicked him in

the head as hard as she could, over and over until, suddenly, people were screaming and frantically rushing around the base of the Ring platform, and she realised that Jeremy's hold on them had ended. He was, at best, unconscious, at worst... she couldn't think about that now, couldn't consider the possibility that she'd just ended a man's life.

Instead, she stumbled over to where Raj lay. He'd managed to move enough to prop himself against the ropes of the Ring, but one of his arms and at least one of his legs were definitely broken, and there was blood on his lips. As she knelt down beside him, he coughed, sending blood spattering over his bare chest, the floor, and onto Maggie's clothes.

For a moment, they just stared at each other.

"I've been... an inexplicable fool," Raj gasped, sending himself into another bout of coughing.

"Don't you dare quote *Pride & Prejudice* to me right now, Rajesh Lewis," Maggie said, trying to hold back her tears. She fumbled for her phone. "I've got to call an ambulance."

"The spells... will stop you," Raj said between heaving breaths. "Can't talk about... this place... with anyone. You won't be... able to give them... an address."

"Then, what do I do?" she cried, wanting to drape herself over him but scared of hurting him more. A stray tear dripped on to his chest.

"Oi," came a rough voice from behind them. "Come on. We don't have long."

Maggie turned to see Ace, the useless other assistant who had helped Jeremy the night she'd worked here. He was standing over them and levitating what looked like a large piece of plywood.

"You're a warlock," she said, her words surprising even her.

"Well, they needed a backup for basic first aid if Doc was

unavailable." Ace glanced over his shoulder at Jeremy's motionless body. "Guess he's unavailable. Come on, let me get the big guy on to the board. I've got a van we can take him to the hospital in, but you'll have to keep him alive until we get there. I'm a warlock, and I know a few things, but I'm no doctor."

"Do it," Maggie begged, leaping to her feet.

Ace clearly wasn't the most skilled of warlocks—Raj seemed to be trying not to scream for most of his transfer on to the board—but the crowd of milling people, which had somewhat thinned by now as they fled, got out of his way as he levitated the board through them and down a series of passageways that Maggie knew from her last visit led to the warmup areas. They sprinted out an unmarked door and up a flight of stairs—Maggie thanked all the gods for the presence of unexpected warlocks—that opened up outside the building. The promised van was right there, engine running, and Ace opened the doors with a twitch of his fingers, lowering the board on to the floor of the vehicle. Maggie clambered in and the doors slammed shut.

"Where to, boss?" the person in the driver's seat asked, sounding surprisingly calm, considering they had a man bleeding to death in the back of the car. Perhaps Ace had done this before.

"Hospital," Ace said without hesitation. "And step on it."

His body seemed too large, lying out in front of her, for her to be able to keep it alive under her own power.

"Heart's getting slower," Ace said, sounding as panicked as she felt. She glanced over to see that he had his fingers over Raj's pulse, bracing the broken arm to stay still even as the van tore around corners.

"You have broken ribs," she heard her own voice say to Raj. "If I do CPR on you, one of them might puncture a lung."

"Doesn't CPR normally break ribs?" Ace asked. He was starting to sound desperate. "I've seen that on TV—it's meant to break ribs if you're doing it right. Right?"

"If his heart actually stops, I'll have to do it," Maggie said, feeling the knowledge that she might kill the man she loved while trying to save him settle on to her shoulders, bowing them forwards. "A hole in the lung is better than a stopped heart."

"It'll be... fine," Raj said, but his voice was getting weaker.

For the first time, Maggie focused on his face rather than his wounds. "It might kill you," she said.

"It might not," Raj offered with a grin that was a bare ghost of his usual smile.

The tears began to rise in her throat. She bit her lip and turned to move away, but she knew when she felt the pressure on her knee that it was his hand.

"Don't leave me... on my own now," he gasped out, pain and struggle colouring his every word. His eyes added the rest of the thought. *Not when I don't know if I'll see you again.*

"Why didn't you tell me I was your mate?" she asked, the words barely comprehensible under the sobs she was trying to suppress.

He stared at her for a long moment. "I never wanted you... to be pressured... to be mine, just because... I was already yours," Raj said. He coughed, and there was more blood on his lips. So much blood.

Without taking her eyes off Raj, still tamping down on the tears as hard she could, Maggie yelled, "How far away are we?"

"Five more minutes," the driver called back. The words, and their implication—*you just have to keep him alive for five more minutes*—reverberated in the back of the van.

"I felt it too," Maggie told Raj, tears escaping to slip

down her cheeks. "After I got over being scared of you, that is. I couldn't stay away from you. Somehow, I knew you were mine."

"I'm so glad... you didn't... stay away." Raj's voice was even weaker this time.

"Please stay with me," Maggie found herself saying, fighting the tears that fell onto his skin. "Please, Raj. We haven't had enough time. There are so many more books to read. I want to see my name on your skin. Please, Raj. I love you. Don't leave me."

"I'd do it... all again," he said, heaving in breaths in wet wheezes. "Even this... just for the time... I got with you."

"Please," she sobbed, both her hands wrapped around his much bigger one. "Please. Please."

He didn't say anything more, just slowly pulled her hand to his mouth with his good arm and pressed a kiss to her fingers. She could feel his grip loosening degree by degree, and when the doors of the van slammed open and everything was lights and noise, she had to force herself to release him and try to answer the questions thrown at her about his condition. She felt the phantom touch of his lips and his hand on hers, even as they frantically shifted him to a hospital bed and raced him away.

The doors to the Emergency Department slid closed behind the bed, and Maggie sat down on the curb and gave herself over to sobs so deep and heavy that they shook her to her core.

"Whoever is out there," she whispered through her tears. "Whoever is listening. *Anyone.* Please, please, don't let this be the end. Please don't let me lose him. Please, *please,* bring him back to me."

But the night was cold and dark, and no answer came from the sentinel stars.

Chapter 15

THERE WAS PAIN. He couldn't breathe. There was pain. Something was holding him down. There was pain.

There was pain.

There was nothing.

Chapter 16

HAD someone been of the inclination to take out the Blue Crescent command structure, they would have had no trouble over the next few days. Leo and Emmett were at Raj's bedside almost as much as Maggie was, and she only left when the nurses, many of whom she knew personally, insisted. This did not happen often. She was one of their own; they would allow her some leeway as she waited to see whether the man she loved would survive.

The police came through, curious to know the origins of this extreme trauma case, and she told them that her ex-boyfriend had done this to her current one out of mad jealousy. She gave no more details. She had left Jeremy with a pulped skull on the floor of the Ring, but even if she had wanted to give the police that information, the secrecy spells prevented her from telling them. She played up the distress of her situation—it was not difficult for her to bring tears to the surface at this point—and promised the police she'd come by the station in the next few days. They pressed that this was too urgent for them to wait until Raj woke up, that Jeremy could be fleeing the country or committing more crimes while they waited for her mate to regain consciousness. They left out the comment, delivered gently by the doctors when Raj came out of the first surgery, that he might not. The unspoken words hung heavy in the air.

He had to be taken back to surgery twice. Maggie didn't ask for details, and the information she would normally have been able to follow about heart damage and brain swelling and internal bleeding dissolved in the face of her frantic fear. All she retained from those conversations was that, had he not been blessed with werewolf healing abilities, he would have died several times over. She took the time he was in the operating theatre to go home, shower, change her clothes, and inform her work that she was not ready to come back yet. They were kind; for once, the hospital administration was prepared to give her some leeway. She suspected they felt guilty that one of their most admired surgeons had tried to murder her mate. As soon as she could, she returned to Raj's room. At least one or two of Leo, Della, Emmett, and Petra were always with her, even overnight. Once, she came back to find Leo and Emmett leaning heavily on each other as they stared down at Raj's motionless face, machines beeping in the background. That was when her hope took the biggest hit. If even they weren't confident that Raj could survive this, then how could she be?

The sun rose, and the sun set, and Maggie waited. She ate hospital food, or one of the others would run down to the cafeteria to collect supplies. She held his hand sometimes, but it felt wrong for it to be so still.

After a few days, she started reading to him. Maybe he could hear her, maybe not, but she figured if there was anything that would bring Raj back to her, it would be a good story. They filled the silence of the hospital room and pushed the cloud of fear that surrounded them all to the edges for a while. One of the nurses found her a battered copy of *A Tale of Two Cities* when she asked if there were any books around, and then when Leo asked if she needed anything, she gave him a list of books she could remember talking about with Raj, in those all-too-brief coffee dates. She wasn't game to try Shakespeare, but Dickens was, she thought, within her range. She read *Martin Chuzzlewit* and *Hitchhiker's Guide to The Galaxy* and *Matilda*, Dr Seuss stories and *Wuthering Heights*. When her voice gave out, one of the others took over. Eventually, Della brought her the entire paperback collection of *A Song of Ice and Fire*, and she almost cried looking at the size of them; it felt like the huge number of hours required to read him all these books was somehow ill-wishing his recovery. Like she was cursing him to stay unconscious, just by keeping herself prepared in case it happened. But what else was she supposed to do to fill the endless hours by his bed? Was she just meant to wait there in silence, time measured out by the beeping of the monitors displaying the feeble numbers measuring his life?

Still, unable to think of anything else to do, she picked up the first book.

She read the first chapter, trying to return to the flow of the story and get a feel for each character, and by the second, she was beginning to feel the enthrallment that had led her to read the entire long series in the first place. She fell into the story, and hours ticked by, the sun sinking towards the horizon.

She was too engrossed to hear the change in the rhythm of the machines beeping, but she definitely noticed when Raj said, in a voice like ground glass, "Magnolia."

In that moment, it felt like it had been her heart that stopped, her heart that was suddenly resuming beating. That all the light in the world had been dimmed, and now, it had become bright again, and she could see.

"I'm here," she managed, trying not to choke on her

tongue as she threw the book aside, uncaring of where it landed, and reached out to take his hand. His face looked haggard, but his eyes were open, and she couldn't drag her own gaze away.

She listened to a few of his gasping breaths before he spoke. "I'm sorry," he managed, still wheezing between words, "that I didn't tell you."

"You don't have to be," Maggie said, tears spilling down her cheeks. "I don't care about that now."

"I still am," Raj rasped. "Should have... told you... sooner."

"I don't care," Maggie said. "I'll be mad at you for the mate thing when you're not six inches from death."

"Don't be ridiculous," Raj said with what looked like a pained grin, "I'm at least eight inches away by now." Maybe it should have made her laugh, but instead, Maggie felt more tears welling up in her eyes.

"I thought I lost you," she managed. "I was so... I was so mad at you, for not telling me, and I went to the Ring to rip you a new one after your fight because I needed to know the truth, and then, suddenly, I was just trying to keep you alive." She strangled a sob.

"Doc?" Raj rasped.

"I don't know if I killed him," Maggie said, "But he wasn't moving when I left, and with that many boot marks in his skull, I don't think he would have got far. And I doubt the people who run the Ring are likely to look kindly on him after an attempted coup."

"They're dead," Raj said. "He killed them, burst their skulls open. But I'll bet their organisations took care of it."

"I hope so," Maggie said. "I told the police it was he who hurt you, but I didn't give any details."

"Can't tell anyone the truth," Raj managed, and Maggie cracked a smile.

"My lips are sealed," she said, squeezing his hand. "I have no wish to admit to whatever multiple felonies were committed that night. No going to jail for me. I'm going to be right here while you get better."

"Will you stay?" Raj asked, and Maggie felt her heart seize as his gaze met hers. He took a long moment to breathe deeply, and then the words seemed to rasp out of his damaged throat in a rush. "I promise we can talk about all of it; I promise I will tell you every thought I had about whether it would be better to tell you or not. I will answer any question you ask. Will you please stay?"

"I'll stay," Maggie said and tried to ignore the part of her that followed her words with a deep, heartfelt, *forever.*

Epilogue

RAJ WAS in physical therapy for two months. Werewolf super healing was apparently a powerful tool. Still, it took a while for him to get back to full function. Jeremy had broken both his legs—one in multiple places—and one arm, had put holes in his heart, one lung and several of his abdominal organs, had shattered his rib cage, and had torn apart several of the major blood vessels in his brain. He'd had to regrow a significant chunk of his spinal cord. But he couldn't stand being kept in bed, and even with all the books in his entire house at his disposal, he was climbing the walls within days of regaining consciousness. He consistently disobeyed his doctors about how much exercise he could tolerate, but it seemed he knew his own limits better than they did, because apart from being in constant pain as he pushed his body further than they recommended, he didn't seem to suffer any long-term effects of his refusal to remain in the wheelchair or on crutches for as long as they suggested. He was militant about doing the exercises prescribed to him, desperate to get back his health and fitness as soon as possible. Still, it was two months before the doctors signed off that his body was once again healthy enough to shift into his wolf form and join the pack on a full moon run.

The draw of the moon was something that had never been fully explained to Raj. He'd never needed it to be. He felt it in his body and his soul and knew that he was at his strongest when the moon was full. His wolf had been desperate for release for weeks. This was the longest break he'd ever had from shifting. His eyes had been silver for a week. He'd been back at the library since he was able to walk around on crutches, but his boss hadn't let him do story book hour this past week, as she was concerned his constantly shifted eyes would unnerve the children.

Raj walked up the steps at the front of Leo's house without aid and knocked twice before letting himself in. Emmett called his name from the living room.

"You're late!" Em said when he walked through the doorway.

"Sit down," Della said, ushering him towards his usual seat in the big sofa. "Do you want more of that painkiller tea? My grandmother delivered a new batch—grudgingly—but that's how she does everything."

"I'm fine, thanks," Raj replied, smiling up at her.

"Maggie coming?"

"She was just getting home when I left," Raj said. "She'll be here soon." By which, he meant he'd jumped on her as soon as she walked in the door from her morning shift, and she had told him to leave before her, since she knew full well that if he watched her showering their combined sweat off her body, they'd just wind up in bed all over again. Plus, she'd said cheekily, for once, it was *she* who needed some time to recover before joining them at Leo's house.

He couldn't have helped himself. She looked rumpled when she got in from work, just minutes after he did, so he made her tea and rubbed her shoulders, and when she looked up at him from her seat at the table, those big eyes had melted his heart, not to mention hardened his dick in a matter of seconds.

"I think there might be a better way to get this day out of my head," she'd said. "Want to distract me?"

"If I ever say no to that, put me in the ground," Raj had growled, and then she'd been in his arms and racing through the buttons of his shirt. She'd shoved him backwards onto the sofa and undid his belt and teased every inch of him with her tongue and lips until he couldn't stop himself from tearing off her clothes, dragging her onto his lap and driving inside her. She'd ridden him with hard, rough, deep grinds, her moans filling the air around them, her nails digging into his shoulders. He'd watched as she placed her hand over the place on his heart where her name marked his skin and dragged her down for a kiss that only broke when she increased the pace of her riding. When he felt her clench tight around him, he couldn't help but let himself go at the same time.

"See?" he'd asked once he was holding her close, feeling her racing heartbeat slow as her breathing gradually returned to normal. "This is what you can look forward to if you move in. Every day. Every night."

"Raj," Maggie said, still slightly breathless, "we've been together for barely two months. I am not moving in with you."

"What are you worried about?" Raj asked, though he knew the answer from the many times they'd had this conversation. "You're my mate. It'll happen eventually. Why not now?"

"It'll happen eventually," Maggie countered. "Why rush?"

"So, the 'every day, every night' argument didn't convince you even slightly?"

She'd laughed, and he'd felt it reverberate through his

body as well as hers. She looked up at him. "I already get this every day and every night," she said with a cheeky grin. "What kind of weight did you expect it to carry?" She pressed her fingertips to the place her name now marked the skin over his heart and whispered, "'You must allow me to tell you how ardently I admire and love you.'"

"Too easy," he said with a lazy grin. "You always choose *Pride & Prejudice* for love quotes."

"I'm happy to be predictable." Maggie grinned up at him.

"How's this? 'I love thee to the depths and breadth and height my soul can reach'."

"Shakespeare," Maggie said immediately, "and you were lying about not knowing the sonnets."

"Sonnet 43," Raj confirmed. "But I only remember the ones that mean something to me."

Her smile was soft and sweet. "'You should be kissed and often, and by someone who knows how'."

He pressed his lips to hers. "No denying you know how. Where's that from?"

"*Gone With the Wind*," Maggie said, "Which is what we need to be if we're going to get to Della and Leo's less than an hour late!"

She went to rise, but he wrapped his arms around her and pulled her close, curling his body around hers and running his hands over the front of her torso, circling her nipples in the way that always made her gasp. This time was no different, and then she sighed, relaxing against him. "Later, baby. I promise we'll come home together."

"But not to the same home?" Raj teased.

"Both of us, together, in one of two different homes at various times," Maggie said, a smile evident in her voice. She craned her neck to see his face, and her face went soft as their eyes met. "For now."

Raj managed to drag his mind away from the sense of utter contentment he'd felt at hearing those words for long enough to catch Della's reply. "No worries! As long as she's here before you all run off at moonrise."

"Petra here too?"

"Out the back, supervising Emmett's barbecuing. I told you we'd make it a party."

"I'm just looking forward to shifting. And the run. I've been dying for a good run."

"I'm sure you'll have it tonight," Della said. "Can I grab you a beer instead?"

"I won't say no to that," Raj said, "But in a second. Can I ask you something first?"

"Of course," Della said, perching on the armrest.

"Has Maggie said anything to you about being nervous about this?" he asked. "She hasn't seen me in my wolf form yet. I don't want it to stress her out."

"I think she's more excited than nervous," Della said. "Look, Maggie loves you. She knows you're a werewolf. I don't think she's going to suddenly change her mind because she sees what your other form looks like."

"She still won't agree to move in with me," Raj complained. He'd had this conversation with Della several times.

"Give her time," Della said. "You werewolves like to rush things. Humans are a little different. Let her do it in her own time."

"Time it is, then," Raj said with a rueful laugh.

But as Maggie walked through the door, her hair still slightly ruffled from the way he'd wrapped his hands in it earlier, he knew he'd give her all the time she needed. Every second he had was hers to spend, as long as she spent it with him.

Acknowledgments

This is the longest book I've ever written, defying all my attempts to cut down the word count, and it's taken place over a period of time that has been fairly challenging in my life. I won't go into detail, but suffice to say I rarely had the energy to write, even when I did have the time. Fortunately, when you're writing a book, it's pretty much always there for you to come back to when you can, and sometimes you even come back to it with fun new ideas, and some of those sometimes mean you then have to rewrite the whole thing. Repeatedly.

I started writing this book towards the end of Australia's 2021 COVID lockdown. I had just finished *Bonded to the Wolf* and was trying to work out how Raj's story would play out. For some time, I'd known he was going to be mated to Maggie, but despite the fact that I created him, and other writers will relate to this, I actually didn't know much about Raj other than the fact that he was a joker with a heart of gold and a penchant for a) talking without thinking first and b) enjoying a good romance novel. In a lot of ways, Raj is a character whom I see a lot of myself in; in a lot of other ways, I very strongly relate to Maggie. I am, of course, a book nerd of the highest degree, and I have friendships where much of our interactions are just talking about the books we love. One of these treasured relationships is with one of my sisters, who, while expressly forbidden from reading this novel, is Raj's #1 fan. I am pretty sure she's going to read this even though I've asked her not, and if so—

gotcha. (Sorry about the sex scenes. Not really. You knew what you were signing up for.)

The first conversation I had about this book was at the dinner table with my family. They know that I write somewhat spicy romance novels and occasionally even suggest fun character pairings, which I love, and we all pretend the story we're discussing won't involve a bunch of particularly explicit sex scenes. My brother came up with the nickname of "The Warlocktor" (a warlock-doctor portmanteau, for pronunciation) for Dr Jeremy that night, and I've been calling him that in my head ever since. While I will continue to insist my family do not read the books I write, I could not write them without their support. They love me and challenge me and make fun of me and accept my weirdness, and hold me together each time I think I might fall apart, and there's nothing more I could ask for.

This book is, in large part, for all the Rajes in the world, people who took a while to find a place they fit, or are maybe still finding it, who don't always say the right thing and maybe have some unusual interests—hopefully, not many of those interests relate to illegal fighting. It's also for the Maggies, the people who feel sometimes like the only human in a room full of supernaturals, who have to fight to be taken seriously and put all their heart into taking care of people in whatever way they can. I think many of us have at least some of these characteristics, and if that's you, this book is for you. Stay weird.

There are too many people to whom this book in some part belongs for me to list all their names here, and knowing me, I'd forget someone. Everyone with whom I've laughed about Raj and Maggie's story, or come to with queries about fighting or nursing or librarian-ing, or questions about what a relationship with a big height difference feels like, or suggestions for tattoo ideas, or lists of quotes you love, you are a part of this story. Everyone who has visited me in hospital or put up with my rambling about how to hide a supernatural underground fighting ring or let me spam them with potential quotes to be included in the quote game, you are the heart of my story. It only grows because you help me grow it. Writing can be both a particularly isolating experience and a deeply communal one. I might do the words part myself, but everyone I've spoken to about my stories or who has made comments or suggestions has left a mark on the way the story plays out.

Finally, I want to thank you, gentle reader, for picking up this book and for sticking with it and also for reading all the way to the end of the acknowledgements. Well done! The first job I ever wanted was to be a writer, and with the Blue Crescent series, I finally can hold a copy of a book that I've written in my hands. It makes me so happy to know I have fulfilled the dream that my six-year-old self had when she was drawing crayon pictures to illustrate the books she wrote.

And thank you to all the people who did not laugh when I announced I was going to start writing my romances as featuring smitten werewolves and their slightly confused, sometimes belligerent, but overall wonderful, mates. I swear, Mum, it's not werewolf porn.

Well, kind of.

Don't tell Dad.

Sophia Martin

Sophia grew up in Australia as part of a big family. She started telling stories before she could write, and writing before she could spell. Her early works consist almost entirely of misspelled fairy stories. As a teenager she would hand-copy the steamy scenes out of her favourite books to enjoy later, and this naturally led her to romance.

After a brief stint in non-fiction writing with a university paper, she returned to her origins and started writing fiction again. When not writing, she can be found pole-dancing very poorly, completing her university degree or terrorizing her two dogs.

Find her on Instagram: @sophiamartinwrites

Don't miss these exciting titles by Sophia Martin and Eclipse Press!

Blue Crescent
Bewitching the Wolf
Bonded to the Wolf

Shepherd's Creek Series
He Comes Home - Book One
Taking His Time - Book Two
Belonging to Him - Book Three
Claimed by Him - Book Four

Stand-Alone Titles
Exposed

Blushing Books

Blushing Books is one of the oldest eBook publishers on the web. We've been running websites that publish spanking and BDSM related romance and erotica since 1999, and we have been selling eBooks since 2003. We hope you'll check out our hundreds of offerings at http://www.blushingbooks.com.

Blushing Books Newsletter

Please join the Blushing Books newsletter
to receive updates & special promotional offers.
You can also join by using your mobile phone:
Just text BLUSHING to 22828.